Mademoiselle Victorine

Debra Finerman

Three Rivers Press · New York

Mademoiselle *Victorine*

A Novel

Copyright © 2007 by Debra Finerman

Reader's Group Guide copyright © 2007 by Three Rivers Press, an imprint of the Crown Publishing Group, a division of Random House, Inc., New York.

All rights reserved.
Published in the United States by Three Rivers Press, an imprint of the Crown Publishing Group, a division of Random House, Inc., New York.
www.crownpublishing.com

Three Rivers Press and the Tugboat design are registered trademarks of Random House, Inc.

Library of Congress Cataloging-in-Publication Data

Finerman, Debra.
Mademoiselle Victorine / Debra Finerman.—1st ed.
1. Meurent, Victorine—Fiction. 2. Artists' models—France—Fiction.
3. Manet, Edouard, 1832–1883—Fiction. 4. Painters—France—
Fiction. 5. France—Fiction. I. Title.
PS3606.I54M33 2007
813'.6—dc22   2006032464

ISBN 978-0-307-35283-5

Printed in the United States of America

DESIGN BY ELINA D. NUDELMAN

10 9 8 7 6 5 4 3 2 1

First Edition

To the two brilliant men in my life, Bill and Alex.
To my beautiful family.
To Paris, my home.

Acknowledgments

I would like to thank Bill, Alex, Bronia, Marcia, Monica, and Michael, whose encouragement and inspiration were never ending. I would like to thank Kevin Callahan, the future head of a publishing house; Danielle Mollet, the quintessential Frenchwoman of style and intellect; Stratis Haviaras; and the Harvard Writing Workshop for their invaluable insights. Thanks to Doug Pirnie for his kindness and WICE Paris for their programs on the cultural and intellectual life of Paris. Thanks to Christie's New York for the academic year of art history lectures, particularly those of Professors Kenneth Silver, Carol Armstrong, Shelley Rice, and Jack Flam, which led to the idea for this book. I wish to thank Philippe de Montebello and the Metropolitan Museum, where Manet's portraits of Victorine Meurent and the photographic exhibition of the tempestuous courtesan the Countess of Castiglione were the inspiration for Mademoiselle Victorine.

I would like to thank my brilliant and beautiful agent, Erin Malone, for her enthusiasm and special love for this project. I thank my editor, the legendary Allison McCabe, for her intelligent guidance and for her tender relationship with the written word. Thanks to Patricia Nelson for her discerning legal eye. Thank you, Lindsey Moore, for your kind help. Thanks also to Heather Proulx.

Special thanks to my son, Alex Finerman, the Harvard history major, whose tongue-in-cheek title for this book, *The Franco-Prussian Whore,* was greatly appreciated, but unfortunately not used.

We are searching for that modern painter who will
wrest from life its epic side and will make us see and understand
how heroic we are in our cravats and our polished boots.

—Charles Baudelaire, 1863

Prologue
1858

On a humid August afternoon, wedged between her two aunts in the third-class coach of a locomotive, trickles of sweat dripped down Victorine's ribs. Thirteen years old; her first train trip. But the stench of overcrowded bodies and the flies crawling up the windows had dampened the thrill of chugging toward Paris. In the last hundred miles, excitement had puddled into boredom. She studied other passengers to pass the time. A young mother with a prematurely creased, careworn face juggled two babies on her lap, and brushed a stray lock from her forehead with the ruddy, chapped hand of a laundress. Next to her sat an old man with rheumy eyes and open sores blooming purple and magenta across the bridge of his nose.

She noticed another girl, about her age, staring at her. Victorine glanced at the girl's starched dress and smoothed the wrinkles on her own cotton skirt. She tugged the sleeves of her hand-me-down blouse to cover the bruises on her arms. Aunt

Evelyne had a temper, and the proof was all over Victorine's body.

Her aunts discussed her as though she were deaf or perhaps Parisian, unable to comprehend the Alsatian dialect. "At least she's off our hands now," Aunt Gerthe said.

"She'll be someone else's headache," Aunt Evelyne cackled.

"Where am I going to live, Auntie?" Victorine asked.

They ignored her as usual and continued to talk.

"Who am I going to live with?"

Aunt Evelyne pinched her arm so hard, Victorine cried out.

"Stop asking questions. You'll go where you're told."

"I just wondered if I . . ."

Another pinch. "We've fed you and looked after you all these years, haven't we? Since the day you were born. You're on your own now, so you'd better find yourself a way to survive, because we ain't taking you back."

Victorine glanced at the other girl, who had been watching with a smirk.

I'll find my place in this world, she thought. I'll do whatever necessary and I'll never look back.

Chapter One

1862

We always seek out forbidden things
and long for whatever is denied us.

—François Rabelais, *Gargantua and Pantagruel,* 1532–1564

Outside the tall bow windows of the Paris Opera ballet school, dusk embraced the city in a grayish pink veil, settling around spires of cathedrals and draping across bridges of the Seine. Inside the cavernous rehearsal hall, Victorine Laurent's fellow students practiced pliés under the critical eye of their pudgy dance master, Monsieur Jules. The violinist yawned as he scratched out a listless Chopin nocturne. The girls' middle-aged mothers nested on folding chairs, gossiping and clutching tattered shawls against the evening chill.

In the bright vestibule, Victorine cupped her hands against the glass-paned French doors and scanned the room for Edgar Degas. Was she too late for their appointment? No, there he was in his sketching corner, but not alone. Another gentleman stood with him off to the side, observing the girls in the flickering gaslight. When Degas caught sight of her, he nudged his companion and nodded his chin toward her. Victorine smoothed her dark curls. She tugged the décolleté of her crimson taffeta frock just a touch lower, took a deep breath, and threw open the double doors, slicing the room with a shaft of light.

As she approached, Victorine's gaze riveted to the other gentleman.

Degas introduced her, and Victorine lowered her face in the charming way she had practiced a thousand times in her cheval glass. Then she glanced up at the stranger, held his gaze a moment longer than was proper. The shine of a silk top hat, the sparkle of a gold watch chain, and the polish of leather boots spoke to her of affluence.

"So! This is the gentleman from Marseille you told me so much about." She smiled sweetly, extending her hand.

There was a moment of confusion before Degas realized the mistaken identity. "No, no, this isn't the banker chap. This is Edouard Manet! He's an artist, Victorine. He wants you to model for him."

She kept her smile, murmured it was a pleasure, then turned to walk away. Edouard Manet grabbed her wrist. "Wait a moment. What's wrong with artists? They can't afford to buy you a carriage and pair?"

So he understood where her priorities lay.

"I've never heard of you, Monsieur Manet. Have you exhibited in the Salon?"

"He has," Degas said. "Just not very often."

The yearly Salon competition sponsored by the prestigious Académie française held the entire city of Paris enthralled. It was ostensibly open to all artists, but everyone knew that the conservative jury was notable for rejecting work deemed too iconoclastic.

"I'd wager you've never seen paintings like mine." Edouard scribbled an address on the back of his calling card. "Come to the studio, judge my work, then decide." He watched her face closely. "I pay my models well."

A flicker of interest lit her eyes. "I'll consider it. But if I agree to model for you, I insist Monsieur Degas be present as chaperone."

"You flatter yourself, mademoiselle," Edouard laughed. "When I choose a model, it's for the music inside them."

She was taken aback by the poetry of his remark. "Do I possess music?" Her tone turned soft.

"Perhaps."

Victorine pulled her thin wool mantelet closer around her shoulders as she and Degas sipped crèmes in the cool morning air. They chatted under the green canvas awning of her favorite café near the cathedral of Notre-Dame-de-Lorette, in the quartier where she and many young women of her social class lived. They were called *lorettes*—not quite as debased as streetwalkers, not quite as exalted as courtesans.

"After boarding school, Manet could have followed his father's wishes and become a barrister or chosen a position in banking or the stock exchange," Degas said. "But he has a talent that will propel him higher." Degas sat back. "He has the hands of an artist coupled with the passion of a revolutionary. With paintbrush and canvas he's going to change the way the world's perceived." Degas named obscure artists Victorine had never heard of—Monet, Renoir, and Cézanne—who had chosen Edouard Manet as their Apollo. "Of them all, Manet has the cool, analytical intelligence to be a painter of his own time."

Victorine swirled the spoon in her cup, contemplating Manet. "Tell him I'll come tomorrow afternoon at three."

The next day at the scheduled hour, Victorine knocked at the black lacquered door of Edouard Manet's flat. As footsteps approached inside, she glanced down and noticed her hem splattered with the reddish brown mud of Paris's ubiquitous construction pits. And it was her best dress, the only one made of silk satin. Her side-laced ankle boots were caked with mud as well. Too late now to regret walking to save six sous on omnibus fare.

The door swung open and Edouard bowed with an exaggerated flair.

Victorine paused under the shimmering gas jets of the foyer chandelier to untie the lilac satin ribbons of her cabriolet bonnet and placed it with her fringed parasol on the marble-top bureau. She knew that even within the modest budget of a *lorette* she looked as delectable as a candy box in a confectionery shop; her luxuriant dark hair, swept back into a sophisticated chignon, had taken her hairdresser painstaking time to accomplish. The faux pearl—and-rhinestone earrings pulled the eye to her expertly powdered and rouged face, pink and white as a Fragonard *galante,* perfect in every feature. Except. Except for a cruel oval scar below her left cheek, which marred the flawless surface. Sensing Edouard appreciatively scanning her from behind, she swayed a bit more seduction into her hips, a cascade of lilac satin ruffles sweeping the dusty floorboards with each step. As she approached the parlor, she glanced at the fine upholstered furnishings, the damask drapes tied back with tasseled silk cords, the gleaming mahogany end tables, and puzzled over the incongruity of these treasures residing in an obscure young artist's studio in the seedy Batignolles district.

In the parlor, she met Degas with a quick kiss to both cheeks while two other gentlemen rose from the crimson velvet divan. The older, distinguished-looking one was a Corinthian column of a man exuding a powerful presence and intimidating demeanor. The other, a willowy chap with vaguely feminine features, was shorter than Victorine and slight of build. What a comical picture they created standing side by side.

Edouard introduced the younger man as André, the Marquis de Montpellier. He adjusted his cravat and slicked back a stray lock of fine, blond hair. The soft peach fuzz on his cheeks and the spray of freckles across his nose hinted that he could be no more than her age, seventeen, or eighteen at the most. She commented that her favorite shopping street in Paris was the boulevard de Montpellier, no doubt named for his illustrious ancestors? He replied that he was just a humble writer, and could take no credit for his family's storied past. Judging by his threadbare suit of clothes, Victorine surmised that the family had moved out of the ancestral château and into the caretaker's cottage several generations ago.

The older gentleman waited patiently for his turn. Edouard introduced him as Monsieur Baudelaire. She instantly recognized the name of Charles Baudelaire, the poet and author, esteemed as one of the greatest thinkers of the age.

"Monsieur Baudelaire, this is an honor. I'm a great admirer of your work."

Not one to be as inveigled as the young marquis by flattery, Baudelaire questioned her as to which, if any, of his "humble scribblings" she had read?

She wanted him to know that she had a good education, wasn't some vulgar cocotte from the streets. "I loved an essay you published recently about women. I committed a phrase to memory: 'Woman is a divinity, a star which presides over all the conceptions of the brain of Man.'"

"Quite right, my essay in *Le Figaro* last week!" He seemed impressed. He asked how Victorine had come to meet Manet.

"I pressed Degas for an introduction after seeing her in one of his pastel sketches," Edouard said.

"I can't blame Manet for being intrigued by your beauty." Baudelaire smiled at Victorine.

"Not mere beauty," Edouard said. "Beneath the surface, there's light and shadow."

The four gentlemen fell silent and scrutinized her. Victorine felt like a display at Le Bon Marché department store.

"Such opposites warring in one human being, that's the entire matter right there, isn't it? Chiaroscuro," Edouard said.

Victorine asked the meaning of that foreign word.

"Light and shadow. It's Italian," Edouard explained.

"Victorine, you told me your parents were famous Italian musicians. Didn't you say they toured the Continent performing for royalty?" Degas asked.

"You must have me confused with someone else. I was born in Vienna. My father was fencing master at the Habsburg court."

By the looks exchanged between the gentlemen, she could see they didn't believe her. After all, it was common knowledge that girls in the corps de ballet hailed from poor working-class backgrounds. The junior ballerinas were amateurs chosen for their beauty, not their dancing skills, to perform in the short ballet entr'acte. They supplemented their meager salaries by becoming the coddled mistresses of rich married bankers, real estate speculators, and industrialists. No sophisticated person believed that a love of Wagner or Verdi brought these nouveaux riches to the Opera every Thursday; they came solely to admire their mistresses' long legs in short tutus. Gossip in the dressing room usually centered on ballerinas who had been passed around by wealthy protectors for years, only to resort to common street prostitution. But Victorine had no intention of following that downward spiral. She was seventeen and knew she had only a few good years left. She took Edouard's arm. "Where are these masterpieces of yours, Monsieur Manet? If I'm to sit for a portrait, I'd better see what I've gotten myself into."

Edouard led her to the hallway lined with canvases. There were landscapes, cityscapes, and portraits of women. Many women. One after another, she surveyed the paintings without comment, twisting her gloves in her hands as she evaluated the intense colors and the thick impasto slashed on the canvas by palette knife. Edouard followed one step behind.

"Well"—she turned to him at last—"thank you."

"Don't you like my work?" He seemed crushed.

"I don't want to say they're good or bad." She chose her words as thoughtfully as a woman trying on hats in a millinery shop. "I can only say I don't understand them. This one." She pointed to a group portrait of outdoor concertgoers in a shady garden setting. "Some faces in the crowd have features, while others are blurred. And this one." She indicated a portrait of an old peasant. "They say one judges an artist's talent by how he depicts the hands. Those hands look like lumps of raw dough. I don't wish to insult your art, but . . ." She turned back to his pictures with a shrug.

"Mademoiselle." Baudelaire stepped forward. "Consider for a moment. Why do you feel uncomfortable? Critics feel uneasy because it's too radical. But should a modern artist imitate the ancient world, model the human figure after a classical Greek sculpture? Do we stroll the streets of Paris in togas?"

"No . . . but an artist should paint subjects as he truly *sees* them."

"That's precisely what he does! When one looks, one sees refracted light, not colors. Light is a symbol of our time, and Manet is a master of that light."

"Baudelaire, please . . . ," Edouard protested.

Baudelaire held up his hand for silence. "Leonardo taught his students *saper vedere*—knowing *how* to see. Manet is the Leonardo of our times. Someday his talent will be recognized."

She glanced at the pictures lined up across the wall and calculated her options. They didn't know her yet, could little fathom that she was preoccupied with one thing: the search for a wealthier, more powerful replacement for Dr. LeBrun, the married dentist who currently paid her rent and dress-maker bills. She deliberated that being associated with Manet and his odd painting style might damage her reputation. Yet it was also possible that with a portrait on display at the Salon for all to see, her image would be exposed to a wide audience of potential suitors and she could rise faster up the ladder of success. She had read about a man named P. T. Barnum in America who used this phenomenon—"advertising"—to profitable effect. "Yes, I will sit for you, Monsieur Manet."

They drank some fine Veuve Clicquot, and Victorine felt Edouard's gaze luxuriate in the curves of her shoulders and slide down the nape of her neck. She caught his glance, evalu-ating her skin tone, cream of custard, and tracing her mouth, the aspect of angel's wings, and lingering over the scar. He reached out to touch it. "How did you—"

"Don't ask me about that." She jerked her head away. "To-morrow morning, ten o'clock. We'll begin work."

He grasped her hand, but she recoiled.

"Don't expect anything more." Her voice had the sound of a door slamming shut. "You're not what I want."

"Not what you want?"

"Not what I need." Her voice softened.

"As you wish," he said. "A strictly professional relationship."

She allowed him to escort her to the hallway as the other men watched, and felt his gaze following her as she walked down the four flights of marble steps. She wanted him to un-derstand from the start that there was to be no love affair, nothing to distract her from her goal: financial security. As Victorine stepped onto the boulevard des Batignolles, dusk was falling and the lamplighters with their long poles illumi-nated the streetlamps. How difficult would it be to keep Manet at a distance while engaging in the intimate act of posing for him? Judging from the numerous portraits of women in the studio and the tender way he touched her face, he was accustomed to females succumbing to the Manet charm. But she was accustomed to balding heads, middle-aged paunches, and the financial benefits an aged mouth on hers could provide.

Chapter Two

'Tis to create, and in creating live.

—Lord Byron, *Childe Harold's Pilgrimage,* 1812

*V*ictorine knocked for several minutes and began to doubt that anyone was home. As she turned to leave, the door creaked open to reveal André de Montpellier cinching closed his silk dressing gown. He smoothed down a cowlick of fine, blond hair and welcomed her in, waving a brown bottle of elixir and mumbling about his delicate constitution and a devilish bout of dyspepsia.

"Do you live here?" Victorine asked, glancing at him as he weaved down the foyer behind her.

"My rent's in arrears and I'm houseguesting with Manet until payday next week at *Le Moniteur.*"

Victorine considered this new tidbit. "You work for a newspaper?" she asked.

"I'm writing a literary masterpiece, but I make ends meet with a weekly gossip piece you may have seen called 'La Vie Parisienne.'"

Indeed she had. It was indispensable reading for young *lorettes* like her, the primary source for rumors involving socialites and their straying husbands. She was about to inquire more when Edouard stumbled into the hallway, clutching a blanket around his naked waist.

"Am I early?" Victorine glanced at the clock in the foyer. "Our appointment was for ten o'clock."

"Appointment?" Edouard ran his hands through his bed-tousled hair as though that would clear his mind.

"My sitting," Victorine said.

"Oh, the sitting. I was out late last night and I——"

Edouard watched, quite fascinated, as she unbuttoned her short kid gloves, one button at a time, and slid them off. In a slow, deliberate fashion, she unfastened the black braid froggings of her brown wool cape and shrugged it from her shoulders. After removing her black velvet bonnet, she adjusted her white cotton basque and smoothed the fifteen yards of gray-and-white windowpane broadcloth that made up her crinoline skirt. With a glance in the hallway cheval glass, she smoothed her sleek hair, tucking a few stray wisps into her chignon.

"Duckie? Who's there?"

Edouard winced. A waiflike girl with a halo of tangled blond curls sauntered out of his bedchamber, yawning. The girl stopped short when she saw Victorine in the hallway and self-consciously tugged her chemise over her small, exposed breasts. "Are we expecting company?" she asked, and stared suspiciously at Victorine.

Victorine scooped up her gloves, cape, and bonnet, and turned toward the door. "Apparently, I'm interrupting," she said.

Edouard grabbed her arm. "No, please stay."

The mophead shrugged and sauntered back to the bedchamber.

"I'm so sorry about"—his thumb jerked toward the bedchamber—"that."

Her gaze inadvertently drifted to the blanket slipping lower down his waist. "I am *not* staying if she does. Either that little tart goes, or I do."

"Yes. Of course. As you wish."

He returned to his bedchamber and gingerly closed the door.

Victorine headed into the parlor, the tip of her shoe sweeping aside a pair of wool trousers crumpled on the floor. She sat on the red velvet divan, thinking about the girl soon to be tossed out. A few years ago, as a newcomer to Paris, she never would have made such a demand; she had arrived from the provinces unprepared for competitive city girls. When wealthy gentlemen had first noticed her in the ballet's Green Room and invited her for "supper" after the performance, she had no idea the other girls would flirt and connive to steal her admirers. She learned quickly enough; other women were not to be trusted. She would tolerate no rivals to distract Edouard Manet, considering how useful he and his art could be in furthering her career.

As she waited in Edouard's parlor, she noticed the smell of stale cigar smoke clinging to the drapes and wallpaper. Ashtrays overflowed with cigarette butts, and half-empty wine and whiskey glasses littered the side tables. Various garments skittered across the floor; one lace petticoat, she noted, was draped over a lamp shade. Her gaze traveled up two walls of bookshelves. Edouard's collection of books was prodigious: the classics, poetry, history, art theory, optics. André reappeared, dressed but still pale as an ocean-liner passenger rolling with the pitch. He suggested they pass the time waiting for Edouard in the studio.

One step inside, and she entered an enchanted world, a chaotic universe of props, of spangled costumes lying about in heaps like tired dancers, of animal-skin rugs sprawled across the bare wooden floor, of dusty wine bottles cluttering the tabletop, not for the purpose of drinking, but for painting. But mostly, of pictures lining the perimeter of the room and marching up the walls, unseen, unsold, and unwanted.

Victorine peered into an old wooden steamer trunk and selected a silk flowered bonnet. She placed it on her head, checked the mirror, and twirled around for André's approval. He shook his head no. She then replaced it with another, more elaborate creation featuring artificial fruit and a white feathered plume. Nodding her head comically, she swayed the plume to and fro.

They heard raised voices. "But I love you!" the girl whined. Edouard answered, but Victorine could not quite hear what he replied. "The other girls warned me about you! All the nights we've spent together. I thought you loved me!"

Victorine laughed at that, and crossed the room to inspect several portraits stacked against the wall. The women in the paintings were uniformly young and beautiful. But she noted no more than one portrait of each girl. She turned to André. "Does he paint a model only once?"

"Each time Manet discovers a woman who inspires him, he falls in love with the woman in the flesh and the one in the painting. As he makes love to her in his bed, so, too, on the canvas."

"But why does he paint only a single portrait of her?"

André sighed. "As the paint dries on the canvas, the girl fades into past tense."

"I hate you!" the girl shrieked.

Victorine turned her attention back to the mirror and exchanged a smug smile with her own reflection. She picked up a tiara and a scepter, then regally waved the scepter above André's head, knighting him. He was pale, thin-boned, his sexuality a bit of a mystery. But as he grinned at her, she read in his eyes absolute adoration. She wasn't sure whether he wanted to be her or bed her, but one thing was certain: She had made another conquest. This boy could be quite useful, she thought, if he would mention her name in his gossip column.

The door flew open and the girl burst through, startling Victorine and André. Clothes askew, eyes swollen with tears, she glared at Victorine as another crying fit overtook her. She marched to the door, her battered suitcase trailing lace pantalets like a white flag of surrender, and slammed it so hard that paint pots rattled on a shelf near André's head.

Victorine smiled and winked at André.

She flipped through a sketchbook on a worktable and paused at a pastel chalk self-portrait of Edouard. She studied the sandy blond hair curling around the high, aristocratic forehead, the cobalt-blue eyes with their incisive gaze, all captured with searing insight. When she heard Edouard's footfall, she slapped the sketchbook closed.

He wore a fine wool suit in the English style and a silk cravat; even his boots were buffed to a high polish.

"Do you always dress so handsomely in your own studio?" she asked.

"I try to look my best."

Edouard approached and circled completely around her. He raised his pencil to her face, turned it at an angle, and measured from the tip of her nose to the outside corner of her eyebrow. He then stepped back and stroked his cheek with his hand, deep in thought. André stood beside him, as well, gravely commenting to Edouard how nature could have arranged features so symmetrically in a face. An idea occurred to her that would rattle these two serious gentlemen. She began to unbutton her basque and pulled loose the lacings of her bodice. Her gray-and-white dress slipped off her shoulders and crumpled in a curtsy to the floor, crinoline skirt and all. Edouard took a startled step back and bumped into André. "What are you doing?"

"Don't you want to see if my body will suit you?"

"We don't have to start with . . ." His words trailed off.

The whalebone corset came off, the white cotton camisole, the lace-trimmed petticoats, and the chamois pantalets as well. Her nudity was accented by a black satin ribbon encircling her neck and black silk stockings held by lace garters around her thighs. She walked calmly right past them to the chaise longue and stretched out languidly. André excused himself to allow them to work.

Edouard seated himself on a three-legged stool across from Victorine and grabbed his sketchbook. Glancing from her to the page, his fingers moved rapidly in quick strokes. He drew the oval outline of her face, her gray eyes, and then her luxurious chestnut hair caressing her neck and tumbling around her shoulders. His gaze swept over her breasts, pointed upward slightly, nipples the pink of rose petals. He moved down her torso to her hand draped over her pubic area. She noticed his smile of irony at her coy gesture. He continued to draw her plump thighs and long, elegant legs, which ended in beautifully shaped, absurdly small feet.

"Good, good. You've done this before?"

"Never."

The pen nib scratched hatch marks urgently on the paper. Victorine was fascinated by the dynamic arcs of his right arm. No halfhearted gestures from the wrist, his strokes were powerful statements of purpose. His hands intrigued her as well: strong, expressive, tapering to sensitive fingers. She felt his entire concentration focused on her, perceiving her with all his senses. He observed her with his eyes, but she also understood he was "listening to the music" inside her, which he had alluded to the day they had met. She watched as he signed the drawing with a flourish and held it up for her to see.

Victorine clapped her hands with delight. He had portrayed her as she was, a perfect likeness, but with a fantastical headdress and elaborate bracelets and anklets. She truly resembled an exotic goddess. "It's beautiful!" As he handed her the hastily drawn sketch, she felt a window opening on her life.

As Victorine dressed, she heard Edouard call André to join them, then disappear into his tiny kitchen to return with a fine Bordeaux and three crystal glasses on a silver tray. Victorine and André sat side by side on Edouard's red velvet divan and watched him uncork the bottle.

"It's from the vineyard of my mother's family, but I think you'll like it." Edouard handed each a glass.

"A *premier cru* château?" Victorine reached for the forest-green bottle and examined the label.

"It's a small estate. Don't assume I'm a wealthy dilettante playing the bohemian. I don't have millions to support you with."

"Do you imagine that's all I think about?"

André interrupted their contretemps. "Victorine, have any of your liaisons accidentally turned into"—he scanned the room searching for the proper term—"love?"

"Love!" She spat out the word like a lemon seed. "Love fades away. Only one thing survives. That's money."

"You're too sentimental, mademoiselle," Edouard said. "But how can you be so certain?"

She paused for a moment, considering. To tell the truth? For once? She leaned back against the divan cushions and recounted her first view of Paris the day she arrived to join the ballet school. After she and her aunts pushed their way through the crowd-jammed train station, they exited the double doors and paused at the top of the white marble steps opposite the boulevard du Strasbourg. "My first impression of Paris wasn't of elegant shops or fashionable ladies. The first person I saw was a beggar woman rooting in trash cans; she staggered up the steps and tugged at my skirt with her dirt-caked hand, begging for half a sou. I shrank away in horror. I'd never seen anything like that in my little village in Alsace."

"You're from Alsace? You told us you were from Vienna," André said.

She ignored his remark. "The porter shooed her away and explained she was called Queen Mabille. She'd been a courtesan, a great beauty who started her career at the Bal Mabille. She'd become famous for inventing a wild, shocking dance called the cancan. She'd had diamonds, a palace, and carriages, but she made unwise choices ruled by her heart and came to ruin. Love." Victorine shook her head. "It doesn't really exist."

"I beg to differ. I can fall in love ten times a day just wandering the streets. Anyone who says there's no such thing as love has never been in love," Edouard said.

"Well, then love isn't meant for girls like me. I can feign love, and that's sufficient for the men I know," she said softly. She sipped the wine and rolled it over her tongue, savoring the warm glow as she swallowed. "Now tell me, Edouard, are your family from Bordeaux?"

"Some of my mother's family are. I couldn't be more Parisian. I grew up in an apartment on the rue des Petits-Augustins across from the Ecole des Beaux Arts. But I spent my childhood summers at our country estate in Gennevilliers. The landed gentry there have a tradition; they choose a beggar as a child's godfather so we're reminded that the poor are our cousins and sisters."

"How noble." Victorine smirked.

"Sarcasm as sharp as whalebone against rib cage," Edouard said.

"Were you as insufferable a child as you are now?" she asked Edouard.

He said that he never spoke a word for the first three years of his life.

"My family thought I was mentally deficient or, at best, a mute. Then a young maidservant joined our household who changed my life. One day, she sat me down with a sketchbook and a crayon and I began to draw. As she named each item, I repeated every word back to her. The entire family came running when they heard me speak for the first time. I suppose I've been drawing ever since."

Victorine rose and approached a burl wood library table holding a collection of family photographs. Selecting an oval frame, she stared at it intently. "Who are these people?" she asked Edouard.

He hesitated a moment as he regarded the photograph of the chubby blond woman with a boy standing beside her. "She's a woman I've had a liaison with for thirteen years. And the boy's her . . . brother."

"Does she live here?"

"No."

Victorine replaced the photograph and chose another. "And these people? Who are they?"

He answered that they were his mother and father. "What about your parents?"

"I know nothing about my father. My mother died in childbirth. At least that's what my aunts told me. I don't really know." She swallowed the rest of her wine and held out her glass for more.

"Well, who raised you?" Edouard asked, pouring.

"I raised myself." She noted the puzzled expression on both their faces. Should she continue? There was a rule she lived by: Never confide in anyone, least of all men. If she revealed that she was shuttled like an unwanted piece of baggage between the aunts, wouldn't their fascination turn to pity? What if they knew that when she was thirteen years old, the aunts sold her to Monsieur Kaye? He paid them and, in exchange, she moved in as au pair to his children. He had promised to continue her education. Her lip curled with derision at the memory. He gave me an education, all right; in things no young girl should learn. Her fingertips found the scar on her face and caressed it absentmindedly.

"That scar?" Edouard interrupted her thoughts.

"Don't ask me about that. As it is, I can't imagine why I've gone on about myself. How utterly boring of me! Besides, it's not where you come from that matters, it's where you're going." She returned her attention to the picture of his parents. Cradling the frame in her hands, she asked if she might have it.

"What? You don't even know my parents."

She couldn't find words to articulate her feelings. She stared at the picture in her hands. What if she had been raised by parents such as these? How different would her life have been if she were the daughter of this elegantly dressed man and this woman with such kind, deep-set eyes? They would have given her a proper upbringing; they would have arranged a future for her in which sordid acts in shabby rooms like the one she lived in would be a grotesque nightmare, too horrible to imagine. "I don't have any family photographs," she said.

Edouard said that she could have the picture if she wished.

She slipped it into her pocket and willed herself to change her mood.

Although it was close to midnight, crowds of revelers thronged the streets. Pools of green, sulfurous light from newly installed gas lampposts shimmered in a vanishing perspective down the bustling boulevards. Victorine and her "protector," Dr. LeBrun, were jostled by those with a few francs jingling in their pockets and those with a few million in their bank accounts. No matter how much money one had, there was some form of entertainment, of escape, for sale in Paris.

They headed for 11 Grand-Rue des Batignolles. The Café Guerbois was a writers' and artists' hangout in the heart of the Batignolles district. Victorine wasn't surprised that LeBrun had chosen the Guerbois. In a workingman's café, he could enjoy the company of his mistress without running the risk of encountering any bourgeois acquaintances.

Inside the café, the dining room thundered with conversations, the clanking of silverware against plates, and music from an accordion in the far corner whining out popular musical-theater tunes. The mirrors on the amber walls reflected a swirl of waiters in long white aprons bustling between packed tables, holding trays of steaming plates high above their customers' heads.

Once seated across from LeBrun at a wooden table facing the room, Victorine removed her short bolero jacket and adjusted the white lace *chemisette à jabot* that filled in the neckline of her silver-gray muslin basque. She smoothed her crinoline skirt across her side of the wooden banquette, quite engulfing it in yards of gray broadcloth.

She waited patiently as LeBrun studied the menu, adjusting the pince-nez on his bulbous nose and tapping his fingers against the rotund belly of his waistcoat. He ordered two prix fixe dinners and launched into an account of his afternoon spent extracting a particularly stubborn pair of molars. His bushy gray eyebrows flicked up and down to emphasize the most dramatic moments. Despite her best efforts, Victorine's attention wandered around the brightly lit room, alert to a loud burst of laughter. She saw a rowdy group of scruffy-looking young men; she recognized Edouard Manet, right in the center of this group.

She watched him as he recounted a story until suddenly, feeling the pressure of her gaze, he turned toward her. Spying her, he stood up and waved her over. She vigorously declined by shaking her head no. To her horror, he approached her table, introduced himself smoothly to LeBrun as Victorine's cousin, and asked if he might borrow her for a moment to meet his friends. She felt his grip on her elbow as he steered her away from the fuming LeBrun.

"I'm not leaving him to sit with you and those paupers." She tried to pull her arm out of his grasp.

"Don't worry, Grandpa will be fine for a few moments without you."

She protested the entire length of the room, but he steamed her through the crowd until they reached his table. One side was introduced as "the enemy," with an ironic laugh. They were art students of the Académie française who upheld the status quo. The others—he pointed to his side of the table—were his compatriots, "avant-garde" artists at the forefront of the charge into the future.

She reluctantly sat down at a spot he indicated between himself and André.

"So, how's work progressing, Edouard?" asked one of the Academy students.

"Can't complain; I'm preparing an exhibit at the Galerie Lamont with Monet." He pointed to a young artist in his mid-twenties with a red beard and head of wild hair, who raised his stein in a toast.

"You fellows are a bunch of dabblers," said an Academy student, pointing his fork at Edouard. "Your paintings are nothing more than a train wreck on canvas." Victorine noticed the tips and nail beds of his chubby fingers were stained with green paint. "You destroy the past and everything that's beautiful."

"Absurd," Edouard said. "A true artist never abandons Beauty. We revere Beauty." He glanced around the crowded café. "Our age is rife with hypocrisy. Look at that married fellow over there."

All attention followed his hand as he pointed to LeBrun.

"Polite society looks the other way at his having a mistress, though he attends church each Sunday with his family and pretends he's a fine, upright gentleman."

Victorine defended her dentist and their mutually beneficial arrangement. "His marriage was planned by his parents. He'd never met the girl until a week before the wedding——"

"That's the sad tale he told you. How many times have you heard the same story from your married admirers?" He turned to the table. "This bourgeois hypocrisy permeates every level of society, right up to Napoléon III and his cronies."

"What does the emperor have to do with this?" Victorine asked.

"*Le petit* Napoléon"——Edouard used a derisive term coined by left-wing critics——"is the epitome of the 'new man,' the 'self-made man.' I should know; most of my friends from the Sorbonne are such. They build fortunes, marry wives who spend ostentatiously, groom sons to join their thriving businesses, and purchase love from beautiful young courtesans, the most exotic commodity for sale in this great free-market economy of ours."

Victorine had read dozens of editorials extolling the new capitalist spirit in Paris. The newspapers were full of articles citing the treaties and alliances of the Napoleonic Wars and the resultant shift in populations as responsible for the massive changes sweeping Europe.

"You chaps don't understand our modern world," Edouard said, pointing toward the Académie française students. "Things are changing fast." He waved his cigar in the air, where it created a circle of blue smoke. "Scientific discoveries buffet us at every turn. We can barely assimilate them before something newer slams into us."

Victorine noticed a beautiful waitress, her rouge too bright, her neckline too low, approaching the table. She leaned down, revealing an ample décolleté, and kissed Edouard on both cheeks. His arm slipped easily around her waist in a proprietary hug. All the artists gave their dinner orders, except for Monet, who checked his pockets and declined, insisting he wasn't hungry.

"He'll have what I'm having," Edouard told the waitress.

"It's the third time this week you've paid for my meals. I can't allow you to support me this way—"

"You'll pay me back when you've made it."

A general murmur of encouragement for young Monet traveled down Manet's side of the table. Then a man called Cézanne asked, "Haven't you noticed the astonishing speed of trains?" Victorine noted his southern accent. This one must be from Provence, she thought. "We follow timetables now to get ourselves from here to there. Even the way we perceive time has changed!"

"Consider the changes faced by women today," said a man called Pissarro.

"The manner in which society treats women fascinates me." Edouard sat back thoughtfully and contemplated Victorine.

She glanced at LeBrun, engrossed in conversation with a diner at the table next to him. She knew she should get back. "I'd better go." She half rose, but Edouard gently pulled her back down.

"Stay and listen. You'll learn about the ideas behind our pictures and understand better what you're going to be a part of."

She hesitated. In truth, these ideas whirling about fascinated her. An intriguing world existed among these artists, one that piqued her curiosity. She turned back to the conversation.

"The Paris of Victor Hugo, of our fathers and grandfathers, is gone. These new streets with perspectives as straight as railroad tracks did away with the old labyrinth of streets and neighborhoods flowing into each other," André said.

She smiled at him, and he raised his champagne glass in response. He may be penniless, but a marquis must have some powerful acquaintances, she thought.

"Remember when you only knew the people on your own street because it was too tortuous to get to the ones nearby? Now other classes mix with us and bring their ideas and way of life to us," another artist, called Bazille, said as he was served another absinthe. Victorine watched as he balanced a sugar cube on the silver slotted spoon and poured a small bit of water over the strong green liquor. Absinthe was called "the green parrot"; it eventually rotted the brain. "I can't stand this infernal tearing down of familiar landmarks and the deep pits surrounding us everywhere," Bazille continued between swigs of his drink. "I've moved addresses ten times in my life thanks to that devil Haussmann."

Baron Haussmann was the creator of Paris's massive urban-renewal project; Victorine knew him as the protector of the girl who danced beside her onstage.

"How can we hide from the upheavals in our lives when each day we contend with upheavals of dirt and masonry?" Edouard said. "Change is everywhere, and either we learn to master it, harness its power, or like Sisyphus, we're condemned to struggle with it over and over each day."

LeBrun approached the table and insisted that Victorine return to dine with him. She rose and bid good night to her "cousin" and his friends, then hooked her arm through LeBrun's. As they walked away, she glanced back and caught Manet's gaze following them as they receded into the haze of cigar smoke and gaslight.

Chapter Three

In art there are only revolutionaries and plagiarists.

—attributed to Jean-Auguste-Dominique Ingres (1780–1867)

ictorine stood beside André on the platform of the Gare Saint-Lazare and watched the locomotive from Argenteuil lumbering through the train yard, hissing and lurching closer, funneling lavender-and-gray steam up to the vaporous sky.

The plan was to collect André's cousin, a pupil of Manet's, deposit her luggage at her lodgings at the Grand Hotel, across from the construction site of the new opera house, then go on to Edouard's studio to preview the nearly completed portrait of Victorine. As the train pulled closer to the platform, André mentioned how his cousin had come to study with Manet. Since the prestigious Ecole des Beaux Arts was out of the question for a woman, she had enrolled in the School for Women in the Arts. Sketching at the Louvre, she had noticed Edouard Manet working nearby. Aware of his burgeoning reputation, she had summoned her courage and inquired if she could join him on a sketching expedition. After a few days, an inspiration came to her: to study with Edouard Manet.

"As a rule, he never accepts students," André said, "but after much persistence, including letters from her art tutors back home, he relented and took her on."

The doors opened and crowds began to pour from the carriages. A young blond woman on the step of the first-class coach hopped down. Cheeks cherry red with excitement, she waved her parasol in the air, rushed toward André, threw her arms around his neck, and squealed as he lifted her up and swung her in a circle. When he set her down, André introduced Victorine to Mademoiselle Julia Stanhope-Morgan.

Victorine instantly sized her up. Everything about her appearance announced that she was up to date with the mercurial Parisian fashions and, equally important, able to spend as much of her trust fund as she pleased to look stylish. Like her cousin André, she was as pale and fine-boned as a Sèvres porcelain figurine, and so tiny she had to tilt her chin to meet Victorine's gaze. Her face was unexceptional, as dull as a Sunday school lesson.

"Mademoiselle Laurent, I've seen your beautiful portrait, and am so pleased to meet Monsieur Manet's inspiration," she said, offering her hand politely.

Silence hung between them. For several awkward moments, Victorine made no move. Finally, she swept aside her brown wool cape and extended a kid-gloved hand to Julia. "I'm happy to meet you, too," Victorine said. "Monsieur Manet's spoken of your skill, and he's a good judge of talent."

She heard André exhale a sigh of relief.

Once outside in the bright Parisian sunshine, they took the rue de Londres up the hill toward the place de l'Europe. The two cousins traded stories about family members, strolling arm in arm, obviously elated to be in each other's company. It had not been initially apparent to Victorine that Julia Stanhope-Morgan was an American. Julia's accent was as natural and flowing as any Parisian's; she carved each syllable as elegantly as the curves of a fleur-de-lys. The only clue was her poise and confident gait; there was something free and healthy about the way she walked, an unapologetic curiosity.

Julia showed Victorine a wrapped package. "I have a little housewarming gift from Argenteuil for Monsieur Manet."

"You mean 'King Edouard'?" André slid the girls a playful look.

"What?" Victorine said.

André recounted how at the Opera, he was seated behind two elegant married beauties whom he declined to name. They were extolling the many charms and fascinations of Monsieur Edouard Manet.

"Well, go on, what did they say?" Julia said.

"It seems a friend of theirs called Dominique—"

"Countess Dominique de Saint-Pierre?" Julia interrupted.

"I don't know, they just said 'Dominique.' Her parents commissioned her portrait, but there was more going on between the bedsheets than on the canvas."

Victorine rolled her eyes, but urged him to continue.

"As is his habit, Manet finished the portrait and immediately lost interest in her. When informed that their 'friendship' was over, the jilted girl threatened to commit suicide."

"Good heavens! The poor thing," Julia said.

"Naturally, she didn't succeed," André said, "as one can't really die from slitting one's wrists with a manicurist's file. But she left a dramatic note declaring her love for him. I overheard one of them say that Edouard Manet has a nickname: 'King Edouard.'"

"Why that?" Julia asked.

"Apparently all the women who've been in his bed call him Edouard the Great."

Victorine burst out laughing, and noted that a scarlet blush had crawled up Julia's face from neckline to hairline.

"I wouldn't know anything about that," Julia said. "He's a brilliant teacher, and I admire his talent. That's all."

Victorine was delighted by Julia's tortured expression.

"After our visit to Monsieur Manet's studio, I'm off to the Salpêtrière Hospital to visit a charity case," Julia said.

Victorine had heard of the notorious Salpêtrière Hospital, the women's mental asylum where all manner of flotsam and jetsam, prostitutes, the poorest of the poor, and the certifiably insane were incarcerated.

"Why must you constantly minister to madwomen and beggars?" André asked.

"I've been assigned a patient named Mademoiselle Marie by the charity committee. There's no better nourishment for the soul than good deeds."

Victorine tried, but she could not suppress a laugh.

"We'll leave the 'good deeds' to you saints. Sinners have more fun," André said as he took Victorine's arm.

"André, that woman with the boy in the photograph at Edouard's studio. Who is she?" Victorine asked. Julia nodded, indicating she was aware of that woman.

"Suzanne Leenhoff. She gave piano lessons to the children in the Manet household. He began a casual affair with her when he was a young art student. That boy isn't her younger brother; he's the son she had out of wedlock. When she became pregnant, she convinced Edouard, who was twenty at the time, that he was the father."

"So he supports her out of duty?" Victorine asked.

"I would say out of chivalry," André replied. "The child's paternity is unclear. But . . ." André shrugged. "He fulfills his obligations to Suzanne and the child, Léon, in the most perfunctory manner. She isn't allowed into his studio unless he specifically invites her. And that is never."

As they finally reached the top floor of Edouard's new studio, out of breath from the long climb up four flights of stairs, they entered the vestibule, where the odor of linseed oil, sharp and acrid, assaulted their nostrils.

Victorine gave the door a gentle push and squinted from the bright northern light flooding the studio from a wall of windows. She saw from across the room that Edouard was concentrating intently on a small corner of the canvas, adding daubs of white highlights with a long-handled paintbrush.

"I hope he's in a pleasant humor," André whispered.

In the two months since she began posing for him, Victorine had heard stories told of how Manet went through months of being his usual charming self, when for no discernible reason a dark mood seized him. He ceased painting and brooded in his room, withdrawn and paralyzed by self-doubt, riddled with inner turmoil. André believed that his moods were related to the seasons. They always seemed to strike in March and September. Baudelaire, she was told, called it "spleen" and posited that it was a component of a genius's mind.

They tiptoed closer for a better view of the painting. Most shocking was its huge size; it was of epic proportions, with a dimension traditionally reserved for history paintings commissioned by the state. The subject was a modern woman of the lower classes, a guitar singer, exiting a shabby cabaret. Victorine remembered how precisely Edouard had posed her clutching a guitar and a fold of her charcoal-gray cotton dress in one hand, the skirt slightly raised to ensure a hint of white lace petticoat peeking out. In her other hand, Edouard had instructed her to hold a small bunch of cherries to her mouth. The lace petticoat was intended as a subtle hint of her loose sexuality, and the cherries were a coded message of the sexual delight to be tasted by those lucky enough to make her acquaintance. He had painted a man leering at her from the shadows of the cabaret. Edouard intended to raise the desires of men by a certain message they read in her eyes. She had understood the part she had played, but now she saw that a part was played by the artist and the viewer as well, that of voyeur.

"Hello, may we come in?" Victorine called out.

Edouard, so absorbed in his work, seemed astonished that he had an audience. He wiped his paint-stained hands and welcomed them in. Julia followed him to the sink, stood by watching as he scrubbed his hands, and then held out a linen cloth for him to dry them. "I brought a little present for you from Argenteuil," she said, and extracted a rectangular box from her purse. "Just a small token."

"This is totally unnecessary . . ." He flicked the clasp on the ornately carved rosewood box and opened it slowly. He held up an extravagant paintbrush set for Victorine and André to see. "This is much too generous of you. I couldn't possibly—"

"No, I insist you keep it," Julia said.

Victorine caught the dubious look on his face.

Julia attempted to deflect the moment by turning attention to his painting. "Mademoiselle Laurent's portrait is magnificent."

"I plan to finish it in time for the Salon deadline. If those cowards dare accept it."

Julia mentioned a family friend, Monsieur Durand-Ruel, an art dealer who might be able to help him sell his work.

"That's kind of you, but I'm not interested in selling. Art is for art's sake. My goal is to educate the viewer. Open his eyes, albeit one eye at a time." He laughed.

Victorine was ready to leave and asked André if he would escort her home. They stepped outside onto the boulevard de Montmartre into a light spring rain shimmering on the cobblestones, sheathing the city in a silvery mist. Victorine hooked her white-gloved arm through his elbow and swayed her body seductively against his hip. "André, that society column of yours is very popular with rich gentlemen. I've noticed them at the smartest cafés; it's the first thing they turn to in the newspaper."

From his puzzled glance, he seemed to be wondering what she was leading up to.

"If you were to write about Edouard Manet's fascinating new model and mention my name in your column, I'd be very grateful." If only he'd agree, Victorine thought, she could use him to promote herself to a higher class of clientele.

"If I can help you in any way, I'd be happy to."

"Oh, wonderful." She smiled into his eyes. "How would you like to come by the boardinghouse tonight, my room around midnight, for a little visit?" she asked sweetly.

"Why, no. I mean, that's not necessary," he stammered.

"Oh, thank goodness." She turned to him, assessing him. "This makes our friendship perfect. You'd probably rather have Edouard, anyway."

She felt his body stiffen as he stopped short. He seemed astounded. She guessed he was worried that it was obvious to everyone, including Edouard. Her arm encircled his shoulder tenderly. "The only men who've ever been kind to me were the ones like you. You have nothing to be embarrassed about."

He turned to her, grasped both her hands, and raised them gently to his lips. At that moment, a visceral bond connected them unlike any she had ever felt. The moment passed, they dropped hands, and continued their stroll. André expressed pleasant surprise at her polite reception to his cousin Julia. "She's quite infatuated with Manet, you know," he said.

Victorine laughed. "She's no competition for me, if that's what you're hinting. She can't take my place." She took a few more steps, then turned to face him. "He'd ravish me in a moment if I gave him the chance, but I won't. Ever."

"Why not?" he asked.

"If he made love to me, it would end the tension he channels into his painting."

"Hmm, Samson shorn of his locks," André said.

"Something like that," she responded.

"You care for him, for his art, that much?"

"I don't care a thing about him or his art. I care for myself." To lighten the mood, she steered him toward a doorway. "Now, let's go inside this store and find a beautiful fan. I'll need it tonight when I go with you to the Opera."

She heard a sigh of resignation. He knew who would be paying for it; there was always a price for her company.

Several weeks later, Victorine walked among the flower stalls of Les Halles marketplace. Flowers were an extravagance she could little afford, although someday, she promised herself, she would have fresh flowers delivered every day to her *hôtel particulier*. When she was a grand lady, she would have a bouquet in every room. For now, every Saturday she came here and endured suspicious looks from the flower vendors, who recognized her as a voyeur, not a buyer.

The sun shimmered through the glass-and-iron roof, glistening on the green satin ribbons trailing from her bonnet. She leaned down to steal a whiff from a bunch of peonies in a tin bucket and jumped as she felt a tap on her shoulder. When she turned around, Edouard Manet stood behind her, grinning.

"Oh! You startled me," she laughed, clutching her heart in mock surprise.

"For you, Mademoiselle Victorine," he said, using the pet name he had taken to calling her lately. His cobalt-blue eyes seemed to laugh as he pulled a bouquet of white gardenias from behind his back.

"Flowers!" She reached for the bouquet and inhaled the heavenly scent.

"I've been watching you flit from stand to stand like some kind of bumblebee."

She laughed with him, and told him she was on her way up the rue de Turbigo to meet André for lunch. Would he like to join them? He was otherwise engaged, but he would accompany her part of the way since he was heading that direction as well.

As they began to stroll past the church of Saint-Eustache together, she stole glances at him. Edouard Manet carried himself so elegantly, touching his walking stick on the pavement with every step. It was unusual for a man to move with such masculine grace. And as he talked, his beautiful, large hands cut the air, expressing more emotion than many men could with a torrent of words. Another girl might be charmed to notice how his hair curled in an endearing way around his collar. Luckily, all this meant nothing to her. They reached the boulevard Sébastopol, where they were to take separate paths. She said good-bye, raised the bouquet of white gardenias to her face, and thanked him again for the flowers.

Lucky thing she wasn't a bit attracted to Edouard Manet.

Victorine and André lunched at a window table at Café Tortoni; Baudelaire joined them. "So, young lady. Now that you've been modeling for Manet, how do you like it?"

She confided that she loved it. While posing, he amused her with droll anecdotes and tales of his adventures in exotic ports of call as a young naval officer in the merchant marine.

"How do you manage to overcome the tedium of sitting in one position for so long? Frankly, he's asked me to do it, and I've refused."

"I'm accustomed to sitting very still and being quiet," Victorine said. She told Baudelaire that when she was a little girl, her aunt worked as a laundress for the Dominican sisters in a boarding school. Aunt Evelyne often took Victorine to work the days her boyfriend slept off his hangovers. Her aunt hid her in the laundry room under a table and demanded that she stay "quiet as a mouse," so as not to be discovered by the mother superior.

"Do you mean to tell me that you were forced to keep silent all day?" Baudelaire asked. "Is this another one of your fables, my dear? You needn't construct marvelous walls of defense against me. I have no ulterior motives."

She felt his large hand engulf hers, and genuine warmth flowed there.

"No, it's true, Monsieur Baudelaire. I discovered a reading primer lying around and taught myself to read under that linen-folding table."

He stared at her in disbelief. "You attended school, didn't you?"

She heard an almost fatherly concern in his tone.

"Yes, one day I was discovered by Mother Superior. It turned out to be a lucky thing, because she allowed me to enroll as a charity student with a tuition waiver. I attended for seven wonderful years until . . ." She stopped. "I'm sorry to go on about myself. I'm boring you."

"I don't believe you're capable of boring any man," he said with a laugh. "But do be careful. Parisian men are wolves, mademoiselle."

"I'm not naive. I understand men only too well. I'm sure of my goals, and I plan to conquer Paris."

"Well, I do worry about you. And I don't know which is worse: to achieve one's dream here, or not to."

Edouard finished his portrait of Victorine. It was accepted for the Salon exhibition in May along with another gem of his, a beautiful little still life of peonies in a vase.

On the opening day of the Salon, Victorine rode in Edouard's brougham carriage along with Baudelaire and André, down the Champs-Elysées toward the exhibition site, the Palais de l'Industrie. She glanced at André seated beside her, squirming in his seat. He had sprouted a case of the hives in anticipation of the controversy regarding the painting. The other two exchanged inanities as though nothing extraordinary was happening that day.

"It takes three or four lovers to support the lifestyle of the Countess de Castiglione. No one man has the fortune of five hundred thousand gold francs to support her palaces, jewels, and servants." Baudelaire leaned back against the tufted leather of the carriage. "I also heard that Madame de Jeumont charged two hundred thousand to attend a ball with one of her admirers! The emperor drove up her price by paying her one hundred thousand gold francs for a night of pleasure just the week before." He laughed.

Victorine loved hearing these stories about the famous *grandes horizontales.*

"My friend Princess Isabelle uses the same couturier as Madame de Jeumont. She told me Madame de Jeumont buys three hundred sixty-five pairs of kid gloves and wears a new one each day," Edouard said, adjusting the gardenia in his buttonhole.

"André, my dear boy, whatever is the matter with you?" Baudelaire pointed his gold-fobbed cane at André. "The way you're scratching, one would think you had fleas."

"I don't see how you two can joke and laugh at a time like this," André said.

"A time like what?" Baudelaire turned to Victorine. "Can't you just imagine those curmudgeonly art critics this very moment, their spectacles perched on their noses, circling Edouard's pictures like vultures, scribbling clever insults in their notebooks and cackling to each other like crones? They're little old ladies in gentlemen's clothes."

André clucked his tongue and said they would both be

worried if they had any common sense. After all—he wagged a finger—Edouard had been rejected so many times, he had not exhibited at the Salon for years.

Edouard affected a singsong voice. "How dare that mad-man Manet paint a canvas the grandiose size of a history painting yet with a subject as quotidian as a common cabaret musician? And she's clearly a woman of low morals, judging by the visual cues in the painting. This is unabashed radical-ism thrown in the face of the august academicians."

Victorine laughed, and Baudelaire said, "You may well ridicule them, Manet, but they're right to be worried about the threat you pose. The damage by the sweep of your paint-brush is greater than that of my pen. After all, prose appeals to the intellect, while art hits square at the emotions; is this not the most powerful weapon of all?"

The coachman whistled and tugged up on the lines, direct-ing the quartet of horses to turn off the Rond Point into the gravel driveway of the Palais de l'Industrie. They approached the venue of the Salon, a massive three-story neoclassical stone structure topped by an iron-and-glass barrel vault run-ning the entire length of the building.

As they waited in a long line of black carriages inching to the front entrance, Victorine felt a twinge of nervous excite-ment to see her portrait exhibited in public for the first time. She had never attended an opening day of the Salon, as it was a major social event with reserved tickets costing a premium. Wealthy Parisians considered it the ideal opportunity to engage in the spectacle of theatricality they adored, the men preening in their finest frock coats and top hats while the women showed off their newest creations straight from the dressmaker's. Victorine glanced down at her ensemble, a simple light-blue serge dress and white lace fichu. She wished that she had a beautiful new frock to mark this occasion, but Dr. LeBrun had been stingy lately, and she had to make do with what she had.

Edouard prepared her for the onslaught. "To them"—he waved his hand at the public streaming up the steps—"the art is just a background for society on display here. It's just another diversion, along with the theater, racing, endless balls, and adulterous love affairs, that helps them escape from their vast inner emptiness."

They pulled to a stop. Victorine paused as Edouard stepped down, then turned to offer his hand. She read in his gaze a reassuring calm; was her anxiety that obvious? But she felt elation as well. It was a combination of joy and dread, sweet and tart.

Edouard guided her up the marble stairs of the palace to the main entranceway, shaped like a triumphal arch. As Victorine gazed up, she saw on either side a bas-relief angel holding a trumpet to his chiseled mouth. In the space between the curve of the barrel vault, the words PALAIS DE L'INDUSTRIE were carved in the architrave. Atop that towered a statue of France crowned with a halo of stars and holding a victory wreath in each hand. As she passed under, she felt as though that sculpture was glancing down, evaluating her as she entered the building.

Edouard led her through the vast doors to the central hall, flanked by a double row of exhibition galleries. He explained his plan was to first search for Victorine's portrait, then his other entry, the still life, and meet up with a good pal, an avid art lover who was sure to be present on opening day.

"Manet, over here, old chap!"

Victorine saw a stocky, muscular gentleman bustling toward them, pushing himself through the throng. He was impeccably turned out in a fine wool frock coat, clutching a shiny black silk top hat in his hand. He was shorter than average and compensated for his lack of height with ramrod-straight posture, giving him the appearance of a military man. She supposed he was handsome; he seemed possessed of a jovial nature as he greeted them with an easy smile.

Edouard introduced him, but Victorine was distracted by a scuffle nearby. A guard was dragging a derelict out by the collar, a freeloader who had snuck in without paying admission. Victorine turned her attention back to Edouard's friend.

"So this is your muse? It is a great pleasure to meet you." He raised Victorine's gloved hand and lightly touched it to his lips. Turning to Manet, he said, "The crowds are impossible. I've tried to find your pictures, but . . ." He shrugged as he led the way through the foyer packed with the public.

In his conversation, he declared that he had not only inherited a family fortune from his late father, but a connoisseur's eye as well. He mentioned that he collected old master paintings and eighteenth-century European furniture. Victorine moved closer beside him the more he talked, and touched her ungloved hand lightly on his jacket sleeve. Was this cashmere, she wondered. And when he mentioned his Thoroughbred farm near Deauville, she turned up the light of her charm to full glow. "Is it possible we've met somewhere before?" he asked earnestly. She politely allowed the cliché to pass.

"Well, perhaps at the Opera. I'm a junior ballerina."

"A ballet dancer! I imagine you have several admirers?"

"No one special." Her dentist, LeBrun, was certainly no one special compared to an art connoisseur who owned a stud farm in Deauville! Victorine saw Edouard lean toward Baudelaire and whisper something. The two of them were clearly formulating a plan of some kind. She ached to hear what they were saying, a frustrating impossibility over the din. They passed through several crowded rooms trying to find the gallery with Edouard's portrait. She gazed up at the walls literally jammed floor to ceiling with row upon row of paintings, two thousand pictures in all, crammed against one another like passengers on the five o'clock omnibus. Finally, after fighting crowds in one corridor after another, they at last entered a small back room where Edouard gave a shout and pointed to *The Street Singer*. It hung at the very top, right below the crown molding. Even from this odd perspective, it was an arresting sight.

"My God, it's brilliant!" Baudelaire said. "The gaze of that woman. How she holds the cherries so seductively to her lips. It's mesmerizing."

"You can barely see it from down here," Edouard said.

"What an enchanting beauty!" the other gentleman whispered, and turned to Victorine, comparing her to the portrait. "A masterful likeness, Manet."

"What do you think of the painting? Never mind the girl for the moment," Edouard said, nodding to Victorine.

The gentleman contemplated the painting, his hand stroking his beard with a bristling noise, the intensity of his concentration palpable. "Edouard, you know my ideals are the Renaissance masters. This modern style is unfathomable to me . . . yet, there's something hypnotic about that painting. I can't explain it."

As they discussed the picture, Victorine gradually became aware that people were congregating around her and staring. A few began to whisper, to point at her and then at the portrait. More spectators began to jam the gallery as word bounced around that the painter Edouard Manet and his model were in the room with his controversial entry.

"You modern painters are ruining great French art," someone cried out.

"That monstrosity up there must be your idea of a joke!" someone else shouted.

"Let's get out of here before they string us up." Edouard grabbed Victorine's arm and led the way toward the exit. André and Baudelaire followed close behind; Edouard's friend was trapped among the hordes. They continued through the exhibition, past rows of treacly subjects—adorable sloe-eyed children; buxom, lush Venuses stretched out on ocean waves or emerging from the sea; military heroes on rearing white stallions—searching for his other entry. They finally found the still life and, evaluating it, a man introduced to Victorine as Maxime Du Camp. André whispered to her that he was a conservative art critic for *La Revue des Deux Mondes*.

"Manet, I saw your huge portrait of the guitar singer. Exactly what is she supposed to represent?" he asked.

"The end of your world, Maxime, and the beginning of a new one," Edouard said.

The following week, Edouard Manet's painting was the primary subject of discussion among every stratum of the populace, from fine drawing rooms to vegetable stands in the outdoor markets of Les Halles. Strangers recognized Victorine on the street and in the shops, and treated her like a minor celebrity.

She was shocked and delighted to open *Le Moniteur* and read an editorial in which she was mentioned as an archetypal "new woman," one unashamed of her own sensuality. A journalist from *L'Artiste* had learned Edouard's pet name for her, Mademoiselle Victorine, and had printed the sobriquet for all of Paris to read. In a fashion weekly, she learned that a dress designer, inspired by the subtle yet cunning gesture of Victorine holding up her skirt in the painting, had created the Street Singer tunic—a skirt that was looped up with a pannier puff to show a glimpse of lace petticoat. Seamstresses all over Paris were busily hunched over their new contraptions, "sewing machines," turning out copies of this new fad of the moment.

Edouard invited Victorine, André, and a few friends to his

studio as he gleefully assembled a stack of reviews. Victorine perched on the red velvet divan between Claude Monet and Camille Pissarro, who flirted madly with her, cajoling her to model for them. André ensconced himself on the floor at her feet. Baudelaire was there, as well as the young artists from the café—Auguste Renoir, Paul Cézanne, and Frédéric Bazille. She saw two new faces, and was told by André that they were Georges Bizet, the composer, and his wife, Geneviève.

"Listen," Edouard said, as he quoted from an editorial by Maxime Du Camp. "'The painting by Monsieur Manet is at once sad and grotesque. It is one of the oddest you could see. People come to the exhibition and laugh as they do at a farce. It is hoped that the jury will spare us the sight of such lamentable things as this in the future.'"

"Here's one Edouard is too modest to read," Frédéric Bazille said. "This is from Zacharie Astruc's weekly column. It says, 'One must have the strength of two to stand up under the *storm* of fools who pour in here by the *thousands* to jeer with stupid smiles on their lips Manet, one of the great personalities of our time.'"

Applause rang out. It was obvious to everyone that Edouard was thrilled his painting had tweaked the critics.

"The dullards misunderstand Edouard." Baudelaire rose to his feet. "There's a detachment among personal relations that Edouard captures on canvas. Social relations have changed in our modern world. Look at the mass production of goods! We don't have a craftsman turning out a piece of furniture or a pair of shoes, we have identical commodities churned out by drones toiling in factories. We've all become those mass-produced commodities."

Edouard plucked a volume from his bookshelf. "I've been reading a new treatise on the subject by this German fellow named Karl Marx."

A general buzz of recognition met the mention of the name.

"This is Marx's manifesto, commissioned by a socialist group. It's written in German, so I'm having it translated."

"I read German." Victorine motioned for Edouard to bring her the book.

"How is that?" Edouard asked.

"Alsace has been traded back and forth between Germany and France so often, we're bilingual." She opened to the first chapter and read a few sentences aloud in perfect German.

"Victorine, that fellow you met who hated the painting but loved the model. Do you recall?"

"I do." She wrapped her arms around her knees. Her black-and-white windowpane hooped skirt engulfed her in a pouf.

"Do you know who he is? Baron Robert de Rothschild."

"He's a Rothschild? What did he say about me?"

"That he would buy you anything you desire; after all, he's richer than God."

"Well, when are you going to arrange it?"

"Maybe after my vacation in the Alps. Did I mention my family's chalet near Moutiers? It's called Le Refuge. I go hiking in the mountains every summer and——"

"Don't you dare wait that long!"

"All right then, next week. I suggested we all meet at the Guerbois, but do you know what he replied? He said, 'The Guerbois? That dive? Don't be ridiculous. A girl like that should be taken to the Café Anglais.' So, I'll host a supper party. He'll join us and the rest is up to you."

"The Café Anglais! I've read about it in the society pages, but never . . . oh, Edouard!" Posing had brought this stunning opportunity, just as she had hoped.

"Victorine, what did *you* think of Rothschild?" He struck a match on his bootheel, lit a cigarette, and blew the smoke straight up above his head.

"Oh, he's a pompous duffer. But you'll see, I'll absolutely charm him."

"Of that, I'm fairly sure," he laughed. Suddenly, his mood changed. "Victorine, you're determined to be a kept woman, and Rothschild will be good to you. He's not the type to use a girl and toss her to the next customer in line." He narrowed his eyes against the blue cigarette smoke curling an arabesque around his face.

She evaluated him, trying to assess this professed concern for her welfare. It couldn't be genuine. A womanizer like him? What a ridiculous notion. Victorine affected a serious air. "I'm afraid there's a complication," she said. "His current mistress, the Countess Calli. From what I've read in André's column, she's a fiery Italian, considered one of the most beautiful women in Paris." She smiled slyly. "But don't worry, Edouard, she's quite old—thirty, maybe more. She's no competition for me."

He burst out laughing. "You're one in a million, my dear Mademoiselle Victorine. But you're right; there is no competition for the likes of you."

Chapter Four

Almost all misfortunes come from not having
stayed in our room.

—Blaise Pascal, *Pensées,* 1670

The Café Anglais on the rue Marivaux had the
reputation of a spoiled yet ravishing woman. People flocked
to it to be humiliated. By the rude staff, by the grandeur, by
the complicated seating chart, by the indigestible creamy
sauces and gamy meats. They paid obscene sums to say the
next morning, "Last night, at the Café Anglais, I . . ."

Victorine arrived for Edouard's supper party precisely at
midnight, on André's arm. As she followed the maître d'hôtel
down one of the many mahogany-paneled corridors lined with
red leather banquettes, she felt her heart pounding against her
tight bodice, felt small and more insignificant than the wallpaper. Silver-haired gentlemen in full formal evening dress,
seated at tables with bejeweled middle-aged ladies, appraised
her with a connoisseur's glance as she passed by. She knew that
when she looked back upon this night, it would be either the
definitive beginning of her rise on the social ladder or the end

of her dreams. She willed herself to feel as though she belonged, as though she could breathe this rarefied air.

She looked particularly ravishing, knowing it was the exterior of the package that was important. She had cajoled one of the hairdressers at the Opera to smooth her long curls into a sleek chignon and thread in tiny seed pearls, just as he did for the prima ballerinas. Her midnight-blue velvet gown with silver and gold lace appliqués was negotiated from the wardrobe mistress with the bribe of an expensive bottle of perfume, last year's Christmas present from Dr. LeBrun. She nervously fingered the choker at her throat, feeling as counterfeit as her rhinestone necklace.

André sensed her trepidation; he whispered in her ear that the other diners' envy would grow with each step she took to room number sixteen, the most exclusive private dining room, reserved for the chosen few. He told her, in his best gossip-diarist mode, that more naughty acts were committed under the skirts of those starched tablecloths than under the skirts of any brothel up on Montmartre.

They entered a scarlet Fabergé jewel of a room bathed in the golden glow of gas jets. The maître d'hôtel led them toward Edouard's table, past a Turkish pasha's son whose habit was to wear at least three hundred thousand francs' worth of rubies in a lavaliere around his neck. André pointed out the Duke de Brunswick at his customary table in the corner. He dined there with a different young actress every night, except Saturday, the night he brought his wife.

As they approached Edouard's table, he rose to introduce Victorine to his six guests, and seated her next to Baron de Rothschild. She smiled sweetly at Rothschild as he kissed her hand and noticed a scowl from his paramour, the Countess Calli. As the waiter took dinner orders, Victorine drank an entire flute of vintage 1845 Veuve Clicquot, feeling ready now to take on the formidable House of Rothschild.

At the commencement of dinner service, the waiters brought in gold-rimmed plates of pâté de foie gras. Conversation among the eight guests grew lively. "So, Mademoiselle Laurent, you're Parisian by birth?" Baron de Rothschild asked, leaning his elbows on the white damask tablecloth and gazing down the front of her bodice.

"Oh, no. I was born in Saint Petersburg," she said, taking a sip from her third glass of Château Lafite. She didn't look at Edouard, but felt him shoot her a glance.

"How did you come to live in Paris?" the baron asked.

"I ran away to join the ballet against my parents' wishes. I came here to follow my dreams."

She was annoyed to see Edouard stifle a laugh behind his hand.

"What a colorful life you've led!" the baron said.

"Saint Petersburg? Won't you grace us with a few words in your mother tongue?" Edouard said. "I adore a woman who can be pleasing in more than one language."

"Kack ve pashaviatii? Ya te lublu."

Victorine rattled off the only two phrases she knew, savoring Edouard's shocked expression. One of her former admirers was a midlevel bureaucrat attached to the Russian embassy, and she had picked up "How do you do?" and "I love you."

As the lids were lifted off the main course, a steaming pheasant under glass, the countess noticed Victorine's hand under the tablecloth massaging Baron de Rothschild's ego in the vicinity of his thigh. When the cheese boy rolled around his glass-domed cart, naming each type of cheese and its region in a grave, self-important tone, Countess Calli interrupted to announce that she felt ill, and asked the baron to take her home immediately. He didn't budge when she threw down her napkin and headed to the exit. The smitten Baron de Rothschild didn't even bother to escort her downstairs to his carriage. At the conclusion of dinner, when the dessert of flaming cherries jubilee arrived, the baron whispered to Victorine that he was very happy to have met her and looked forward to seeing more of her.

After enjoying some very pleasurable evenings in Victorine's modest room in her boardinghouse, Rothschild wanted her closer to his own home, a mansion in the newly developed Parc Monceau neighborhood on the fashionable west side. He found the perfect location at number 90 boulevard Malesherbes, a chic building of creamy Loire limestone and black wrought-iron balconies exactly five stories high, conforming to Baron Haussmann's strict regulations.

The leasing agent escorted them inside the tall wooden gates, through the cobblestone courtyard, and up four flights of stairs, opening the front door of the flat with a flourish. Victorine drew in her breath at the sight of the drawing room of verdigris wood paneling and gold-leaf boiserie. Her heels tapped against gleaming Versailles parquet floors leading to the entrance of an ornate boudoir. In the bedchamber, double French doors, tall enough to bathe the room with sunlight, opened onto a balcony facing the apartment building directly across the street.

"Do you like this one, my love?" Rothschild laid down his top hat and walking stick on the floor as they stood in the empty bedroom. The agent waited discreetly in the hallway.

"Only if you'll come to me here every night." Her lips grazed his ear.

Her gaze roamed the room, even as she nibbled his earlobe. She could scarcely believe that she would be living here! Events were proceeding so much faster than she could have ever imagined. His arms encircled her waist, and she felt his beard tickle her cheek. As he pressed her against his body, she looked over his shoulder. On the other side of the boulevard Malesherbes she saw a maidservant in the third-story window just opposite, arranging scarlet roses in a vase. Just like me, she thought, arranging events in the bouquet of my life.

"Monsieur le Baron," the agent called out.

As they discussed financial details, Victorine peered down from the third floor to the empty street below. She pressed her nose against the glass, idly wondering how far it was from here to Edouard's flat. What would he think of her new home? she mused, as she imagined furnishings and wall hangings.

It quickly became common knowledge that Victorine Laurent was Rothschild's new mistress, having supplanted the Italian countess. Victorine created a stir every time she sat in his box at the Opera, or went for a drive with him through the Bois de Boulogne in the new open carriage he had bought her. When she entered the Théâtre Français on his arm, they literally stood on their seats for a better look.

Through Rothschild's circle of friends, she was elated to gain two new admirers, a minor Russian prince and a wealthy munitions dealer. She was now officially a courtesan with several gentlemen calling at her apartment and sending expensive gifts, but Baron de Rothschild remained her primary protector.

In keeping with her new status, Victorine engaged the wardrobe mistress at the Opera ballet to design all her dresses. Victorine insisted they display the best of taste, although the necklines were cut a little lower than everyone else's, the better to show off her magnificent shoulders and décolleté. The fabrics were sumptuous silks and taffeta, with capes and jackets trimmed in fur. The bills were sent, as were all her expenses, to the Rothschild bank and conveniently settled by the devoted chairman himself, the head of the House of Rothschild.

Rothschild indulged her with luxuries she only dreamed of in her days with Dr. LeBrun. In addition to the beautiful apartment, he insisted that she have a maid, as all proper Parisian ladies should. So one rainy afternoon Victorine struggled to interview candidates, as André watched with amusement. She had requested André's help because she had heard that he grew up in his family's *hôtel particulier* attended by a staff of twenty servants. Sadly, he explained, they were reduced to just four in help after the palace was sold to pay off debts. An unimpressive parade of domestics continued, until a young woman breezed through the door rustling her orange muslin skirt and flooding the room with the Caribbean sunshine of her smile. She said her name was Toinette.

"Your references?" Victorine asked, as Rothschild had instructed.

"I worked in the governor's mansion in Martinique as an assistant pastry cook, ma'm'selle. I can bake galettes and tarts that will make your mouth water." She handed Victorine a letter of recommendation.

"Any experience cleaning, polishing, making beds?" Victorine read off a checklist prepared for her by Rothschild.

"Not really. But I guarantee if you hire me, you won't care if your beds are made or your silver polished because you'll be happy, singing a song all day eating my delicious madeleines!"

She was the one.

A few weeks later, her apartment was ready for its official unveiling for Edouard. Victorine nervously bustled about the living room, plumping pillows on brocade armchairs, obsessively arranging and rearranging Sèvres figurines placed prominently on a Louis XVI marquetry rosewood table. She glanced around for one final inspection and smiled with satisfaction at the eighteenth-century wood and ormolu furniture, the yellow silk damask drapes held back with heavy fringe tiebacks, the collection of green Moroccan leather-bound volumes of

Balzac, George Sand, and Stendhal, perfectly lined up on the bookshelf like soldiers standing at attention.

She heard a knock at the front door and gave a quick glance to check her reflection in the cheval glass. She had chosen a morning dress of coral shot silk, a Watteau robe richly embroidered with floral appliqués featuring a square neckline that dipped to display a new coral bead necklace courtesy of Rothschild. Her coral silk shoes and coral silk hose matched the entire ensemble.

Toinette announced that a gentleman was here, and threw a wink at her mistress. Edouard's gaze appreciatively scanned Toinette's face as he passed by, lingering over the beautiful bone structure. Victorine was annoyed to catch the alluring look Toinette gave him before dropping a quick curtsy and retreating hastily.

Edouard handed her a bouquet of white gardenias and set down a rectangular wrapped package on the floor behind him.

"Well?" Victorine waved her hand around the salon.

"Beautiful, Victorine. I see Rothschild's spared no expense."

"I adore the Louis XVI settee over in the corner, don't you? And the eighteenth-century Sèvres cachepot on the mantel, my absolute favorite."

"You and Louis XVI are very well acquainted, I see. And as for Sèvres porcelain, I'm *very* impressed." He smiled.

She opened a rectangular velvet box, extracted a pair of tan calfskin gloves, and pulled them on with a flourish.

"Do you know what these are?" She spread her hands and wiggled her fingers.

"Driving gloves, of course," Edouard said.

"Yes, and who has a carriage and pair? Me. I'm going to take the lines myself and drive you all around the Bois de Boulogne, and every single woman will be jealous when they see me driving my own carriage."

"I used to know a simple, provincial girl called Victorine. Now I find a grand lady has taken her place."

"What's wrong with beautiful objects? They make me happy. What of it?"

"Some people find pleasure from more enduring things. From friendship and love, for example." He watched her closely.

"Rothschild adores me. He buys me expensive presents to prove it."

"Love has a price?"

"Of course," she answered.

Edouard sighed and returned his attention to her new home. His gaze fell on an object that caused him to burst out laughing. There, in a place of honor, was the daguerreotype of his parents that she had taken from his studio on her first visit.

"My mother and father! Do you intend to tell people these are your own parents?"

She placed her hands on her hips, poised to descry this slander, but stopped. Why bother? He knew her so well. She smiled and changed the subject. "What are you hiding behind your back?"

"I've brought you a little housewarming gift."

She was immediately aware that it was a painting and tore off the paper wrapping greedily. It was the still life of peonies in a stemmed vase that remained unsold after the Salon.

"It's so beautiful, Edouard." She gazed at it lovingly, then set about to find the perfect spot for it. She held the painting over the fireplace, then took it to the opposite wall to see if he preferred it over the piano. "Here or here?" she asked.

When she turned around, he was staring intently at her.

"What is it?" she asked, startled.

"Here, come stretch out on this divan."

She was taken aback by his tone, yet followed his instructions and laid back, allowing him to place her arm behind her head, and cross her legs at the ankles.

"Yes, just so. Superb!"

At that moment, Toinette brought in a tray laden with a sterling-silver tea service and a plate of freshly baked, warm madeleines, diffusing the aroma of lemon and vanilla throughout the room. She set the tray down and beamed at Edouard.

"You may go now, Toinette," Victorine ordered.

"No, wait a moment. Come here." He grasped Toinette by her shoulders and steered her behind the couch, then pulled a bouquet of flowers from a vase and placed them in her arms.

"Edouard, what is this all about?" Victorine asked.

"Toinette, you may leave now. Thank you," he said, and waited until she had gone. "I've been thinking about the next Salon, searching for inspiration, and found myself considering Titian's *Venus of Urbino*. What if I portrayed a Venus of today? Not an allegory or a mythical deity. A nude portrait of a modern woman. It's never been done!"

"What exactly do you mean?"

"I envision you, lying supine on a couch. No, better yet, your bed. Your beautiful African servant stands behind, holding a bouquet of flowers a lover has sent. You gaze boldly at the viewer. Naked."

"What is the allegory?" she asked.

"Victorine, you're not listening—a *modern woman*, not an allegory. Proud of her sexuality, her nakedness. The look in your eyes will say to hypocrites: 'Go ahead and condemn me all the while you're desiring me.'"

An awkward silence settled between them.

"Who is it exactly you're labeling as hypocrites?" she asked.

"All of them, from the emperor down to the bourgeois banker."

"A banker like Rothschild?"

"Victorine, are you willing to stand with me against them, or are you just another common cocotte?"

"I'm the mistress of a baron, and a Rothschild at that. I don't want to do anything I'll be ashamed of."

"The only thing to be ashamed of is to be ashamed," he said.

As he rose to leave, she fought an urge to beg him to stay.

After the door had slammed, she glanced at the painting across the room and noticed a small change had been added since its display at the Salon. A calling card had been painted in attached to the bouquet. She approached the picture and saw that the card bore a little poem. She read aloud:

To Mademoiselle Victorine:

In her gaze, a fire ablaze,
In her eyes, the Paris skies.

—Edouard Manet

Chapter Five

Self-love is a part of love just as self-interest
is a part of friendship.

—George Sand, *Marguerite,* 1852

*V*ictorine hurried past the jewelry shops on the rue de la Paix. She'd been invited to tea by Julia Stanhope-Morgan at a fashionable new café called Le Chouchou. Taking tea was a chic new pastime copied from the British. It was de rigueur to be seen at tea between the hours of three and four thirty, followed by a carriage ride at five o'clock around the lake in the Bois de Boulogne.

As she walked she wondered why she felt curious to know Julia better. She reminded her of someone, but who? She had no female friends, relied only on men, yet Julia recalled someone from her past. Victorine entered the crowded tearoom to a farrago of chattering voices. Le Chouchou was decorated in the latest style, glowing with pale-pink lacquered walls. The same hue graced every visible surface, from the little pink cushions on wrought-iron chairs, to the waitresses' pink-striped uniforms, to their starched pink aprons. Victorine spotted Julia seated at a tea-rose pink banquette engaged in conversation with two elegant society doyennes at the next table. She hurried toward them, then stopped short.

"And her dress! The bodice was so sheer you could see right through the lace," one woman sniped.

"She and Baron de Rothschild disappeared from the party for an hour. It didn't please his wife much."

"I believe you're jealous." It was Julia's voice.

"She's a common streetwalker flaunting her wares. Look at that portrait of her in the Salon. Scandalous. Victorine Laurent is a glorified trollop. She entrapped a man to get jewels, furs, and—"

"How is she so different from any of you? You married to acquire those same things."

Victorine had heard enough. She stepped from the shadows and came forward.

Julia offered her cheek to Victorine and was taken aback when Victorine hugged her so warmly that she quite knocked her bonnet off.

"You're a darling to defend me," Victorine said.

The waitress interrupted with a silver platter of Viennese pastries. Julia eagerly dove into the sweets. Her manners were perfect, but her enthusiasm seemed odd compared to the French custom of restraint.

"Julia, last night at Baron de Rothschild's, I chatted with a fascinating woman who said her late husband was a Stanhope-Morgan. She introduced herself as Madame Jeanette McMillan. Is she related to you?"

With her mouth full, Julia could only nod. She brushed crumbs from her lips, and told Victorine that Madame McMillan had outlived three husbands, a Bonaparte, Julia's great-uncle Stanhope-Morgan, and her last husband, a Scottish laird.

"Well, she told me the oddest thing," Victorine continued. "She cautioned me to build strong defenses against gossip and betrayal. She said that Parisian charm dazzles as it plunges the knife in your back."

The two girls turned to gaze at the table next to them.

"Parisians can be so cruel."

"Especially to outsiders," Julia said.

"Alsatians like me," Victorine said.

"Americans like me," Julia sighed. "I always intended to leave Boston and study art here. I'm famous in my family for being rather strong willed. I was teased because I was different. I wanted to sketch and be left alone. When I was nine years old, I decided I'd become a great artist. And I mean to do it, too."

"So, we both came to Paris to escape our pasts," Victorine said. "We're more alike than I knew."

"And we share Edouard," Julia said.

Victorine thought, I never share a man.

They sat in silence for several moments.

"Edouard asked me to pose for another portrait, but I declined because it's too controversial—a nude."

"He would paint it brilliantly."

"But it's not an allegory. It's a modern-day woman; a challenge to the hypocrisy in our society," Victorine said.

"Those are the values I reject. That's why I adore Edouard's modern style of painting," Julia said. "My advice is, sit for the nude portrait, Victorine."

"You're right. I'll do it. I *hate* them." She nodded at the table next to them.

"Oh no, darling." Julia placed her hand on Victorine's. "We mustn't hate, but love our enemies. The Golden Rule."

Victorine stared in utter disbelief. A memory flashed through her mind. That remark brought to mind Mimi, a little girl she knew years ago. She and Victorine had played together and shared a precious brief friendship before the girl moved away. That was who Julia resembled.

"May I ask you something I don't understand? Why do you volunteer at the Sâlpetrière Hospital and minister to that insane woman?" Victorine asked.

"I take care of Mademoiselle Marie because I hope someone would do the same for me," Julia said.

"But what do *you* gain from it?" Victorine could not fathom it.

Julia laughed. "I've helped someone less fortunate. That's all."

"I'll never forget the way you defended me to them," Victorine said softly, and indicated the society doyennes.

"But of course, that's what friends do. It's normal," Julia said.

I wouldn't know, thought Victorine.

Victorine was eager to share her decision with Edouard. As she climbed the stairs to his studio, she heard his voice above. She leaned over the railing, looked up, and spied him kissing a woman in his doorway.

"Don't go, darling."

"But Edouard, my husband . . ."

"Stendhal said, 'Beauty is nothing but a promise of happiness.' Promise me happiness and stay." His voice was a caress.

Victorine felt a pang of jealousy. She stepped back to see who would come down the staircase. Probably one of his little waitresses or a shopgirl from the painting-supplies dealer. The woman descended the stairs, and Victorine looked straight into the exotically slanted eyes of the fifty-year-old Princesse de Bourbon-Parme, "La Chinoise." Her career as a courtesan had culminated in a royal marriage proposal; such was not unusual in Imperial Paris. Several generations of aristocratic families boasted a former courtesan as a decorative flower on their family trees. The two women instantly recognized each other as they passed on the staircase, nodded an awkward greeting, and parted.

Victorine steamed up the stairs two at a time and banged on Edouard's door with her parasol. When it swung open, she swept past him into his flat and whirled around. She could barely control her anger as she sensed the pleasure that had taken place in these very rooms before her arrival. "So! Now it's Princess Isabelle you're screwing."

"What have we here, the green-eyed monster?" he asked in a laconic tone.

"What was she doing here?" Victorine was appalled at the words tumbling out her mouth, detesting her own shrill voice, yet unable to control herself.

Edouard glanced at a canvas covered with a drape. Immediately, Victorine flew past him and lifted the muslin cloth. She gasped. It was a nude portrait, only partly finished, of the beautiful Isabelle, who had just left this very room.

"She commissioned me to do a private portrait. It's a professional relationship."

"Am I to be replaced by her?" she asked, rage in her voice.

He sat quietly, the suggestion of a smile hovering at his lips.

As the moments passed, she felt confused. Why was she doing this? She was fully aware of how attractive he was to women, of the palpable charge of his sexuality; that he could have any woman he desired. "I don't care whom you're sleeping with. But I, alone, am your model, and I won't stand for competition!"

He continued to sit silently. Exasperated, she slammed her parasol against the arm of his chair. "Well, aren't you going to answer me?"

Finally, he uncrossed his long legs and stood up. He walked toward her, gently tilted her face up, and gazed down intently into her eyes.

"No one," he said softly, "no one could ever replace you, Mademoiselle Victorine."

He grasped both her hands tenderly, walked with her to the doorway of his bedchamber, and stepped aside. When she entered the room, she gave a little cry of surprise. The walls were literally covered with *études* of her, studies of individual compositional elements, tacked up all around. He had drawn her in profile and full face, charcoal studies of her hands, her back, her delicate feet, views from the posterior, from the anterior. There were sketches of her exotically portrayed in the costume of a Spanish matador, erotically posed as a nude bathing, and in many other imaginary roles.

"Now, do you think anyone else could inspire me to this?" He waved a hand around the room. "I can close my eyes and sketch you. I know every centimeter of you."

"I'm so sorry. I acted like a fool." She encircled her arms around his waist and hugged him. She heard the thumping of his heartbeat against her ear and felt suddenly very safe and at peace. It was an unfamiliar feeling that she wanted to make last. "I came to tell you that I'll do that nude portrait for you, the Venus."

"I'm not going to call it *Venus*. I'm calling it *Mademoiselle Victorine*."

Chapter Six

A painting is something that requires as much trickery, malice,
and vice as the perpetration of crime.

—Edgar Degas (1834–1917)

*V*ictorine stripped off her corset as Edouard pulled on
his painter's smock. She slipped out of her pantalets as he
dipped his brush in paint pots. She bent down to unbutton
her ankle boots as he reached up to fasten the drop cloth. She
clicked shut the clasp of her seed pearl necklace as he flipped
open the cap of his turpentine bottle. She stretched out,
completely nude, on the chaise longue, arched her back, and
checked her pose in the full-length cheval glass, where she
caught Edouard's reflection watching her for an instant before
he turned back to his paintbrushes and palette.

Adjusting his little stool, Edouard seated himself. He immediately rose and approached the chaise longue to re-
arrange the folds of the white bedsheet before returning to
his easel. He regarded her for a moment, approached again,
and turned the couch forty-five degrees toward the light. His
boot toe tapped a staccato rhythm on the floor. After several

moments, he spoke. "This portrait will change the direction of art forever, Victorine."

She asked if that wasn't a good thing.

"For art, yes. For you, I can't say." He gazed at the canvas. "This painting will be in art history books and so will your name. Immortality . . . are you ready for that?"

She teased him to stop being so serious. "Isn't controversy good for business?" she said, but the grave expression on his face unnerved her. "How devastating could this painting be?" she asked. She knew his strict policy: never show models a work in progress because their subjective opinions interfered with his creative vision.

"They'll blame you for all sorts of evil things, like bringing down bourgeois values and decency and even the flag of France. Your identity will be linked forever with this portrait."

"I had no identity until you gave me one."

"I simply portray the woman I see."

"No, I've become the woman you portray."

He stared at her from his stool. She realized that she had opened her heart momentarily to him. It was a slip; she hadn't meant to.

"Well, then, Mademoiselle Victorine," he said, "let's turn the world upside down."

Two months later, the exhibition of Manet's scandalous nude portrait caused a social earthquake that rattled all layers of Parisian society from its top hat down to its lace undergarments, precisely as Edouard had predicted. In addition to depicting the sexuality of a contemporary woman, he had achieved maximum shock value by painting Victorine reclining at eye level to the viewer, staring boldly back at him. Amusing sexual jokes played hide-and-seek in the painting:

a small black cat curled on the corner of the bed punned the rude slang term for a woman's sexuality; bedsheets rumpled in such a way as to mimic the female vaginal opening. Victorine's hand demurely covered her private parts while blatant references to her sexuality confronted the viewer. All of it was meant to underscore the hypocrisy of Second Empire values.

Naturally, the critics missed the point and reported that the artist had completely lost his mind; they questioned his sanity in painting a female nude in a contemporary context. She was clearly not a classical goddess, nor an allegorical wood nymph, and this represented blatant rebellion against the elite canon of the Academy. The general public reacted viscerally, and branded the painting an insult to morals. Clerics and conservative politicians used their respective pulpits to warn of the dangers of modern ideas and the decline of civilized French values as represented by this young woman in the painting, this Mademoiselle Victorine.

A week after opening day of the Salon, André dropped by. Victorine greeted him in her drawing room with tear-swollen eyes. "André, I'm ruined." She dabbed a handkerchief across her lashes, smearing her cheek with black mascara. She handed him a note from Rothschild. "'Baroness de Rothschild demands that I immediately cease illicit relations with you or face divorce proceedings, due to the public humiliation brought upon her and the children,'" Victorine repeated from memory as André read the note. An enclosed solicitor's letter warned her not to contact Baron de Rothschild at the bank or his family home, and gave her until the end of the month to vacate her beautiful apartment. She had expected this *might* happen, but the abstract concept and the shock of reality were two quite different things.

André dropped down beside her on the yellow silk divan. "What about your other admirers? That Russian prince who's mad for you. Or the cabinet minister who sends exotic flowers?" André pointed to an arrangement of hothouse lilies in a crystal vase.

"*No one* will want me after this," she sniffed.

"Don't worry, Victorine. I'll support you."

She burst out laughing through her tears. This was not the response his brave gesture deserved, but it was so preposterous. "With what?" she said.

"My allowance and my earnings from the tabloid."

"You're very sweet, darling André." She shook her head and tenderly took his hand. "But I'm afraid your allowance and earnings . . ." Her voice trailed off.

"Then Edouard. He's wealthy enough to pay your expenses."

"If I sleep with him, I'll be like all the rest. I'd mean no more to him than that—" She snapped her fingers. She saw from the puzzled look on his face that he did not understand. He didn't know sex like she did.

"Then what shall you do? Haven't you any savings?"

"Oh, you're a fine one to talk about savings."

"I have gaming debts." He shrugged. "If you'd only allow him, Edouard could—"

"No! I don't want to hear that again."

André repeated office gossip: Empress Eugénie's circle, particularly her dearest friend, Baroness de Rothschild, were celebrating Victorine's demise. They encouraged the tabloids to publish editorials disparaging the painting as a warning to other ambitious *lorettes* with designs on their husbands.

⁓

Toinette held up a fistful of bills: the florist, the draper, the coal merchant, and a reminder of overdue livery-stable fees. Victorine would have faced eviction from her home if Edouard had not stepped forward and temporarily assumed the lease, and Baudelaire had not "lent" her two thousand-franc notes.

Toinette dropped a curtsy and left Victorine to ponder the time she had resorted to earning a little extra money at Madame Goulue's. It was a drastic step; up until then, Victorine had only been mistress to three Parisian gentlemen sequentially. She had been supported discreetly by their largesse, but each had moved on to other girls and left her no option but to knock on the door of Madame's Goulue's establishment. The madam had checked her teeth and her posture, and thrust her hand down the front of her pantalets. When Victorine had recoiled, Madame Goulue had explained that it was just a precaution to screen out the male prostitutes who dressed as women. "I don't service *that sort of* clientele," she had said. Victorine stared wearily at the pile of mail stacked on the bureau. One looked curiously like an invitation. Could this be? The invitations had stopped abruptly after opening day of the Salon.

She unsealed the ecru envelope and extracted a calligraphed card requesting her presence at a seventy-fifth birthday celebration for Madame Jeanette McMillan. She skimmed to the end of the invitation. The host of the ball was the Duke de Lyon. Who was that? She didn't recall ever meeting a Duke de Lyon.

~

"Who is this Duke de Lyon?" Victorine asked, as she showed André the invitation.

"The duke? He's a member of Emperor Louis-Napoléon's privy council, rumored to be the illegitimate son of the Comte de Gabbay, a dashing military hero of the first Napoléon's Grande Armée," André said.

"I've read about Philippe de Lyon in the newspapers. Isn't he a politician?"

"De Lyon spearheaded Emperor Louis-Napoléon's coup d'état in 1851. As reward for his loyalty, he was appointed vice president of the legislative body."

"So he's a politician," she said in a disappointed tone.

"He also was an early investor in the railroads and owns the lucrative Paris-Bordeaux line, and the railroad station as well. His fortune includes sugar beets, newspapers, and real estate," André said.

Victorine brightened up at this last bit of information.

André continued: "De Lyon has several enemies, but the most powerful is Empress Eugénie. They're bitter rivals for the emperor's favor."

Victorine stared at the invitation in her hand. "Why did he send this to me? I don't even know him."

André said that he would make some inquiries and return.

A true gossip diarist can't succeed without "anonymous" sources. André returned only a short while later with the full story. According to witnesses, the Duke de Lyon had accompanied Emperor Louis-Napoléon to the opening preview of the Salon for the imperial family. He had paused in the gallery before the shocking portrait, captivated and oblivious to the condemnatory buzz of courtiers and invited guests. With a snap-of-the-fingers disdain for Empress Eugénie, Baroness de Rothschild, and all the rest, he had sent Victorine the invitation.

Word spread of the duke's gesture. Victorine suddenly found the interdiction against herself lifted. Former admirers began to send bouquets of flowers, invitations to social events stacked up on the mantel in her drawing room, and even Rothschild sent a note of apology offering to resume his financial support.

While all of Paris rollicked to the white-hot scandal of the duke's interest in Victorine, Monsieur Boucheron, society jeweler to the haut monde, sent a note congratulating her. He mentioned how thrilled he was that the only thing covering

Mademoiselle Victorine in the infamous painting was the choker of triple-strand seed pearls and diamonds of his very own design. Boucheron offered Victorine her choice of jewels to borrow for the upcoming fancy-dress ball at the Duke de Lyon's palace. She asked Baudelaire and André to accompany her for their good advice and excellent taste.

As the threesome strolled past the jewelry shops on the place Vendôme, Baudelaire galanted Victorine on his arm. She glanced at their reflection in the shop windows and noticed that he was tall and graceful in a masculine way, an exact mirror to her physique in a feminine form. She paused under the domed cupola of Boucheron's jewelry shop.

"Look, it's her!" A shopgirl nudged another.

"Is that Baron de Rothschild?"

"Don't be ridiculous. That's Charles Baudelaire, the writer. You really are so ignorant." The shopgirl pointed at André. "The little man with them is her manservant."

"So how do *you* know all this?"

"From the newspapers, silly."

Victorine glanced at the two girls whispering, heads bowed together, as she passed their counter. "Good morning, Ma'm'selle Laurent," they cried in unison.

Boucheron bustled toward her and kissed Victorine's hand lightly.

"Mademoiselle Laurent! You are more beautiful and charming than ever! Marquis." He offered a polite bow to André. "Monsieur Baudelaire, always a pleasure," he said as he bowed once more and waved his hand toward his private office.

His assistant scurried to place three chairs at the reproduction Louis XIV desk in the inner sanctum. "Look at these magnificent suites. Diamonds and emeralds. Or do you prefer rubies and pearls?"

"It's very kind of you to entrust me with such an extravagant loan, Monsieur Boucheron." Merely two months ago, she had placed orders with no thought to cost. Today, she was dependent on his largesse.

He shrugged. "You've been a loyal customer. I'm pleased to do a very minor favor for you, mademoiselle." He tugged back his lace shirt cuffs and placed a black velvet box before her, lifting out a magnificent diamond-and-emerald necklace with matching bracelet and earbobs. "Just the thing to set off your beauty at the Duke de Lyon's masked ball," Boucheron said. "This birthday celebration will be the party of the year! *Everyone* will be there."

"'Wearing anklets as well as bracelets is trying too hard to be splendid,'" Baudelaire quoted.

Boucheron was unacquainted with Longinus, the Greek critic of the first century A.D. He muttered that this fellow's sayings were bad business for jewelers as he dipped at the knees and clicked the clasp of the dazzling diamond-and-emerald *collier* around Victorine's neck. In his opinion, courtesans were roughly interchangeable with one another. He draped the diamond-and-emerald bracelet around her wrist as she held out her arm. But never, at least not to his memory, was there such a phenomenon as young Mademoiselle Laurent here. She was back in the running, he predicted, a safe horse upon which to place his bet. If she came charging back to success, he, Roland Boucheron of the place Vendôme, would be swept along with her.

They heard a commotion at the front of the store and an assistant burst in.

"Her Majesty the Empress is arriving! She's early, Monsieur Boucheron!"

They rushed to the window. An imperial procession approached; Victorine drew in her breath at the sight of outriders in green and gold preceding an open calèche with postilions in powder and tricorn hats. A squadron of palace guards cantered behind to bring up the rear. The empress was surrounded by two handsome equerries and several gorgeously dressed ladies. Bystanders on the pavement doffed their hats and cheered as she regally waved to the crowd. Though she was a tiny figure, she descended from her carriage with the gravitas of one who has played this familiar scene for all of her adult life.

"Oh my God. Oh my God!" Boucheron trembled. He scurried through his shop barking orders and nervously smoothing his balding head.

"Look away, Victorine, it's Medusa herself," Baudelaire said, turning from the window.

"Why, Baudelaire, what do you mean?"

"Don't you remember the vicious stories planted about you in the tabloids after the Salon? She's the devil, Victorine. Just accept my word for it."

Victorine remembered reading that Empress Eugénie routinely spent fifteen hundred francs on a dress; her aunt Evelyne earned two francs a day as a laundress.

Eugénie smiled and waved to the sales staff as she entered. She was engulfed by her entourage, her ladies-in-waiting, her burly guards. Boucheron pranced through his shop, bowing obsequiously while directing her to the private viewing room. As they reached the doorway, Boucheron suddenly clapped his hand to his mouth as a horrified look flashed across his face. It was too late. Eugénie locked eyes with Victorine, startling her with an expression of pure contempt.

"I beg your pardon, Your Majesty," Boucheron stuttered. "You're acquainted with the Marquis de Montpellier and Monsieur Baudelaire . . . and may I present this young lady—"

"I know who this *lady* is," she said. "I've heard tales of her from Baroness de Rothschild and I've seen her portrait at the Exhibition. I believe we've all seen entirely too much of this *lady*." She turned on her regal heel, and the entire imperial party left the shop in an uproar of confusion, with Boucheron trailing them out the door flinging apologies.

Victorine was stunned. Tears of humiliation stung her eyes, but she fought them back, determined not to show such emotion in public. She accepted Baudelaire's proffered arm and the three exited through the back door.

The evening of the Duke de Lyon's masked ball, Victorine performed the ritual of her toilette in her dressing room. Baudelaire was to be her escort for this evening. When he arrived, she greeted his reflection in her mirror with an affectionate smile. He radiated elegance in evening clothes of the finest cut, a handsome sight from his silk top hat right down to his patent-leather evening slippers. In one hand he clutched a gold knobbed cane, in the other a fanciful mask with a Punchinello nose.

"Why do you always arrive early? Don't you know it's very rude?" she teased.

His gaze skimmed the soft curves of her face, recalling the lines of his own poem comparing the graceful, long necks of Parisian women to those of a beautiful, doomed bird. "Why do you say it's rude, my love?" he asked.

"I don't want my escort to see the artifice, the little secrets I have for improving on nature," she laughed.

He responded very seriously, oblivious to her jovial tone. "Nature? How ugly and animalistic is nature. Nature makes us look after our own self-interest. It has nothing to do with beauty or goodness." He kissed her cheeks lightly as she offered up her face and sat down on the settee opposite her vanity table.

She picked up her pot of rouge and turned around. Her Oriental dressing gown parted slightly and revealed the swell of her bosom. "But natural beauty is valued by all cultures, except the savages," she said.

"On the contrary." He was playing the orator now. "Those savages adorn themselves with feathers and fabrics and have more depth to their souls than all our philosophers. Women should astonish and charm us. When women use makeup, corsets, all sorts of tricks, they lift themselves above nature, the better to conquer hearts and rivet attention!"

"Baudelaire," she called out from behind her coromandel screen, "I've never met a man who adores women more than you do, yet despises the power they have over men!" Baudelaire had lost his father at an early age. He had been coddled by his young mother, whom he adored, until she "betrayed" him and remarried. Since then, he had harbored a love-hate relationship with her and projected that feeling onto all women. Baudelaire would only have sex with prostitutes: They required no pleasure, and no dangerous expectations of commitment deluded them.

"Women? Diabolical creatures, all of them, the symbol of modern Paris. There's only one I adore—Victorine Laurent," he said.

A playful throw of her silk stocking meant for Baudelaire hit André square in the face as he entered the boudoir. He raised it to his lips and kissed it. "Ah, I shall treasure this forever." He stuffed it in his breast pocket in place of his silk square.

"André, tell me more about the Duke de Lyon," she called out.

"He's simply the wealthiest man in Paris. Maybe all of France. He's a social lion, Victorine, a charter member of the Jockey Club. What a contrast to the emperor, that balding, short dumpling. The ladies tell me de Lyon is quite the Don Juan," André said.

"The ladies? Is he a famous lover?"

"Is he! De Lyon publishes sonnets under a pseudonym and writes for the theater. You've heard of Jacques Offenbach, the producer and songwriter? He's one of his theatrical pals. They sometimes collaborate, mounting productions in the private theater of his palace for the entertainment of his friends. He's an avid art collector whose collection of Rembrandts is so famous, he has public viewings of it once a month in his home."

The hairdresser arrived, a young Spaniard named Raoul, and began to set up the tools of his trade. He carried a leather satchel that resembled a doctor's bag, out of which he extracted brushes, combs, and a curling iron. Victorine seated herself in front of the mirror and continued the conversation.

"This is going to be a most important night," she said solemnly. She caressed the magnificent diamond-and-emerald necklace nestled between her collarbones and turned to face Baudelaire and André, but the hairdresser sighed his displeasure.

"We must hold our head steady, Mademoiselle Laurent." He hunched over, meticulously threading clusters of small rhinestones through her thick hair.

Victorine looked intently into Baudelaire's eyes. Although he had been born into wealth and comfort, she adored him for his empathy. "The Duke de Lyon's worth more than all the rest combined," she said.

"Be forewarned, my dear. This man could be the first to break your heart."

"What heart?" she laughed.

"Nevertheless, be cautious, Victorine," Baudelaire continued. "You're venturing into an entirely different world. I worry for you."

Victorine attempted to brush off this mood. "I can take care of myself. Always have, always will."

She was ready for her ball gown, and called in Toinette. While the gentlemen exited to wait in the hallway, Toinette steadied her mistress as she stepped into a pair of long pantalets trimmed with lace.

"On my island, when a woman wants to entrap a man, she wears a locket holding the fur of a captured animal. The scent of the prey has the magic in it," Toinette said. "I have a locket like that."

"Have you been eavesdropping?" Victorine raised an eyebrow.

"I never do!"

Toinette opened the double-door armoire to choose the undergarments Victorine would wear: a corset trailing ribbon lacings, a stiff wool petticoat, a second petticoat padded from the knees down, a three-layered petticoat of Alençon lace trim and a muslin underskirt.

Toinette placed the undergarments down carefully on a silk tufted bench, then helped Victorine with every layer until she was ready for the ball gown. Victorine bent at the waist and stretched her arms forward as Toinette pulled the bodice over her head and knelt on the floor to smooth the voluminous skirt. Victorine checked her reflection in the full-length cheval glass and adjusted the blue velvet fichu framing her shoulders and skimming her famous breasts. The dress was made of ten yards of sky-blue silk velvet striped with white silk satin with a lovely scattering of pink brocaded carnations draping the bodice and garlanded across the skirt. White Chantilly lace bordered the flounced hem, which fell to the floor in graceful folds.

Toinette handed her mistress a pair of elbow-length white evening gloves and a handmade blue silk moiré mask trimmed with white ostrich plumes.

"You're a goddess, ma'm'selle." Toinette squeezed Victorine's hand. "I'll run to my room and fetch the locket."

Baudelaire and André watched from the doorway.

André exhaled a long whistle at the sight of Victorine.

"Good God! You're a vision of loveliness," Baudelaire said.

"Thank you, my darling." She smiled up at him as she handed him her cloak to drape over her shoulders.

Toinette reappeared and placed a trinket in the palm of Victorine's hand. She also handed her a tiny silk bag containing a crunchy substance. "Wear the bracelet on your wrist. See, it's engraved with the seal of the moon, a powerful aid to lovers. This little bag is filled with dried rosebuds. Tuck it into your bosom, ma'm'selle, and the next man you meet will become your lover or husband."

Victorine smiled at Toinette and allowed Baudelaire to fasten the clasp around her wrist. Her skirt was too wide for Baudelaire to escort her through the door, so he and André simply followed behind like dutiful acolytes.

Chapter Seven

> Pleasure and Pain are represented as twins,
> since there never is one without the other.
>
> —Leonardo da Vinci (1452–1519)

As they inched through the insufferable traffic jam of the carriage-clogged Champs-Elysées toward the Duke de Lyon's palace—known as *le petit coin d'amour,* the little corner of love—rain clattered on the metal roof of the coach like artillery fire. Victorine sat next to André and across from Baudelaire in the brown leather interior of Baudelaire's carriage, fidgeting with her fan and jostling André every time she readjusted the folds of her voluminous skirt.

"So he asked me if I'd ever been Madame George Sand's lover. And I replied, 'Of course, hasn't everyone?'" Baudelaire roared with appreciation for his own wit.

"Why are we crawling along like this!" Victorine cried, interrupting Baudelaire in the midst of his monologue. She had not heard a word; her mind churned on one objective—how to orchestrate her first meeting with Philippe de Lyon. "Baudelaire, I need your advice—tell me what to do to capture him."

"That would be like giving Manet advice on how to paint."

André pointed out that the Duke de Lyon was considered the most eligible man in Paris. "The duke has the most fascinating women available to him, from the aristocracy to stage actresses. They pursue him relentlessly."

Baudelaire tapped his fingertips together in a pyramid. "Use the tactics of Napoléon: ambush and entrap. Intrigue him by seducing and rebuffing, exactly the opposite of what he would expect."

"The old charm-and-harm maneuver." André gave her a playful poke, but she didn't laugh.

"Try to display the utmost sangfroid to his power and wealth. You'll have to be a good actress this evening, my dear," Baudelaire said.

She gazed out the window at the slanted sheets of rain beating against sputtering gas jets in the streetlamps.

"Just look at this crowd! They're all headed for the duke's palace," André remarked.

"The most aristocratic nobility and the wealthiest arrivistes find their names side by side on his guest list," Baudelaire said.

"Why would financiers and real estate speculators be invited to dine with a duke?" Victorine asked.

"He needs their capital, that's why. Financiers have always acted as intermediaries between the bourgeoisie, from which they spring, and the highest nobility, which they aspire to join. They lend money to the crown or the state and marry their children into the highest ranks, managing to erase the stigma of lowly birth for subsequent generations. That's how new blood and fresh ideas circulate through the corpus of the ruling class."

They finally reached the rear facade of the palace fronting the boulevard. The carriage lumbered through the wrought-iron gates and passed under the palace along a circular driveway that led to a formal courtyard. Victorine leaned forward and peered up at the edifice, which was set back on a raised terrace. Every window was ablaze with light and music poured out the front doors, held open despite the rain. Liveried servants in eighteenth-century-style frock coats, knee breeches, and silk stockings held umbrellas over the elegantly coifed heads of guests scurrying up the white marble steps. As they pulled up to the palace and the carriage doors opened, Victorine felt her stomach muscles tighten like a fist.

Once inside, she clutched Baudelaire's arm and drew in her breath. It was difficult to suppress her impulse to marvel. Formerly the official residence of an Orleanist prince, this palace was more ornate than any private home she had ever seen. Her gaze rose to the ceiling by Boucher, court painter to Madame de Pompadour, featuring an azure sky and putti frolicking among pink clouds. A sumptuous double marble staircase swept up to a wide hallway of sparkling crystal chandeliers and gilt-edged mirrors, where servants directed guests to the Grand Salon.

They entered through double doors to a semicircular room surrounded by half columns and rococo floral scrollwork. Victorine lowered her sky-blue silk moiré mask and stared at hundreds of flickering tapers shimmering over the crowd of men and women unrecognizable behind feathered, spangled, sequined masks. Their dark reflections in smoky mirrored eighteenth-century piers created an atmosphere as mysterious as engravings she'd seen of Carnivale in Venice. Waltz music flowed from the adjacent ballroom, punctuated by the occasional laughter and humming of guests as they whirled around the dance floor. The ladies' ball gowns of lapis blue, ruby, and canary yellow dazzled against the gentlemen's black evening tailcoats and military regalia.

André nudged Victorine. "Look, Princess Rimsky-Korsakov."

A woman passed by wearing a Russian court dress sewn with precious rubies and diamonds in floral garlands. He pointed out an Anglo-Indian princess in an ensemble covered with feathers escorted by an Eastern prince in a pink satin tunic wearing a necklace of jewels so heavy that he stooped as he walked. Another woman came dressed as the Queen of the Forest in a dress appliquéd with green emerald branches and a faux fur squirrel dangling from her belt.

When the guest of honor arrived, she was greeted by an enthusiastic burst of applause. Madame McMillan entered through the double doors escorted by two young men, one on each arm. She smiled and waved brightly. With the light step of a coquette, she traveled around the perimeter of the room, greeting guests and thanking them for coming to her party. When she spied Victorine, she motioned for her to approach.

"Happy seventy-fifth birthday, madame, and may you enjoy many, many more," Victorine said.

"You are ravishing tonight, my darling girl!" They touched cheeks lightly. The dowager flashed open her fan. "Have you met my nephew, the Duke de Lyon?" she asked.

"Not yet, madame."

"I predict he'll fall madly for you."

A buffet supper awaited in the dining room on several banquet tables of astounding abundance. André rubbed his hands and headed straight toward them. "As mangy journalists of every era know, there's nothing more thrilling than a gratis meal. Locusts would envy the skills I've developed," he said.

Victorine and Baudelaire watched with amazement as he swarmed over the spread, plate in hand, building a tower of pâté de foie gras, *salade des légumes truffés, galantine de gibier, poulet à la glace*, grapes, and fresh peaches, accompanied by a crystal flute of champagne.

"You're first on my dance card, André, but will you be able to move after you've gobbled all that?" Victorine laughed.

He handed his plate to Baudelaire.

"I would rather dance with you than drink nectar of the gods." He bowed.

She accepted his arm as he pulled his mask down over his face.

When they passed into the adjoining ballroom, all heads turned. The men stopped in midsentence to admire, while the women exchanged glances of disapproval.

Victorine carried herself with the perfect poise drilled into her at the barre. Shoulders thrown back, posture perfectly straight, hips thrust forward slightly, she glided through the crowd, a majestic swan on her sylvan lake. "Who is that young woman? Is she a duchess?" Victorine overheard a woman whisper to her escort as she passed by.

As she scanned the room searching for de Lyon, she spotted Edouard behind his mask. He looked unmistakably dashing in his black frock coat, white tie and waistcoat, and white dancing gloves. She saw him flirting with a girl Victorine judged to be about twenty, with frizzy dark hair and an indecently low-cut gown. As she watched, he leaned close, brought his lips to her ear, and whispered a remark that elicited a honking laugh. Victorine pointed her folded fan at them. "André, who is Edouard's quarry over there?"

He squinted for a better look, then said he didn't know. André grabbed the elbow of Lady Smith-Adams, a notorious gossip, and inquired the identity of the young lady with Edouard Manet. The old bat whipped off her mask, peered through her lorgnette, and announced that she was a young stage actress by the name of Sarah Bernhardt, currently starring at the Comédie Française.

Victorine and André exchanged shrugs. Never heard of her.

"Let's dance, shall we?" Victorine pulled André onto the dance floor.

"The conductor"—André pointed with his chin to the orchestra—"That's Johann Strauss, the composer of these beautiful waltzes. And that"—he nodded toward a flamboyantly dressed woman with synthetically red hair—"is Princess Mathilde Bonaparte. She's cousin to Emperor Louis-Napoléon. At least she's dancing with a male partner tonight. She can go either way, if you know what I mean."

Victorine sensed a ripple of whispers floating from lips to ears. Rothschild and his homely wife had appeared at the entrance to the ballroom. This was the undisputed highlight of the evening, the very epitome of the Parisian moment. All attention was riveted on them, but Victorine willed herself to focus her gaze firmly on André, blissfully dancing with her and completely unaware of the opéra bouffe unfolding behind him. The Baroness de Rothschild, dressed in a gorgeous ball gown and weighed down with jewels, greeted friends and waved a carefree hello to several people around the room. All the bit players, the cream of society, acted their roles as well, feigning ignorance that Baron de Rothschild and his wife stood only a few feet away from the woman whose nude portrait had been the cause of his worst marital woes.

Several dances later, Victorine was tapped by Edouard, who was awaiting his turn on the dance card.

He collected her in his arms and began to waltz her around the ballroom, their bodies in perfect rhythm. She simply had to admire how dashing he looked tonight, a perfect paragon of masculine elegance in his exquisitely tailored evening dress. She wasn't even aware that her white-gloved hand caressed the nape of his neck or that his arm firmly encircled her waist. "Well, look who's angling to win you back." He nodded to Rothschild, tripping over his wife's train as he tried to dance closer to Victorine.

She dismissed Rothschild with a shrug. "Edouard, have you ever seen such opulence?" she asked, casting a glance around the ballroom.

"There isn't one thing here that isn't vulgar or hopelessly ostentatious. Don't be dazzled, Victorine. Philippe de Lyon's got all the charm of a snake slithering through the grass, so don't be the little bird he swallows tonight."

"That's not what Madame McMillan told me." She spotted the dowager in her place of honor on a dais, conducting the music with her fan.

"He's powerful and coldly calculating, a man who knows how to manipulate anyone to get anything he wants," Edouard said.

"And just how do you know all of this?"

"I've seen him in action. I'm acquainted with him through the Jockey Club, and I have friends who've had business dealings with him. He gambles only when he knows he'll win. He races his own Thoroughbreds, speculates in dubious government land deals, and he's the real brains behind the throne."

"What's wrong with a man who has power?"

"It's how he uses it."

"What exactly does that mean?"

"Allow me to give you a little example of his tactics. On the eve of the emperor's coup d'état, de Lyon was seen at the Opera seated between Victor Hugo and the legislative leader, Adolphe Thiers. At dawn the next morning, these two gentlemen were dragged out of their beds in their nightclothes and hauled away by policemen on orders from de Lyon to arrest all opponents of the coup."

Nothing he said could intrigue her more.

As the waltz ended, Rothschild caught her attention and signaled to her. Victorine turned away. A few moments later, a servant slipped her a note in which he begged for a meeting in the music room. She agreed with a discreet nod of her head, then crossed the gleaming black-and-white marble expanse of the hallway. Now her task was to decipher which of the many doors led to the music room in this labyrinthine palace. She continued, past another hallway lined with marble columns, until she found herself in a quiet wing of the palace. Her heels echoed down the hall until she stopped to peek in the next doorway and gasped. She stepped into a private art gallery lined with masterpieces. This was the famous personal collection of the duke's Rembrandts.

Suddenly, the door slammed shut behind her. Victorine whirled around. "I wouldn't be a proper host if I didn't introduce myself. I'm Philippe de Lyon." The deep, warm timbre of his voice resonated.

"Honored to meet you, monsieur le duc." She removed her mask. "My name is——"

"Mademoiselle Victorine. Yes, I know," he said. His gaze caressed her face and traveled down her body.

Her heart hammered in her chest so loudly, she was sure he could hear it. "I should go, someone's waiting for me . . ."

"Please stay. I'd like to show you something. It will only take a moment." The music grew faint as he led her past the paintings down a narrow hallway toward private apartments. They approached a heavy mahogany door that led to a small, wood-paneled study lit by a fire roaring in the fireplace. An ebony cabinet of curiosities at the far end of the room held a collection of ancient gold antiquities. Philippe raised the gas flame in the globes on the wall sconces.

"Napoléon brought these back from Alexandria as tokens of love for Empress Joséphine, spoils of war from Egypt," he said. "These necklaces and earrings are more than three thousand years old." He studied the reflections of firelight flickering across her face. "They're objects of adoration from the pharaoh to his mistress. The lovers died centuries ago, but his devotion lives through this beauty," he said.

She smiled at him and he smiled back, but she saw something else in his eyes that frightened and excited her.

"The beauty of works of art, like the beauty of the soul, are immortal. There's a beautiful Venus on display at the Salon that I intend to possess."

"Manet's paintings aren't for sale."

"I said I want the Venus, not the painting."

She was taken aback by this remark.

"What would you give to own her?"

"It all depends. I'm a pragmatic man; I would do anything for her as long as I receive returns on my investment."

"What? No talk of love, of flowers and romance?" She smiled.

"Very good, Mademoiselle Laurent. You're dispossessed of those foolish romantic notions most of our young beauties are saddled with."

His tone changed and turned serious.

"But you would be mine, exclusively. I won't share you with Rothschild or Manet or anyone else."

"I don't have a romantic relationship with Edouard," she said.

His silence expressed his skepticism.

"I don't," she insisted.

"If you become my mistress, I'll give you the best of everything and spoil you as you deserve to be spoiled. But I won't be a cuckold. I wouldn't relish the gossipmongers having a good laugh at me behind my back."

This was curious. Here was the Duke de Lyon, one of the most powerful men in France, worrying about drawing-room chatter.

"Why does it matter what small minds think?" she asked.

His manner stiffened perceptibly. "When one is born without a name, one spends his whole life protecting it."

She was stunned. With all his accomplishments, de Lyon was still driven by the shame of his illegitimate birth.

"I don't know . . ." She feigned disinterest, just as Baudelaire had instructed her.

De Lyon stepped closer and removed his mask. He was more handsome than she had expected. He took both her hands in his and turned them palms up. Slowly, he raised them to his lips and kissed the pulse points on her wrists. She felt an unfamiliar stirring of passion within her. Then he raised her chin with one hand, and ever so slowly lowered his mouth to her lips. She swayed into his body and felt his physical desire. The crackling fire behind them sputtered and the rain beat against the heavy paned French doors. She told herself sternly to stop this immediately. She pulled away from him so suddenly, it startled him.

"I must go." She tried to turn away, but he held her wrist firmly.

"Mademoiselle Laurent, I always get what I want."

She met his gaze and gently unclasped his grip from her wrist.

"As do I."

As she hurried back to the ball, her smile spread into a delighted laugh. He wanted her, exactly as she had hoped! She spotted Julia and André, flushed from dancing. Julia was dressed magnificently in an elaborate gold lace gown and wore makeup for this occasion. Even so, her face recalled gently rolling New England foothills, white clapboard houses, and neatly planted fields. Powder and rouge could never veil her wholesome visage.

As Victorine approached, Rothschild hurried to her. "What happened? You never came," he whispered urgently.

"I . . . I got terribly lost. I'm sorry," she lied.

He spotted his wife giving him the evil eye and scooted away. She grabbed a champagne glass off a passing waiter's tray.

"Victorine Laurent? Is that you?" She heard a familiar voice and was surprised to see Anne Arlette. Anne performed an elaborate show of greeting Victorine with kisses and hugs. "My dearest Victorine! Oh, how wonderful to see you again." Her cheap eau de toilette wafted around her like a cloud of gnats.

"Lovely to see you, Anne. Are you still at the ballet?" Victorine asked.

Anne waved her hand dismissively. "Oh, no. I'm retired. I've a protector now. He's extremely generous and won't hear of me working anymore." She pointed in the direction of an octogenarian sporting a crooked toupee. "His name is Walter LeCochon, and he plays an important role at court: adviser to Empress Eugénie. He wants to meet you, Victorine. Would you say hello to him?"

Anne signaled, and the deformed troll eagerly limped toward them.

"Enchanted, Mademoiselle Laurent." He bowed comically. "Your beauty on the canvas is only matched by your beauty in the flesh," he gushed and bowed again. When he straightened up, Victorine felt a vague discomfort, but dismissed the feeling. After some small talk, they drifted away.

The rest of the soiree whirled by Victorine. She danced with various partners, all the while trading glances with the Duke de Lyon, who chose not to dance, but chat with his guests.

By three in the morning, the last waltz was played and the guests bid fond farewells.

She had mentioned to no one that today was her nineteenth birthday.

The next morning, Victorine rolled over in bed with a headache pounding in her temples and an ominous foreboding in the pit of her stomach. Toinette knocked softly on her door. "Are you awake, ma'm'selle? This just arrived for you by messenger." She handed Victorine a small package. As Victorine turned over the enclosed note card, Toinette craned her neck for a better view of the sender's crest.

I just want you to know . . . I'm still smiling.

With love and devotion,

    P de L.

She reread it twice and untied the ribbon. As she opened the package, she gasped. One of the priceless Egyptian artifacts she had admired the night before, an ancient bracelet of braided gold, lay nestled in the black velvet box. She slipped it on and admired its perfect fit, as though made for her wrist. She closed her eyes and imagined herself wearing a beautiful dress, tilting a silk-fringed parasol against the sunlight, dazzling in a vulgar display of jewels, as she strolled beside the Duke de Lyon through the Tuileries Gardens. She wouldn't forget her ordinary friends: André, Edouard, Julia. They would be welcome in her salon, right beside European royalty and the crème de la crème of Paris. Then she leaped up and began to rummage among the bedclothes, scattering wrapping paper and ribbons as she searched.

If he intended to visit, where was his calling card?

Chapter Eight

In matters of the heart, nothing is true
except the improbable.

—Madame de Staël, 1766–1817

*B*etween New Year's and Lent, Parisians basked in six bacchanalian weeks of revelry culminating in Mardi Gras. It was "the season for the seduction of the senses." There were fourteen masked Opera balls beginning at midnight and lasting till dawn, debaucheries of every depraved sort to satisfy all appetites, hordes of pretty *lorettes* strutting the streets, crowds of merrymakers, Punchinellos and buskers, choral singers and prostitutes.

Victorine's diary was crammed with invitations: Rothschild, as well as a stable of other admirers, escorted her to masquerade balls, dance musicales, and glittering social events. Victorine held her salon each Wednesday evening. Baudelaire was her star attraction, reading poems from his own scandalous *The Flowers of Evil* to illustrious writers like Victor Hugo and young unknown ones like Emile Zola. While Victorine's reputation as a hostess grew, Toinette's reputation as a pastry chef grew as well. Victorine served warm chocolate *macarons* and scintillating conversation to Prince Dmitri, a Russian émigré, and to various ambassadors, artists, and leading industrialists, who coveted the opportunity to meet in her lemon-yellow parlor for musicales, literature readings, and discussions of current events. There were plenty of brilliant distractions of all types, but Philippe de Lyon gnawed at her mind, and spoiled her enjoyment. One evening, as she sat in the magenta silk interior of her carriage next to Julia, her melancholia became obvious.

"Something's troubling you," Julia said.

Victorine was startled out of her quiet mood. "Not at all." She feigned a bright smile.

"Please tell me."

Victorine sighed with resignation, lifted her wrist, and displayed the gold bracelet, which she wore every day and never removed. "Philippe de Lyon."

"Don't forget my brother. He's crazy for you," Julia laughed. Angus Stanhope-Morgan fit Victorine's qualifications, being a millionaire many times over, but his goal was marriage. He had confided to Julia that his Christian ways could tame Victorine's independent nature. He believed he was just the fellow to mold her into a devoted wife and mother, if he could only get her back home to Beacon Hill.

The carriage veered off the Pont des Invalides and onto the rue de l'Université. A short three blocks off the Seine, they arrived at Madame McMillan's *hôtel particulier*. Victorine stepped down from her carriage, conjured up her usual joie de vivre, and prepared to make her entrance.

André, his wool evening cape draped over his arm, awaited them in the entryway of the ancient mansion. He escorted them up the wide stone staircase, revealing the special treat in store that night. Hector Berlioz himself had consented to conduct selections from his *Symphonie Fantastique*. André whispered a rumor that the aging composer had been Madame McMillan's paramour half a century ago.

They followed a footman to the music room, where a rock crystal chandelier and huge bronze torchères bathed the entire room with shimmering candlelight. Rows of gold bentwood chairs faced a shallow stage at the front of the room. A quartet of elderly musicians tuned their instruments as the guests murmured above C major and G minor trillings. The dim light created a challenge to find Baudelaire, but Madame McMillan forbade the use of gas lighting in her home, convinced that hidden dangers lurked among all scientific novelties. Victorine finally spotted him. He waved a program and indicated three seats beside him a few rows behind the hostess.

Madame McMillan looked resplendent in a magenta taffeta frock and a matching *collier* of rubies and diamonds buried in the folds of skin encircling her neck. Her gaze swept the room approvingly from her perch in the front row as she surveyed the luxurious dresses and elegant ensembles. She rose and motioned enthusiastically to a new arrival. "My Mathilde's here!" she cried. "Over here, my darling girl!" She waved her folded fan in a circle above her head.

"Oh, look, the famous 'aristocratic bohemian,'" Baudelaire said.

"What sort of beast attacked her hair?" André asked as he nudged Victorine. It was dyed an unearthly shade of burnt orange, and frizzled into a crow's nest. The woman's coiffure drew the unabashed stares of the entire audience.

Victorine watched her wave to various faces around the room.

"That is Princess Mathilde Bonaparte," André whispered into Victorine's ear. Princess Mathilde was called the "bohemian princess" in the tabloids, and was the undisputed goddess of the hostess pantheon. She considered herself better educated, and better suited to reign over the realm of art and intellect, than anyone in Paris, including the empress.

"Mathilde staked out a special place in Louis-Napoléon's heart from the time he was just a pretender-in-exile. She was actually considered a marriage candidate for him when they were both in their twenties. But the Bonaparte family didn't expect him to amount to much and married her off to a wealthy Russian prince forty years her senior."

The princess despised her abusive, drunken husband, André said, and began a liaison with the handsome Count Alfred-Emilien Nieuwerkerke. The fact that Mathilde and Nieuwerkerke were lovers was an open secret, conveniently overlooked by both their spouses. André recalled overhearing a British diplomat, a most proper Victorian gentleman, confront Princess Mathilde about the French imperial family's public displays of adultery. She had famously answered, "But darling, upper-class sex isn't vulgar!"

Victorine shushed André's gossiping as Mathilde and Madame McMillan approached. Mathilde kissed André, and greeted Baudelaire with a handshake. "You haven't met my darling friend Mademoiselle Victorine Laurent," said Madame McMillan. "She's the goddess of beauty you've heard about, Mathilde. Isn't she divine?"

Mathilde warmly, almost lasciviously, kissed Victorine's cheeks and held her hands apart, appreciatively evaluating the curves of her body. "Mademoiselle Laurent, I've heard tell of your salons. I'd love you to attend one of *my* literary gatherings. Promise you'll bring that luscious Edouard Manet with you! Next Monday, eight o'clock?"

"That's the night of darling Philippe's homecoming," Madame McMillan said.

Victorine tried not to betray any particular interest at the mention of his name.

"Oh, Aunt Jeanette, I'd forgotten. I hope that Romanoff woman isn't following him back to Paris. They say"— Mathilde leaned toward her aunt—"she lives on cigarettes, absinthe, and idle chatter. I declare, that adventuress is the Russians' revenge on us for Napoléon. Have you heard . . ." She whispered in Madame McMillan's ear. The older woman burst out laughing.

Victorine tried to recall where she had heard the name Romanoff. Yes, she thought she remembered it from a new novel Baudelaire had recommended called *War and Peace*. She longed to hear Mathilde, but the cacophony of noise and laughter all around made it impossible. Applause rolled across the audience, and the elderly maestro wobbled to the podium to take his bow.

Victorine didn't hear a single note of the magnificent music for the turbulence swirling in her own mind. So *this* was why he had been incommunicado for these many months! She glanced around. Rothschild and his checkbook were back in her life, and there were plenty of wealthy and powerful men to be charmed, right in this room. There was a prince of Luxembourg over there. And that one, gazing at her across the aisle, wasn't he a famous American tycoon? She smiled seductively at him, then sat back smugly satisfied. If the Duke de Lyon wasn't fascinated by her, there were many in Paris who were.

She snapped open her fan fiercely.

After all, she was the famous Mademoiselle Victorine.

Victorine and Edouard had developed a working relationship so seamless, she rarely needed instructions. She had found a way to express the promise of sex in her gaze, the arch of her back, the parting of her lips. She usually left the studio by noon and met Julia on the stairway as she arrived for her lessons. Sometimes their sessions overlapped when Edouard ran overtime.

On just such a day, Victorine was changing out of her costume in the small dressing area off the studio when Julia arrived and set up her easel. She glanced out and saw Edouard watching Julia as she untied the ribbons of her bonnet and tossed her cape across his divan. Just the other day, he had remarked to Victorine, "Isn't she quite graceful for such a diminutive girl?" Victorine knew the French admired women of talent and intellect, writers like Madame de Staël and painters like Elizabeth Vigée-Lebrun. Julia had told Victorine that Americans found it bizarre that she expressed her opinions and engaged in intellectual discussions. She confided that she was well aware that her looks were ordinary, but didn't agree with her own father, who said that men could not be attracted to her mind. Well, Victorine thought, watching her, she may be a sophisticate in the intellectual sphere, but in the sexual realm, she's a wanderer without a map.

"Julia, I want to show you something," Edouard called out as he extracted a sheaf of papers from a desk drawer. "First lesson of the day: how to look. Here's a photograph by Nadar. What do you see?"

"I'm not sure what you mean," she replied.

Victorine smiled; she knew the answer. It was the absence of chiaroscuro.

"Is there chiaroscuro, any subtle shading?" he asked.

Victorine knew that Edouard eschewed the academic tradition of chiaroscuro, which had dominated oil painting since the Renaissance. He had told her it was artificially created by a single light source from a high, north-facing window, and that northern light was cool and unchanging, carving deep shadows on the body. When Edouard posed Victorine, he utilized natural light from a wall of windows in his studio that fell full face on her, the exact technique used in photography.

"Next, look at these Japanese woodcut prints." He displayed some illustrations of Mount Fuji. "What do you see?" he asked.

"Flatness. Bold, simple design," Julia answered by rote. Victorine saw that she was gazing at Edouard's lips, not at the prints in his hand.

"Very good. And this is similar to . . ."

She was silent.

"Similar to photography," he said. "Julia, don't rely on your optical eye. Trust your artist's eye. Remember what I told you: Bad art is bad because it's anonymous. An artist shouldn't be like anyone he has ever seen or even anyone who has ever existed."

Julia searched his eyes and said nothing.

"All right, then," he said. "That's enough theory. If you're planning to submit that portrait of your sister Edma to the Salon jury, there isn't much time to finish her." He returned to his painting across the room.

Victorine emerged from the dressing room, said she was off to Le Bon Marché for new gloves, and left them to their lessons. As she was about to climb into her carriage, she realized she'd forgotten her parasol. She debated returning all the way up the stairs. But it was her favorite, so she decided she'd best retrieve it before it became mislaid among the props. When Victorine pushed open the door, she stopped before she called out. The conversation between Edouard and Julia gave her pause.

"Don't you like it?" Julia asked, her tone plaintive.

"I want you to develop your own signature, Julia, use brushstrokes individualized by your hand alone. Express more fluidity. Echo the speed and congestion of modern life."

"But I worked so hard on it. I was up till two in the morning!" She sounded exhausted and overwrought.

"Stay up till three! Don't be satisfied with mediocrity. This is cliché art student crap. Fix it."

"How?"

Victorine heard sobs. Unable to resist, feeling like a snooping interloper, she leaned forward slightly and peeked through the archway. Edouard indicated for Julia to move aside and took a seat on her stool. He dipped a rag in linseed oil, then smeared it across one section of the canvas to erase the paint. "Stop!" She jerked the cloth out of his hand. "You'll ruin it!"

"Too much ego, not enough humility," he said.

Julia crossed the room and dropped onto the divan. She said that she had never hated anyone as much as she despised him.

Oblivious, Edouard picked up a brush and blithely painted over the blotched mess, conjuring a beautiful image to the surface. Julia sat forward and observed. He added touches here and there, daubing a bit of lead-white highlights on the hair, the skirt, wherever he felt the need. He was taking liberties with her work simply because he was the master and she, the pupil. After some time, he turned to her.

"You see? Do you see the difference?"

She folded her arms across her chest and refused to answer.

"What kind of teacher would I be if I didn't correct you?"

She continued to sit in silence for several moments, then approached the painting. It was better, of course, she said, but it was no longer hers, and she could not forgive him that.

"I'm sorry if I wounded your pride. Would a cognac cheer you up?"

Victorine had seen enough and began to tiptoe out. But she stopped when she heard the tone in Julia's voice. She sounded almost—*almost*—coquettish.

"Edouard, there is only one way to regain my good graces."

"And that is?" he asked.

Victorine turned again to spy through the doorway.

"Your next Salon portrait, I want you to paint me instead of her."

Victorine's hand flew to her mouth to cover a gasp.

"Be serious," he said.

"I *am* serious." She pressed up close to him. "I'll give you my *total* self."

He gathered both her hands and brought them to his chest. "Julia," he said softly. "Julia, I'm not for you. Please trust me."

"But Edouard, I would take such good care of you. I could make you happy."

"The last thing I want is someone to take care of me. I want someone who'll drive me stark raving mad."

"I love you, Edouard, and nothing can change that!"

Victorine's mind was reeling. How could Julia debase herself this way by throwing herself at Edouard? And how *dare* she scheme to usurp her as his model!

"Julia, let's forget this happened today, shall we?"

"As you wish. But you'll still be my teacher?" Victorine saw the longing in her gaze, and realized it was not the conclusion of this matter.

"Yes, I am your teacher."

Victorine backed out and pulled the door shut noiselessly. Even Julia, the kindest, most principled person she knew, was waiting to steal away what was hers.

By the first week in March, Rothschild had purchased a dark bay mare with excellent bloodlines at the equine auctions in Deauville, and hired a young riding instructor from a top equitation school to teach Victorine to ride. One day, her strapping teacher complimented her in the presence of Rothschild on her excellent "seat" and allowed his gaze to rest on the shapely curve of her booted ankle as she perched sidesaddle on her mount. He was promptly dismissed by Rothschild and replaced by a paunchy, balding ex–cavalry officer.

After an invigorating ride one morning in April, Victorine and Rothschild returned to her apartment, where the aroma of freshly baked *brioches au sucre* greeted them. She was about to serve him coffee when Toinette urgently gestured her to the hallway. She produced an envelope from the pocket of her apron. "This just arrived by liveried courier," she said, and hopped from foot to foot, unable to contain her excitement. Victorine took the thick ecru envelope, turned it over to read the seal, and caught her breath. It was engraved with the coat of arms of the Duke de Lyon. She exchanged glances with Toinette. "I'll open it later." She pointed to Rothschild, waiting patiently in the dining room.

"The messenger insisted a reply was expected immediately."

As Toinette peeked over her shoulder, Victorine tore open the wax seal and read the calligraphed card. It was an invitation to a house party for the opening of hunt season, requesting "the pleasure of Mademoiselle Laurent's company" to spend a fortnight at the country château of the Duke de Lyon in Anjou. Elation swept through her. Then her joy turned to sobriety. Why should she accept? Victorine turned over in her mind the eight long months of silence. The more she thought about it, the angrier she grew. This was unacceptable treatment. She tossed the envelope dismissively onto the pile of rejected invitations. Toinette shook her head, muttering to herself.

Victorine and André were invited for lunch by Baudelaire a few days later at his country club, the Racing Club de Paris, situated in the heart of the Bois de Boulogne. As they strolled the flagstone pathway winding through manicured lawns,

Victorine's white muslin dress billowed in the breeze and André was obliged to hold on to his straw hat. Victorine loved this park, which had been built by Emperor Louis-Napoléon. It really was "a marvel of Industrial Age ingenuity" and imperial ego, as the papers stated. Louis-Napoléon, exiled to London after the fall of Napoléon I, was a great admirer of Hyde Park, and when he returned decided to turn a tangled forest at the edge of Paris, once a royal hunting preserve, into a park fit for "the capital of Europe." Detractors said that Parisians were so enamored of artifice that they preferred this sham imitation of nature to the real thing. But Victorine enjoyed every corner of the park, from the ice-skating rink in winter to the kiosks, bandstands, and outdoor restaurants in the summertime. When she drove her sporty phaeton around the two lakes, she didn't mind in the least that they were actually lined with cement, filled with water piped in from Passy, and decorated with artificial rocks painted to look authentic. There was also the racetrack, Longchamp, which was built by a consortium led by the Duke de Lyon. Victorine had learned from André that de Lyon had exploited his position as Louis-Napoléon's trusted confidant to coerce five commercial sponsors into fronting half the prize money for the Grand Prix, while inveigling the city of Paris to put up the rest. It was rumored he had profited handsomely from the resultant business. For ordinary Parisians, though, the Bois wasn't a calculated financial investment, just a playground for sophisticated adults.

They greeted Baudelaire at his usual table on the canopied terrace overlooking the pétanque field, where older gentlemen in shirtsleeves played a friendly game of boule. In the near distance, two ladies lobbed a tennis ball in a restrained match on a grassy court.

"You can't turn down this amazing opportunity, Victorine," André said. "Entrée to a social event like this—"

"Stay away from him," Baudelaire said.

"But this could be everything Victorine's worked for," André said.

"Is it true? After all my warnings, you still want to land him?" Baudelaire asked.

She nodded.

"Then do as you like." He scowled.

She changed the subject and they enjoyed a lovely alfresco meal. After lunch, she and André bid good-bye to Baudelaire. On the carriage ride home, André suggested that she seek advice from others. "Why not consult Madame McMillan? He is her nephew, after all. And Julia. What does she think?"

"I am seeing Julia this afternoon, but not to discuss this," Victorine said. "We have another matter to settle."

Victorine and Julia strolled under the arches of the rue de Rivoli, their parasols twirling in unison. Carriages rolled by on the busy thoroughfare fronting the Louvre and the Tuileries Palace, and pedestrians jostled past as they perused shop windows.

"How is your latest painting progressing?" Victorine asked.

"Edouard made me so cross. He wiped it down and repainted it. The picture is better, but he didn't have the right."

Victorine was unsure how to proceed. Disclosing her true feelings was unfamiliar. "He's a tyrant of perfectionism," Victorine said. "Sometimes when he poses me, I feel like a contortionist."

"And he forces me to rework a painting until my back aches. I don't understand what he wants sometimes."

"I always know exactly what he wants. He told me that's why I'm his muse." She shot a glance at Julia. "No one has the right to displace me as his model. No one."

Julia stopped and stared at Victorine. "How did you know I asked for that?" Victorine ignored the question. "To you, he's just a convenience to further your career. I love him," Julia said.

"A woman can't will a man to love her. Least of all Edouard," Victorine said.

"He doesn't belong to you. I knew him first." Julia set her lips in a determined line. "We want him for different purposes. I'm no threat to you."

She was correct about that, Victorine thought. Edouard would never be satisfied with Julia while he was still fascinated by her, the one woman who wouldn't have him.

"Let's not allow this to come between us." Julia took Victorine's arm. "I need your advice on an important matter. Come in this milliner's shop and help me choose a new bonnet."

Victorine followed André's counsel and invited Madame McMillan to tea at Le Chouchou.

"Now listen to me, my girl." The dowager wagged her finger and jingled three gold bracelets with portrait lockets of her three late husbands. "You are not to refuse my nephew. Of all the foolish ideas!" She smiled slyly. "Though he doesn't realize it, you're the hunter and he's the stag. Off to my dressmaker's, where you'll order a few properly bewitching outfits. Oh, you're a young version of me, and I can't think of a nicer compliment!"

The next morning, Victorine and Toinette reviewed the weekly household accounts. Victorine placed a fresh delivery of her favorite flowers, white gardenias, atop her piano as Toinette sat on the divan with her account books on her lap.

"Ma'm'selle, our butcher is cheating us." She scanned her account book and quickly totaled the number. "Ten francs this week."

"Toinette, what does it matter? Ten francs amounts to nothing."

"That may be so, but I refuse to be cheated! Even for ten francs."

"All right, what shall we do?" She closed her eyes and inhaled the perfume of the gardenias.

"I suggest we take our business elsewhere. Perhaps that English butcher on the boulevard Haussmann."

"Very well." Victorine waved away the subject.

"Now we need to discuss the stabling fees for the horses." Toinette opened another ledger book.

Victorine sighed and folded her hands. Quite unexpectedly, someone knocked at the front door. "Whoever could be visiting at this hour of the morning without first sending a calling card?"

"I'll go." Toinette left the parlor, hugging her precious household accounts to her chest.

"Mademoiselle Laurent, is it true?" Princess Mathilde burst into the room. "Philippe de Lyon has invited you to a hunt party at his château?"

"Yes, it's true. Will you be there as well?"

"Oh dear God, no. I couldn't stand fourteen days with those vacuous snobs he surrounds himself with!" She waved her hand as if to dismiss such effluvia. Mathilde extracted a cigarette from a monogrammed silver case, lit it, and blew a jet of smoke straight into the air above her head. She sat beside Victorine on the divan. "You must tell me, *chérie,* are you sleeping with him yet?"

"Well, I . . . no," Victorine said.

"Oh, you can't imagine how important it is to succeed with him!"

"Succeed? I don't understand . . ."

"Succeed at becoming his mistress," Mathilde answered. "Oh, darling Victorine—may I call you that? Victorine, it would devastate her. She would just curl up and die. She would be so diminished, she would just melt into thin air!" She gestured wildly, smoke curling in arabesques above her head.

Victorine felt she was witnessing the rantings of a madwoman. "Who would?"

"Empress Eugénie, of course," Mathilde said, as though it were the most obvious fact in the world.

Victorine was stunned, recalling her humiliating encounter with Eugénie at Boucheron's jewelry shop. "Why on *earth* would Eugénie be interested?"

Mathilde perched on the edge of the divan and stroked Victorine's hand. "Darling, the wives of men like Baron de Rothschild know you and hate you. And their ringleader is that Spanish fishmonger's wife we're forced to call 'Your Majesty.' She's been heard to curse your very name."

"But why me? There are more successful and famous courtesans in Paris!"

"Those women come and go." She looked deeply into Victorine's eyes. "You'll be remembered forever, long after all the others have been forgotten. They'll still be whispering in awe a hundred years from now when they stand before your portrait in some august hall. Beauty isn't unique in our circle. But you evoke the Sublime. Do you know what that is? The Sublime?"

Victorine shook her head.

"The Sublime can only be achieved through the suffering that precedes Beauty. You've suffered; I see it. Manet sees it. That's why you're his ideal." She paused, then glanced at Edouard's still life on the opposite wall.

"Manet's talent is acknowledged by the literati. It's only a matter of time before it filters down to the masses." She sighed and turned back to Victorine.

"I don't want to fill your head with too much intrigue all at once. But believe me, darling. Philippe de Lyon's mistress benefits from his reflected power. If Philippe selects you, you can defy Eugénie. And we'll be allies."

"I don't understand."

"You know the adage 'The enemy of my enemy is my friend,'" she said.

Victorine was aware that Princess Mathilde was a close confidante of the emperor; it was common knowledge that she adored Louis-Napoléon as much as she detested his wife. Empress Eugénie, née Eugénie de Montijo, was the daughter of a minor Spanish nobleman and the granddaughter of a Scottish liquor distributor, a fact overlooked by all of polite society, but never by Princess Mathilde. Eugénie was detested by the entire Bonaparte family, but none so much as Mathilde. It was whispered in the best salons that screaming insults between these two women constantly erupted in the halls of the Tuileries Palace.

Noticing the time, Mathilde flew toward the door in a whirl of orange hair, emerald taffeta, and Guerlain scent. "I have a haiku lesson with my Japanese master and I can't be late. For a Buddhist monk, he has a devilish temper. Good-bye, my dear. Good-bye."

That afternoon, André came to call and found Victorine in the parlor reading the morning edition of *Le Figaro*.

"André, listen to this account of a fancy-dress ball given by La Païva at her *hôtel particulier*." She patted a spot on the divan for him. "'The former Thérèse Lachmann—'"

"She's the most vulgar of the courtesans, in my opinion," André said, taking a seat. "Her palace on the Champs-Elysées has bathrooms with walls of Carrara marble, as well as baths and lavatories of solid onyx."

"Vulgar, perhaps, but she's also the richest. Her protector has three million a year that he shares with her," Victorine said, and continued reading: "'The goddesses of Olympus were represented by *la garde,* the queens of their profession. La Païva came as Juno. The treasure of diamonds, pearls, and precious stones scattered over her dazzling tunic were valued at 1,250,000 francs.'" Victorine laid aside the newspaper. "She's the daughter of a poor Moscow weaver. Look how far she's come!"

"I know the daughter of an Austrian fencing master who will surpass her. Or were you the daughter of Italian court musicians?" André smiled.

"Now, stop that!" She laughed with him.

"Victorine, I just came from Edouard's studio. I saw his latest portrait of you as a bullfighter in a Spanish corrida."

Victorine mentioned that she was puzzled by the matador costume.

"I can explain it to you," André said. "Edouard told me he was inspired by watching his first bullfight in Madrid. The matador was you and that noble bull was him. The bullfighter teased with his red cape, distracted with his red cape, then plunged in the sword to sever the spinal cord."

"The red cape? Is that a metaphor for sex?" she asked.

André confirmed that this was Edouard's intent. "He told me that honesty was critical for an artist or a writer; that fear was fatal. Then he asked me a question that made me wince: why I wrote about other people's lives but was afraid to live my own."

"You haven't really had the chance," Victorine said.

"Precisely. I blurted out that I *was* attracted to someone but was afraid to confess it."

"Did he ask who?"

"I told him that sometimes I love you, Victorine, but other times, it was him." André sighed. "He said he was flattered, but it couldn't be. He told me to go out there and experience passion and I would have plenty to write about. When I left his studio, I felt so glum. But as I walked, I felt lighter, freer. I realized I *was* free."

Chapter Nine

The road to Hell is easy.

—Virgil, *The Aeneid*, c. 30 B.C.

Three weeks later, Victorine set off on her journey to spend a fortnight at the Duke de Lyon's country château.

She settled into her private compartment in the first-class train coach and reflected. What could she expect when she saw the Duke de Lyon after such a long absence? How would he react to her? She felt as nervous as the day she met Edouard Manet at the ballet rehearsal hall, expecting a wealthy tycoon instead of an artist. As the train chugged out of Paris, she drifted asleep to an agitated dream of a different train ride several years ago from her village in Alsace. Victorine alternately woke and dozed until jolted awake as the train jerked to a stop. She peered out the window and saw a sign swaying in the breeze over the tiny station: BEAUVOIS.

She detrained, and an officious manservant stepped forward, bowed, and introduced himself as Ariel, head footman in the Duke de Lyon's household. "Bring the luggage to the barouche

waiting out front," Ariel commanded the unfortunate porter, struggling under two traveling trunks custom-made for
Mademoiselle Laurent by the House of Vuitton. "And hop to
it, man!"

As they bustled through the tiny station, Ariel glared at
several workmen staring lasciviously at Victorine and elbowed farmers out of the way to clear a path for her. He acted
for all the world as though he was the official chamberlain of
the imperial court and she, a duchess.

The coach lumbered through the hamlet with Ariel sitting
atop the box, shouting at the driver to slow down for the precious cargo inside. Victorine's nervous stomach churned during
the bumpy ride, bouncing down country roads, jolting toward
de Lyon's château. Finally, a gravel driveway crunched beneath
the wheels as they rolled past two carved stone sentinels marking the entrance. Victorine gazed out the window and drew in
her breath. A double row of two-hundred-year-old plane trees
lined the white gravel driveway, their branches arcing in a leafy
pergola above the long avenue. The scent of freshly bundled
hay swept in on the breeze as they drove by acres of green lawn
swooping down to an ornamental lake. Out the left side, she
could see a terraced hillside of cypress trees; on the right, formal gardens of boxwood hedges tortured into geometrical
shapes. Various outbuildings loomed in the distance: a green-
house, the kennels, and the grand stables, designed to mimic a
château. A low stone wall of rugged rocks laid during Roman
times ran along the entire perimeter of the estate. The carriage
slowed as it rounded a curve to the limestone mansion, then
bumped over the cobblestone drive. Under the porte cochère,
servants busied themselves unloading the boots of carriages,
bustling up the château steps with the guests' luggage.

They rolled to a stop, and Ariel jumped down from the
coachman's seat to hold the carriage door open for Victorine.
She stepped down and gazed up at the house.

"Eighty-six rooms in total," Ariel said. "Monsieur le duc bought this place ten years ago in a state of utter disarray from the Vazoulay family. Shameful how they had it for five hundred years yet let it go to ruin." She followed him through the two-story foyer. "Château de Beauvois was built as a fortress in the twelfth century," he said, as he led her around baggage lined in neat columns on the floor and past garrulous guests toward the double marble staircase. "During the Renaissance, the fortress was torn down and rebuilt as a more elegant château. In 1780, the house was again added onto. The family lost their fortune after the Revolution and the house decayed over several generations until my master bought it. He restored it and spared no expense, overseeing all the improvements personally. It is the crown jewel among all of his homes."

They reached the second floor and walked noiselessly down a crimson-carpeted hallway where each door boasted a brass nameplate.

"Inebriated guests tend to wander these halls during the wee hours of the morning. A wrong door opened at an extra-marital moment has caused more than one scandal here."

They turned a corner and stopped at the solitary door in this sheltered alcove.

"My master instructed me to anticipate your every need, Mademoiselle Laurent. Every possible comfort has been provided." He opened the door and stepped aside.

At that moment, her luggage arrived in the scrawny arms of a young manservant breathless under their weight. Ariel dismissed him curtly and began to unpack her things, expertly folding and hanging her garments in the cedar-lined wardrobe. He mentioned that the chambermaid had drawn a bath, motioning to a bathroom at the other end of the room. "Go ahead, ma'm'selle. I assure you, I won't be a hindrance to your privacy. The bell pull is for your convenience. The lady's maid assigned to your needs is available with just a tug on that sash."

She pulled on the sash, but no one appeared. She undressed herself, and in a few moments settled into the curves of the marble tub, exhaling a grateful sigh. After the dust and grime of her journey, it was lovely to soak in the warm water scented with lime-tree flowers. She gazed up at the Moroccan mosaic all around. As she closed her eyes, all the tension in her shoulders melted away. This is as close to heaven as I'll ever get, she thought to herself, as she floated like a baby in its warm womb of luxury.

In the evening, Victorine prepared her toilette with the help of the countrywoman who served as lady's maid. She fumbled with Victorine's thick, long hair, unable to twist it into a sleek chignon. She could neither pin the loose tendrils gracefully nor place the diamond-studded hair ornaments in an artful curve. Victorine lost all patience and dismissed her. After dressing herself with some difficulty, the corset lacings up her back the major challenge, she glanced in the mirror to check her reflection. The gown she had chosen for this evening was revolutionary in its design, made all in one piece, the latest rage in Paris. She smoothed her hands over the chrysanthemum-yellow satin bodice trimmed with black lace and jet beading. With a glance back over her shoulder, Victorine checked the effect of the tight velvet skirt gathered over a bustle falling to the floor, ending in a short train. She selected a rivière of diamonds and smoky topaz that exactly matched the color of her eyes. Perfect, she thought as she snapped the clasp.

A knock announced Ariel at the door to escort her to the Grand Salon. She followed him down the white marble staircase past tapestries of hunting scenes by Rubens, and through a maze of corridors. The gentle strains of Vivaldi's *Four Seasons* echoed through the hallways.

Victorine paused at the threshold of the Grand Salon to calm herself, and gazed at the coffered ceilings of the outsize room. A gallery of marble columns around the perimeter divided the upper half, decorated with Aubusson tapestries, from the lower half, hung with paintings by Renaissance masters. A fireplace of white marble with ormolu ornaments dominated the far wall. The furnishings in this monumental salon combined Louis XIV and Empire style with Savonnerie carpets, and somehow created a harmonious mix. When she entered, she spotted Jacques Offenbach and Prince Dmitri, both frequent visitors to her apartment on the boulevard Malesherbes. They encircled Victorine and flirted with her as she perused the room for Philippe. How would he greet her? she wondered. They had been strangers for eight long months; would he still want her? As waves of anxiety washed over her, she caught fragments of conversation between two dowagers gossiping behind their fluttering fans.

"Oh, my dear, Victorine Laurent is *here*," one bejeweled matron whispered in the ear of her septuagenarian friend.

"Who is Victorine Laurent?" the other asked too loudly. "I've never heard of her."

"Oh, surely you must have. She's the one in the paintings by that artist, you know, the one who causes all the scandals."

"Edouard Manet," her husband mumbled helpfully through his white handlebar mustache. "But I thought she was Rothschild's cocotte. What is she doing here alone?"

Victorine's gaze slid toward another group nearby, a coven of Empress Eugénie's inner circle gathered in a huddle. She could hear them quite clearly.

"She's shameful. Look at her wearing a dress designed by Monsieur Worth. How dare she patronize the empress's couturier!"

"At least she's wearing clothes. I can't imagine what Rothschild sees in a woman of such low breeding."

Victorine turned away. Those hateful snobs that Edouard loved to pillory. She wished Manet was there to calm her. A ripple of excitement surged through the room as various male voices called out greetings, followed by a crescendo of delighted female cries, and then an arm encircled her waist. She turned with a start and looked straight into a pair of blue-green eyes. Philippe de Lyon casually planted a kiss on each cheek. She responded coolly, mirroring his sangfroid, though a flush of color rushed to her cheeks. He looked so well, so prosperous and dangerously handsome.

"Let's see, it's been six, seven months since we last met?" he said.

"I don't recall." Her tone indicated a yawn, a forgotten name, a lost glove.

They circulated through the crowd as he galanted Victorine on his arm. He introduced her to a slight, balding man with a pair of pince-nez slipping down his nose. This was Professor Louis Pasteur, whose lab was engaged in some amazing experiments, he explained. Philippe said he didn't pretend to understand the work, but was delighted to be a principle investor. Next, they approached a tall man holding court among a group of admirers. The most singular feature about him was a head of unruly dark hair accented by a single white lock falling across his forehead. He was dressed eccentrically in a canary-yellow frock coat and carried a carved ebony walking stick. Victorine immediately recognized James McNeill Whistler from engravings she had seen in periodicals. At the last Salon, his painting *The White Girl* had created quite a scandal. When Philippe introduced them, Whistler bowed gracefully. "Mademoiselle Victorine."

Continuing through the crowd, they greeted a dark-haired, heavyset woman in her midfifties. Philippe introduced her as

Madame Dudevant, but she was famous under her pen name, George Sand. Though she was not beautiful, her luminous dark eyes were mesmerizing. No wonder Chopin had been so in love with her, thought Victorine.

"Mademoiselle Laurent, I'm a great admirer of Edouard Manet. His paintings are reflecting mirrors through which we see ourselves," she said.

As they passed through the room, Victorine drifted beside the Duke de Lyon as though she were watching herself in a dream. When the butler struck the dinner gong, Victorine and Philippe led the procession of guests into a medieval banqueting hall lit by pink-and-yellow gas jets and a blazing fire in the fireplace. Victorine had never before seen a dining table set for such a large number. Silver epergnes, crystal goblets, and porcelain china shimmered in the golden candlelight of gilt candelabra. Serving tables in the corner held steaming silver chafing dishes. Fresh lilies and hyacinths garlanded the entire length of the table. The murmur of guests reading place cards mingled with the rustling of silk and satin as chairs were drawn out for the ladies and each person found a seat. Victorine caught sight of Ariel, in formal footman's regalia, holding her chair in the place of honor, to the right of the host.

Dinner service commenced with a toast.

Philippe raised his crystal goblet and surveyed each face. "I thank you all for coming. I drink to all of you, to a successful hunt tomorrow"—he turned his gaze directly toward Victorine—"and to all that is beautiful and pleasurable in life."

All attention followed his, and fifty-eight pairs of eyes turned to stare at Victorine.

The sumptuous dinner was served by quietly efficient footmen who stood, one behind each chair, to attend the needs of every guest. With each course, the butler refilled goblets, murmuring the names and vintages of each wine.

Baron Haussmann and Prince Dmitri vied to impress Victorine, competing for her attention with droll anecdotes.

Baron Haussmann didn't recognize her from the ballet school rehearsal hall, but she remembered him, the onetime protector of the little ballerina who danced next to her onstage.

"Yesterday, to the great stupefaction of pedestrians on the Champs-Elysées, I saw a mechanical carriage proceeding down the street all by itself. Can you imagine?" Prince Dmitri said.

"Was it a trick of some kind?" Haussmann asked. "Where were the horses?"

The prince shrugged. "Three people rode in it and about three hundred ran along the pavement following after."

Not one to be outshone, Baron Haussmann said, "I'm obliged to leave this charming house party a few days early. I was invited by Felix Nadar to ride in his hot-air balloon next Sunday. We're taking off from the Champs-de-Mars and sailing through the skies to photograph the boulevards and the Bois down below."

There was nothing Prince Dmitri could say to top this. Haussmann smiled triumphantly, though Victorine was oblivious to the repartee. Philippe de Lyon captivated her complete attention. She watched him charm Madame McMillan, flirting with her as though she were a debutante. He entertained his immediate dinner partners with a series of stories, all the while mindful to the needs of all his guests.

A gentleman seated near Victorine remarked that the duke's wine cellar was so huge and stocked with such priceless quality that Lloyd's of London had refused to insure it. An American guest said he was amazed the French could drink so much alcohol yet never become drunk, while in his country, it was common for men and women to act like blithering idiots after merely one glass of wine. Another commented that the duke's chef rivaled the master chef at the Tuileries Palace.

Ariel glanced skeptically at each plate as he removed it, noting that Victorine had hardly touched any of the six courses. He leaned near her ear as he cleared her dessert plate. "Does the cuisine displease mademoiselle, or are we too nervous to eat?"

At the conclusion of dinner, all adjourned to the library for parlor games and conversation. A contest of charades was organized by some guests, while others played backgammon and bezique. Philippe stood before the fireplace, his arm propped against the mantel, surrounded by a group of chattering female guests. His gaze rested on Victorine across the room, watching her intently as she played cards. Presently, he approached and asked for a private word on the balcony.

She hugged her cashmere shawl closer around her shoulders as they stepped out the French doors into the cool evening air. She faced him in bright moonlight, his face half in shadow. "Finally alone. What a relief from that din inside," he said. He stood silently for several moments, drinking in her presence. "You may wonder why I left Paris without saying good-bye."

"You're free to come and go as you please——" Before she finished her sentence, the touch of his finger to her lips silenced her.

"Shhh. Don't waste time with dissimulation. I say what I mean and you'll always know where you stand with me. I needed physical distance to decide what I should do about you."

"Do about me——"

"I told you I always get what I want. I don't mean that to sound egotistical. It's not that I'm lucky or blessed." His laugh sounded bitter. "Quite the contrary. I get what I want because I plan my course of action rationally using logic."

She looked up at him. "So, while you were away in Saint Petersburg, did Princess Romanoff help you come"—she paused—"to rational *conclusions* about me?"

He laughed at her coy joke and acknowledged that she was quite correct. Then his tone turned serious. "I've made up my mind, Victorine. I want you. I'll give you everything, deny you nothing. But I expect the same in return. You will give me everything and deny me nothing."

The crucial moment. Here was a man whose every order was followed, who steered the ship of state with his pinkie finger. She recalled Baudelaire's words: A man steeped in power would be intrigued by a woman unimpressed by it. She said, "Now I'll decide what *I* should do about *you* . . ." She turned and left him alone on the terrace.

Inside her bedchamber, Victorine slipped off her dress and stepped out of her lingerie, leaving it crumpled on the floor. She removed her corset and felt free, released from the whalebone stays. Layers of lace petticoats and satin undergarments lay strewn where she dropped them. She slipped on her peignoir and sat before the mirrored vanity table. The sound of a door latch startled her. She whirled around and to her shock, Philippe stood silhouetted in the doorway.

"What . . . ?" She looked past him and realized that her bedchamber adjoined his.

He grinned like a mischievous schoolboy who had pulled off a good prank. "It seems someone assigned us connecting rooms," he said, walking out of the darkness toward her.

"No. Out, Philippe." She pointed with her hairbrush.

He disobeyed and approached closer. He grasped her shoulders with both hands and kissed her at a spot on her neck that ran shivers down her spine. Never, never, never lose control, she told herself. "Good night," she said.

He watched her reflection in the mirror, his glance traveling down the length of her body, his thoughts clearly urging him to take what he wanted.

She pointed to the door. His shoulders slumped as he turned to walk out. Suddenly, he stopped in the doorway. "I will not play this game much longer, Victorine." The door banged shut with such force that she felt unnerved. She gazed at herself in the mirror and looked deeply into her own soul. She had never in her career, in her life, been so fascinated by a man.

Although her body was bone weary, once she pulled the silk coverlet up to her chin and snuggled into the feather bed, sleep would not come. Unfamiliar shapes loomed in the darkness. The ticking of the clock on the mantelpiece sounded like the drumbeat to a death march. And when she finally drifted off to sleep, the dream she'd had earlier on the train returned. She saw her thirteen-year-old self on a third-class train coach, dressed in a red taffeta party frock, holding an empty gilt picture frame on her lap. She stared out the window at a figure on the platform, the adolescent Victorine, shivering in a tattered wool coat, clutching a cardboard suitcase, waving good-bye. As the train pulled away from the station, Victorine on the train looked back through the window at Victorine left behind growing smaller and smaller until she finally disappeared.

Chapter Ten

My God, if you exist, pity my soul, if I have one.

—Stendhal (1783–1842)

Victorine swept aside the silk damask curtains in her room to a flurry of activity below her window. She rested her elbows on the sill and her chin in her hands as she watched a group of huntsmen and grooms encircle the Duke de Lyon to receive their orders for the day, heads bowed in concentration like loyal vassals gathered around their liege.

At seven o'clock sharp, house staff laid out a hunt break-fast for the riders. Silver chafing dishes offered truffled eggs with Brie, freshly baked croissants, and sliced hams, accompanied by plenty of steaming coffee. Victorine spotted Philippe in the grand foyer as she descended the staircase in her blue velvet riding habit with a tricorner hat perched jauntily on her sleek hair.

"You look charming. I trust you slept well?" he asked, taking her hand and lightly brushing his lips across it.

"Perfectly," she lied.

Still holding her hand in his, he leaned closer to her. "I can't say the same. I barely slept at all, thanks to you, Mademoiselle Laurent."

"I've heard that from gentlemen before. But never as a complaint," she laughed.

In the dining hall, it didn't surprise her that precious few women were present, considering the exceptional skill and stamina required to ride to the hunt. As she perused the room, Victorine noticed Baron Haussmann motioning her to an empty chair beside him at the long mahogany table. "Good morning, Mademoiselle Laurent." He half rose and pulled out her chair. "I was told this is your first stag hunt. Will you be able to keep up with us?"

"Will you be able to keep up with me, that's the question, Baron."

Victorine was aware that the centuries-old "sport of kings" was a privilege enjoyed by the crown on thousands of acres all over France. The wealthy landowners of de Lyon's class adopted stag hunting as a status symbol, perpetuating this august ritual of the ancien régime that they constantly strove to emulate.

The noise level in the room rose as more riders arrived, greeting one another with slaps on the back and jovial gossip about mutual acquaintances. Silverware scraped against plates as they gulped down their hearty hunt breakfasts, nervously watching the clock on the mantel, waiting for eight thirty to arrive. All around, Victorine heard snippets of conversation relating to the temperament of the hounds, the skill of the huntsman at flushing out the stag, and the merits of stags versus the British preference for fox hunting, while Haussmann expounded on the more arcane traditions she could expect to encounter. After breakfast, all riders assembled in the billiards room. Haussmann had mentioned that one of the long-standing traditions at Philippe's hunt parties was a playful game of chance, each hunter drawing a "surprise packet" to determine which horse he would ride. Victorine stood to one side of the cavernous billiards room surveying the other guests, the men loudly bragging to one another about hunts past. Dressed in gorgeous field uniforms, they personified *galanterie:* blue velvet breeches, blue waistcoats with narrow braiding and engraved buttons, some in burgundy, others in black velvet coats with gold facings and trim. It was clear to her that they craved and dreaded the challenges ahead: the clash of egos, the danger of speed, the unpredictability of Thoroughbreds.

Presently, a servant entered carrying a Georgian silver bowl, from which each rider plucked a slip of paper bearing the name of a horse. Giddy children could not have been as excited as these sophisticated gentlemen comparing the lots they drew. Gloves were pulled on, coats adjusted, and the men donned their hats: time to depart.

Only two women were adventurous enough to ride to the hunt, and Victorine was thrilled to see that Madame McMillan was the other. The rest of the ladies preferred to stay behind at the château gossiping and playing cards.

"Good morning, my dear," Madame McMillan called out, standing daintily on a block, waiting for her horse.

"Do you predict good hunting today?" Victorine asked.

"My nephew always provides a good hunt for his guests. And this is my 2,056th stag. I'm determined to die in the saddle one way or the other!"

Presently, a groom rode up on a magnificent black Thoroughbred, jumped down, and walked him up to Victorine. She was awed by the horse's gleaming coat and elegantly braided mane. The majestic animal scrutinized her with a wary look, radiating nervous energy. As Victorine cooed soothing words and patted his muscular neck, Philippe approached with a concerned look.

"Arnaud"—he turned to the groom—"not this one. I'll take him. Go saddle up Lulu for Mademoiselle."

"No, I want him. What's your name?" She turned to the horse.

"His name's Fury. Does that say enough? He's too big for you, Victorine. And a bit wild. Unpredictable."

She took the reins in her left hand. "Just the way I like it." She placed her left foot in the stirrup of the sidesaddle and swung herself up. The horse danced back and signaled his independence by pulling at the bridle, but Victorine held tight.

Attention turned to the huntsman sounding the fanfare. Within a few minutes, all were ready, and the cheerful group of thirty-five riders walked and trotted their mounts toward the kennels. Victorine noted a variable range of horsemanship, and an equally variable selection of horses. There were high-strung Thoroughbreds, sleek Arabians, sedate, heavy Norman hunters, and, finally, stout, gentle cobs, a plodding breed perfect for the heavier, older members of the hunt party.

The jingling of bits and the squeak of fine leather filled the air. Riders exhaled white puffs of breath as they chatted; their horses steamed jets of vapor out their nostrils. Yellow sunlight filtered through trees and melted patches of frost iced on the lawns. Victorine shaded her eyes from the sun and looked toward the horizon, where a hazy blue mist floated above distant foothills beyond the estate.

When the riders reached the open field, the kennel master cracked the air with his whip and the yapping hounds were off, followed by the mounts close behind.

Victorine was awed by the power of the animal beneath her as they cantered across a meadow and jumped a small stream. Her horse was a superb athlete with the excellent balance and uncanny timing of a steeplechase champion. She sat up and forward as they took a low stone wall and landed with perfect form on the other side. He was tall, sixteen hands, she judged, and straining to run. She relaxed her grip on the reins and let him have his head. Horse and rider exhilarated in great gulps of sheer freedom.

Presently, the hounds lost the scent and the pace slowed. Philippe pulled up beside Victorine on his white Arabian charger and the two horses danced around each other, ears and nostrils twitching. "Are you quite all right on that beast?" he called to her.

As though on cue, her horse lunged to bite the flanks of the Arabian. She grabbed the reins tight and jerked back hard to show him who was in charge. Feeling the sharp tug of the bit in his mouth, he fell into place and quieted down.

"I'm managing very well, thank you. Better than you could do, I'm certain," she answered.

"Oh? Do you think so?"

"Absolutely."

"I'll make a wager on that."

"Let's race to that big tree over there." She pointed down the meadow to the edge of an oak grove. "A hundred-franc note says I'll win."

"Make it five hundred. Let's go!" he shouted as he dug his heels into his stallion.

The horses thundered over the ground side by side, hooves pounding, manes flying. Victorine's heart hammered against her chest. Breathing in gasps, hair whipped by wind; the scenery blurred by. They reached the oak grove, but neither slowed. Tied at the finish line, they passed it and crashed through the forest, ducking to avoid low-hanging branches and sailing over dead tree trunks, side by side. Victorine's horse, gleaming with sweat, pulled ahead of Philippe's. She screamed with excitement and flayed his haunches with her crop. "Go! Go!" she screamed. A full head in front, she savored victory.

The forest grew thicker as they rushed deeper. The tangled branches and slippery leaves, still wet with dew, forced them to slow. Presently, they pulled back on the reins and halted as they came to a clearing near a small lake. Victorine slid off her horse.

"I won! I won!"

"You didn't. It was a tie," he panted as he dismounted. He faced Victorine, still gasping to catch his breath. Her hat had flown off, her hair was flowing, erotic and wild. Sweat glistened at her throat and on her chest. Her eyes were feverish with physical exertion and the elation of their contest.

"You cheated," he said.

"I won a fair contest."

"You cheated." He pulled her into his arms and wrapped them around her.

She tried to break free, but he held tight.

"Let me go," she laughed, and tried to pull away.

He wrapped his leg around and tripped her. She clung to him as they lost their balance on the wet leaves and landed with a thud on the muddy forest floor. Wrestling like children, they rolled over and over each other, laughing hysterically. "Get off me," she said, as she felt the clammy leaves soaking her disheveled dress right through to her skin. He pinned her to the ground between his thighs and held her tightly by the wrists. She tried to escape his grip but was laughing so hard, she couldn't breathe.

Suddenly, she was aware he wasn't laughing anymore.

Looming above, he gazed down at her, passionately aroused by the struggle. He hesitated a moment; then his mouth pressed down hard on hers. She offered no resistance. She met his mouth with hers, drawing him in. His lips traveled down her neck, behind her ears, kissing her skin. His deep voice rumbled in her ear. "I adore you," he said again and again. And he whispered other words, pornographic words. To her ears, it sounded like poetry. He took her with more raw passion than any other man ever had. She felt nothing.

Finally, he lifted his head.

"I'm sorry . . ."

"Don't be."

"I'm not usually . . . I mean . . . I lost control and I hope I didn't . . ." The consummate orator fumbled for words. He couldn't seem to bring his eyes to meet hers.

She stifled a laugh. An apology? She had certainly never heard that before.

"May I make it up to you? Tonight?" he asked.

"Yes, tonight," she said softly.

Slowly, very slowly, they collected themselves.

Victorine realized that she was filthy, splattered all over with mud. Her elegant velvet habit was ruined. Her riding boots were caked with mud as well. She tried to shake free bits of leaves embedded in the tangled curls of her hair and searched in vain on the forest floor for the pearl-and-diamond comb that had held it in place. They approached their horses grazing contentedly a few paces away. After tightening straps and martingales, they remounted and found their way back to the meadow, following the sounds of the hunt.

Raised eyebrows greeted their disheveled return, but the group was too distracted to question them. Victorine and Philippe rode up just in time to witness the stag standing at bay. All the hunters struggled to hold their horses still as they danced back, sensing another animal's doom. Victorine locked eyes with the frightened beast. The excited hounds yelped and leaped at the cornered stag. The magnificent deer realized it was conquered, lowered its antlers, knelt on all fours, and surrendered.

The huntsman raised the trumpet to his lips and sounded a fanfare. At the signal, the hounds attacked. They were taught not to bite the head or neck, but joyously ravaged the beast's torso, barking and leaping with victory. Victorine longed to close her eyes, but was so mesmerized she couldn't tear her gaze away. The other hunters cheered wildly while she swallowed hard as the bile came up her throat.

Philippe rode up beside her. "The traditional hunt supper will take place tonight, but the host won't be present. He will offer his most solemn apologies but urge his guests to enjoy themselves in the capable hands of his butler and staff. Then he'll invite one beautiful guest, *the most* beautiful guest, to join him for a private supper. Will she accept?"

"She will."

"Will she come to his room at nine o'clock?"

"Nine o'clock," she whispered.

At precisely nine o'clock, a knock announced her dinner companion. She opened the door connecting their rooms to find Philippe in a black velvet smoking jacket, a white shirt, and dark trousers. On his feet were slippers embroidered with the gold crest of Beauvois.

He drew in his breath at the sight of her. Her hair was caught up loosely, diamonds sparkled at her ears, but her only other jewelry was the Egyptian gold bracelet, his gift marking the first night they met. Her pink silk peignoir skimmed the surface of her body, revealing the contour of every supple curve.

He stepped aside for her to enter the intimate oval salon, bathed in the glow of candlelight. A small table had been set before the chimneypiece in the parlor of the duke's bedchamber. Servants had no doubt scurried to follow precise orders concerning the linens, china, choice of silver flatware, and flower arrangements. The menu differed from the heavy dinner with its many courses served downstairs. A light meal of oysters on the half shell, caviar with blini, and strawberries with chocolate sauce and Chantilly whipped cream awaited on silver platters. The servants had lit a roaring fire in the fireplace, then dutifully disappeared, most likely instructed not to return unless called upon. Victorine heard the familiar strains of a Waldteufel waltz and glanced about quizzically. By way of explanation, Philippe pointed to a coromandel screen. She peeked behind to find a trio performing a private concert for an audience of two.

He indicated her place at the table and poured two glasses of champagne.

"A toast." He raised his glass. "To the hunt and to the capture of elusive prey."

His meaning was not lost on her as she raised her glass to him. "Let us pray for the defenseless prey," she said.

He laughed. "You're a magnificent rider, Victorine. Where did you learn to sit a horse like that?"

"Rothschild. Riding lessons in the Bois."

"You can't learn that kind of grace in the saddle. It comes naturally to you."

"I recall some vague memories of riding bareback when I was a little girl."

"Where was that?"

"In Alsace. That was a lifetime ago for me." She felt a pang of sadness as she gazed into the fire.

"I understand. I prefer not to revisit childhood memories, either."

"You? Your father was a military hero. Your mother, a beautiful aristocrat—"

"I'm the illegitimate son of the Comte de Gabbay. I can't say with certainty whose natural child I am."

We're certainly alike in that, she thought. "But there's royalty in your bloodlines." She studied his face. "And you've a title, monsieur le duc."

"'The Duke de Lyon.' A title invented for me by Louis-Napoléon. Everything I own, everything I built or brokered, I accomplished alone." He drained the champagne and poured himself another. "It was I who should have been emperor, Victorine. My risks and planning, my strategy, put Louis-Napoléon on the throne. And why am I just a shadow? Because I'm the unacknowledged son of an acknowledged military hero."

"Everyone knows France's glory, all her success, is due to you. Even Edouard tells me——"

"Manet!" He scowled. "I want Manet out of your life."

This isn't the time to argue that point, she thought. She rose to bring a tray of strawberries on the sideboard to the table. "Dismiss the musicians," she said.

He did so, and they filed out discreetly.

"I love these," she said as she took a strawberry in her fingers and dipped it in a small bowl of warm chocolate sauce, then in whipped cream. Holding his gaze, she raised it to her lips and licked, flicking the cream with her tongue. "Tonight, you'll have dessert first," she said.

Afterward, as they both lay exhausted, he said, "You are remarkable, Mademoiselle Victorine." At the mention of Edouard's nickname for her, the thought of him flashed through her mind, and an inexplicable longing for Manet gripped her.

"I'll buy you a new house, one better suited to you."

All thoughts of Edouard Manet vanished.

"You'd buy me a house?" She could not quite believe what she was hearing.

"I'm not going to allow you to stay in Rothschild's flat, am I? It could get a bit uncomfortable with the three of us trying to crowd in there." He studied her face intently. "And what else do you want?"

"Well . . . ," she said softly, barely audible, "all I've ever wanted is security."

"Security. How shall I give you security? I'll establish a trust fund in your name and appoint my own banker as your trustee. You'll have a comfortable income guaranteed for life. But in return, I insist you cut all ties with Rothschild and with—"

"Of course I'm yours, Philippe." She realized she might as well have this argument now because it was bound to happen. "I have several protectors I'm fond of, but I'll say good-bye to them, and to Rothschild. But as for Edouard—"

"I won't stand for it. That's over."

"There isn't anything to *be* over. Please believe me. I'm not his mistress."

"Then what are you?"

"I'm his muse," she said quietly.

"I find that very hard to believe. Is he a eunuch? Is he homosexual?" He rose and walked toward a side table. Extracting a cigarette from a silver case, he lit it, and blew out a jet of smoke. She was distracted admiring his nude body. So lithe, every inch muscle. She flashed back to her previous protectors, the paunches, the wrinkled flesh she had closed her eyes against. This was the physique of a man in his prime.

"So, is he in love with you?"

"He loves the woman he creates on the canvas. You can rest assured he is no eunuch, and he certainly has his share of women who adore him."

"So he has no feelings for you. Then what are your feelings for him?"

She opened her mouth to speak, but realized she didn't know how to articulate an answer to that question. Instead, she smiled seductively at him. "I'm very hungry again. For strawberries and whipped cream . . ." She reached over and took one from the tray.

Snuffing the cigarette in an ashtray, he walked toward her, knelt down, and scooped her up. She placed her arm around his neck and felt herself swept away toward his bedchamber. As he set her down on the bed, she took control and treated him to some very exotic talents learned from the legendary Madame Goulue.

Victorine awoke in a royal bed designed for Queen Anne of Brittany. She gazed up at a medieval Flemish canopy supported by four mahogany bedposts. She studied the mille-fleurs tapestry hanging on the wall opposite, a white unicorn in a field of flowers surrounded by a circle of lady courtiers. The phallic horn of the unicorn reminded her of Edouard and his circle of admiring women. Victorine's gaze traced the designs in the stucco ceiling, hazy with chimney smoke, supported by solid black oaken beams, likely hewn from the forest surrounding the estate. She pulled the goose-down counterpane to her chin as she shivered in the damp morning air seeping through the wavy, lead-paned windows.

She turned to watch Philippe sleeping soundly, faced away from her. He had promised her a home and a trust fund. Everything she had worked for led here, to this bedroom in this château. For this, she had denied herself the foolish notions of romantic love, of silly infatuations, so natural to girls her age, while she focused on her goal. Finally, she thought, her goal was here beside her, the tangible result of her arduous, single-minded climb to the top of her profession.

She listened to his peaceful breathing and observed his tousled head of hair. Her gaze traveled to his muscular shoulder rhythmically rising and falling with each breath. His forearm, crisscrossed with blond hairs, lay heavy across her body, as though to guard his possession while asleep. He's as regal as a royal prince, she thought. But for the grace of God, a twist of fate, he could have been emperor. France, its shining glory, its glittering place in the world were reflections of him; she understood that now. She stroked his hair tenderly. At her touch, he stirred and opened his eyes. "Good morning," she whispered.

An impish grin spread across his face. He sat up against the linen pillows, spread his arms, and sang in a deep baritone, "Victorine is in my bed! Victorine, Victorine, Victorine."

Chapter Eleven

The heart has its reasons which reason knows not.

—Blaise Pascal, *Pensées*, 1670

The news that Victorine was the acknowledged favorite of the Duke de Lyon rippled through the château, whispered from guest to guest. Her new status elicited the polite respect of even the most arrogant society doyennes. If they passed her in the hallways, they nodded and murmured deferential greetings. It became the custom for Victorine to ride with Philippe in the countryside in the mornings, then lunch with him privately on his terrace. Afternoons were spent in passionate lovemaking, after which he insisted she stay at his side while he worked in his office. One afternoon, as Victorine sat in Philippe's study trying her hand at a piece of embroidery, he lit a cigar and stared at a stack of documents.

"Is something wrong?" she asked.

"Mexico." He smacked the papers, scattering them across his massive desk. He told her that Mexico had become a throbbing headache for him, that back in 1861, French investors began to lose big money due to unstable political conditions in that country.

"An idiot named Juárez simply canceled all foreign debt. We stood to lose millions. I devised a plan to stabilize Mexico by sending in French troops to overthrow President Juárez." He tapped his cigar ash against a crystal ashtray. "Unfortunately, Empress Eugénie convinced Louis-Napoléon to send an incompetent archduke of Austria, a staunch Catholic, to rule Mexico.

"Those diplomatic dispatches"—he pointed to the papers on his desk—"arrived this morning by courier. It seems the Civil War in America is over except for the terms of surrender. We backed the wrong side; the Confederacy's vanquished. The United States isn't going to look kindly on French imperialism on its borders, and Juárez and his troops are on the attack again, threatening Archduke Maximilian's rule. This is just what the leftist rabble needs to agitate against us in the elections next year." His fingers stroked the furrow between his brows.

Victorine rose and drew her arms around his neck. "You'll think of something brilliant, I'm sure," she whispered in his ear.

The guests usually met in the library at sundown to enjoy aperitifs before supper. Groups chatted together or played bezique at card tables while awaiting the dinner gong. Victorine and Philippe preferred to remain secluded from the crowd, conversing tête-à-tête on a settee in the corner. On this evening, the butler approached and whispered urgently in the duke's ear. Philippe grasped Victorine's hand and led her out the double doors. They followed the butler to the study, where they found a group of hunt-party guests convened for an emergency meeting. They were all high-level ministers, including two members of the emperor's cabinet.

"What's happened?" Philippe asked.

They glanced at Victorine, coughed, and cleared their throats.

"Anything you have to say to me can be said in front of Mademoiselle Laurent."

"But this is state business, monsieur le duc." Minister Blanc bowed deeply to Victorine. "I'm sorry, mademoiselle. Please don't think me rude."

Philippe guided Victorine to a wing chair and seated her, then turned to the astonished gentlemen. "I said she stays. Now, what is this all about?"

A shroud of silence settled over the room, pierced only by the distant sounds of laughter and conversation from the guests down the hall.

"Well? You're wasting my time." Philippe took a seat behind his mahogany desk.

"Very well." Minister Leclerc adjusted his spectacles and tugged his waistcoat. "We want to discuss an urgent communiqué concerning Mexico." He held up a document. His glance shifted from Victorine to Philippe and back again. He cleared his throat and continued. "Emperor Maximilian has sent a plea for more troops and money to defend himself against the Juárez forces. They're closing in on him, and he doesn't have the manpower to fight them off."

"I'm aware of all this. Therefore?" Philippe said.

"This Mexican adventure has deteriorated into an embarrassing failure. We've made our fortunes off the bonds. I say we get out now," said Minister Blanc.

LeCochon, known as Eugénie's mouthpiece, interrupted. "And abandon Emperor Maximilian? The empress would not be in favor."

"The empress isn't making policy here," Philippe said, and glared at LeCochon. "This Mexico enterprise was launched for one purpose: to recoup the debts owed us by the Juárez government. That's been accomplished. The rest of it, the generals in their uniforms, the brave colonial adventures on faraway shores, it's all bullshit." Victorine flinched as Philippe's fist slammed down on the desktop. "I say pull out and do it now."

"But we guaranteed Maximilian our protection," LeCochon whined.

"Well, we're withdrawing it," Minister Blanc said.

A general mumbling and lighting of cigars filled the room with chatter and smoke.

"Her Majesty has a special interest in Mexico. As a Catholic countess—"

LeCochon was interrupted by Minister Blanc. "She's the countess of c—" He suddenly remembered Victorine's presence and stopped himself.

"I call for an informal vote, gentlemen," Philippe said. "In favor of withdrawing from Mexico?" All hands voted aye except one. LeCochon stubbornly voted nay, folding his arms across his chest.

"We're out of Mexico. Meeting adjourned." Philippe offered his arm to Victorine. She dipped at the knees, gathered the train of her dress, and nodded good evening to the gentlemen. As her silk satin skirt rustled by these éminences grises, she felt LeCochon's hatred and endured the sullen stares of the other ministers and cabinet members. Victorine had dreamed of wealth and fame, but never imagined she could also achieve power. How odd it felt to be a participant in this game of ambition and rivalry, the blood sport of imperial Paris.

By the end of the week, Victorine was back in Paris. As her carriage rolled along the boulevard de la Reine, fronting the Seine, she watched the plane trees flashing past, the familiar apartment houses and buildings behind them. How she had missed the sight of the morning sun shimmering off the golden dome of the Invalides, the rattle of the coal carts on the cobblestone streets, the chugging of the garbage barges lumbering down the Seine, even the putrid smell of manure left by horses trotting down the thoroughfares.

Her carriage stopped at her apartment to unload the bags. Without wasting a moment, she instructed her coachman to take her straight to Edouard's new studio on the rue Guyot. So much had happened, she could hardly wait to brag to him and share all her fresh gossip about the society people they both loathed. She arrived at the same moment as André, and ascended the stairs with him. He declared it puzzling that a vacation in the countryside could do such wonders for an already beautiful woman.

"Edouard, visitors," her voice sang out.

"I'll be right there," he called from the studio. "There's a welcome back gift for you. On the table."

She tore off the bright wrapping paper to find a Boucheron jewelry box. She and André exchanged glances. She flipped open the lid: a midnight-blue sapphire ring surrounded by fiery white diamonds lay nestled in its black velvet bed. She slipped it on her finger. Such a gift from one of her protectors would be expected, but Edouard? "It's magnificent," she called out, admiring her hand. "But why?"

"You were gone too long . . ." He came out from his studio wiping paint-covered hands with a linen cloth, but stopped short. "What's happened to you?" he asked.

"Whatever do you mean?"

"Something's different about you." He chucked his hand under her chin and raised her face. "You've fallen in love with him, haven't you?"

"Don't be absurd." She jerked her head away. "There's no such thing as love."

"I warned you. I told you not to go."

"That's none of your business!" she said.

André slapped his hat on his head, wishing to avoid the explosion. "I think I'll be leaving now——"

"André, stay," Edouard ordered. "Look at you." He grasped Victorine by the shoulders and turned her toward the cheval glass. She looked at her own reflection, then at his behind her. "I've lost you," he whispered.

Like a cool gemstone, beautiful but cold to the touch, her features betrayed no emotion. "You don't own me. I'm free to do as I please."

"Your body's been bought by legions, but I didn't know your heart was for sale."

She slapped him with such force that he reeled back a step. The imprint of her hand burned bright crimson on his cheek.

"You've broken the whore's rule, Victorine: Never fall in love with a client."

"How dare you." She was livid and trembling with rage. If she had been a man, she would have punched him in the gut. As it was, she slapped him again. "I'll never sit for your damn pictures. EVER."

"Paris is full of beautiful girls; I don't need you."

"I hate you. I never want to see you again!" she shouted.

"Good. I never want to see you again, either!" he shouted back.

As she ran down the stairs, tears filled her eyes and spilled over her cheeks. How dare he speak to her that way. She hated him. Arrogant, arrogant . . . she remembered the ring on her finger. She turned around and marched back up the stairs, threw open the door, and stopped dead. Her hand flew to her mouth in shock. Edouard had raised a palette knife and was charging toward a portrait of her.

"No, stop!" André bolted after him but was easily pushed off. He stabbed at her face and her bosom, grunting like a madman. His blade gashed the canvas, and each stroke ripped the linen in strips like flesh peeled from a body. "Bitch! Whore!" he shouted with every blow.

"What are you doing?" she cried.

"This is my reward for creating a goddess out of a bitch," he shouted, uncontrollable in his rage, hacking the canvas again and again. "I'm through with you." His voice was a hoarse whisper. He sat down hard on a chair and held his head in his hands. "Conniving bitch! André, stay away from women, this is what they'll do to you." He raised his head and looked at Victorine. "Get out!" he shouted.

She walked to the table and placed the ring on it. "I thought you might want this back." A door slammed, and footsteps sounded in the foyer. "Hello!" Julia's voice sang out from the hall. "I came early to . . . dear me, what's happened?"

Julia glanced at Victorine, then at Edouard, holding his head in his hands. She walked toward Edouard, dropped to her knees, and embraced him. As Victorine watched, Julia stroked his hair gently and caressed him in a way not at all platonic. Then she began to kiss his cheeks. Initially, he pushed her away and turned his face. But she came round the other side and continued to kiss his eyelids, cheeks, chin. Her mouth found his and kissed him deeply. She swayed her body into his, willing him to kiss her back. And he did, with a vengeance.

Victorine felt physically ill as she watched. She stumbled backward, then turned and escaped as quickly as she could. She stepped into the dusky evening, crossed the street, and ordered her carriage away, agitated and preferring to walk. As she glanced back, she saw a glow of gaslight illuminate Edouard's bedroom window. A carriage clattered around the corner and splashed through a puddle, just missing her before she jumped back to the pavement. A cold north wind gusted off the Seine and sliced through her mantle. She hugged her cloak about herself and bowed her head against the wind as she walked homeward.

Chapter Twelve

Tes yeux sont la citerne où boivent mes ennuis.

—Charles Baudelaire, "Sed Non Satiata," from *The Flowers of Evil,* 1857

'm not aghast at Manet's attacks of spleen," Baudelaire said. "I, myself, suffer from the same melancholia from time to time. Madness and creativity have gone hand in hand for centuries. It was Plato who recognized that prophets and poets communicate with the gods through an inspired madness."

"Yesterday I stopped in and found Edouard at work on an enormous painting. The heat in the studio was stifling, yet all the windows were closed. He was bare-chested and wearing paint-spattered workman's trousers. A two-day stubble shadowed his face and a cigarette dangled from his mouth," said André.

"I don't want to hear any more about him," Victorine said.

"I'm sorry, Victorine, but I'm worried. He was swigging from a bottle of Bordeaux at ten in the morning," André said.

"Well, it's a good sign that he was working. That dear boy sometimes won't pick up a paintbrush when the humors strike," Baudelaire said.

"It was a most curious subject, the unrisen Christ and angels ministering to him. It had all the elements of his signature style: the flat lighting, the handling of black paint, the unconventional use of pictorial space . . ."

"But a traditional crucifixion?" Baudelaire said.

"I asked the same question. He told me it was something he's always wanted to paint. He said, 'Christ as a symbol! Heroism or Love as a subject for a picture is nothing compared with Sorrow. Sorrow is at the root of all humanity and poetry.'"

"I don't want to hear any more!" Victorine covered her ears.

"But here's the most intriguing part. The face of the Christ was Manet."

"I'm leaving. I can't stand another word about Edouard Manet." Victorine hailed a hackney cab and left her two friends standing on the jammed pavement of the boulevard Haussmann wearing astonished expressions as they watched her cab clatter away.

~

Victorine was surrounded by swatches of fabric sprawled over her lemon-yellow divan when Julia dropped in.

"I'm here to tell you something important," Julia said. "It's about Edouard."

"Edouard who? I don't know an Edouard anymore."

"I slept with him." The edge in Julia's voice was sharp enough to slice a friendship to tatters. "I'm happy I did."

"You do realize he intends to hurt me by romancing you," Victorine said.

"Victorine! How can you be so selfish? I'm in love with him, and I'm entitled to a chance for happiness!"

"Happiness? With a man who can't respect or cherish any woman?"

"He loves and cherishes . . ." Julia stopped before blurting "you." She picked up a fabric sample and stroked the nap. "I offered to be his model, and he accepted."

"Julia, Baudelaire once explained Edouard to me." Victorine turned to face Julia. "He said there's an inner dance between the man and the artist. They're his demons. Each time he discovers a new model, he falls in love with the woman in the flesh and the one on the canvas. In his bed, he makes love to her body. On his canvas, he makes love to her soul. The very act spurs his inspiration. Yet when the painting's done, the fascination vanishes. As the painting dries, the girl fades into past tense."

"Is that why you've never . . ."

Victorine nodded.

"I'll change him."

Victorine felt betrayal roil in the pit of her stomach.

"He's not yours to change!" Victorine shouted.

Julia shrank back in her seat, frightened by Victorine's fierce tone.

"You're a girl of privilege. Did you ever guard what little you had from poaching? Did you ever sit at a table gulping your meals with your arm encircling your plate? No one steals what belongs to me!"

"I'm not trying to steal anything! I'm in love with him."

"In love with . . . ? I can't comprehend that emotion," Victorine said softly.

"I know he'll never care for me as he does for you. But I'll settle for whatever of him I can have." Julia took Victorine's hand. "There's only one you," she said. "I can never hope to be that."

"He'll crumple your heart and toss it away when he's grown bored of you." Victorine smiled. "Remember, I warned you."

"Nevertheless, I'll take my chances. Are you still angry with me?" Julia asked.

"Of course not. You're my dearest friend. Nothing can come between us."

Chapter Thirteen

Everyone wants a mistress, as everyone wants to go hunting,
frequent watering places and be seen at theatre premieres.

—Maxime Du Camp (1822–1894)

The 1867 Universal Exposition was scheduled to
open the next April, and tourists from all over the world
would descend on Paris. Emperor Louis-Napoléon, a staunch
promoter of commerce and the arts, intended the exposition
to showcase France and all her glory as a tribute to his own
regime. Selling exposition pavilion space was one of Philippe's
business enterprises, and he invited Victorine to a supper
party at the posh Café Riche to lend her charm and enthusiasm to encourage potential British and American exhibitors.

Victorine politely listened to their stories while glancing
around the white-and-gold salon searching for familiar faces.
Café Riche was a place where everyone mixed—writers, bankers, real estate speculators, actors; whoever could afford the
hellish prices for the sinfully delicious cuisine could be seen
from early morning until midnight. The maître d'hôtel was
famous for his technique of spreading sauce on a filet or

barbue au vin rouge. The gesture was so sensual, it was said that diners stopped in midsentence to watch, like voyeurs.

Victorine glanced up at the gilt-edged mirror lining the wall and caught the reflection of Edouard and a small party just entering the restaurant. Three months had passed since they had said adieu forever. He looked handsome, but appeared gaunt, his tall frame less robust than she remembered. He must have stopped by for a late supper after the Opera, for he was dressed in elegant black evening clothes, a white silk scarf dangling around his neck and a pair of white gloves flopping from his breast pocket. A single white gardenia graced his lapel. She leaned a bit to see his companions. She spied André and Degas and two other gentlemen whom she didn't recognize. Although the maître d'hôtel seated them right behind her, they didn't see her. She could see them from a certain angle in the mirror and could also hear some of their conversation.

"Bring me an absinthe!" Edouard called out to the waiter, who came round with a white napkin draped over his arm. The others laughed rather too loudly and ordered the same. Victorine realized they were roaring drunk.

"Here's to all the beautiful women in Paris." Edouard raised his glass. "We'll be the envy of every country at the exposition when they discover our French coquettes."

"Expositions, bah! An homage to capitalism by a conspicuous worship of display," said the young man she didn't recognize. "Have you seen that monstrosity the emperor built over the Champs-de-Mars? He calls that an exposition hall?"

"He ought to have built a structure that reflects the beauty of our art," Degas said.

"Like Manet's paintings that manifest pure elegance," the other stranger said.

"Rochefort, stop flattering me, I'm not buying drinks this round." Edouard threw a balled-up napkin at his friend. "I heard today that the Salon might accept a few of my paintings for the exposition. I've received offers from dealers who never gave my work a second look. And Julia's friends from America! They visit my studio with such open minds and willingness to appreciate my art, it's—"

"You're selling to them?"

"Pictures to see, not to sell." Edouard swallowed his entire drink in one mouthful.

"There's an artist I know who's painting under contract to Durand-Ruel," said Degas, referring to the art dealer. "He's slave to a mortgage now. The fool's bought himself a fancy new house in the Parc Monceau district and churns out pictures like a factory stamping out ceramic ashtrays. I've seen the garbage he produces. What a shame. That man used to actually have talent."

Edouard half rose from his seat and Victorine heard him call out, "Over here, darling." A young woman had just entered the café accompanied by two friends. She was about seventeen years old, with reddish chestnut hair framing deep-set gray eyes. Heads turned to stare as she passed by. She greeted Edouard with a deep kiss and joined his table. She and her friends leaned in toward him, flirting and giggling. Edouard was in his element. After a few moments, he rose and gallantly offered his arm to her. As they headed for the exit, he turned around and signaled a triumphant thumbs-up to his pals. That was when he caught sight of Victorine watching him in the mirror. Their glances met for an instant before she looked away. In her peripheral vision, she saw him stand stock-still, though the girl was tugging his arm. Victorine refused to meet his gaze. She drained her entire glass of wine to calm herself and checked the mirror again; he was gone.

The day Philippe drove her to see her own house—a newly built mansion, an *hôtel particulier,* on the rue Van Dyck, bordering the elegant Parc Monceau—for the first time, he directed his driver to take them from her apartment on the boulevard Malesherbes to the elegant district surrounding the park. As the carriage slowed, he covered her eyes with his hands and did not uncover them until she heard gates swinging open and the sound of water splashing in a fountain as the carriage slowed to a stop.

"Mademoiselle Laurent." He took his hands away. "Your new home."

Her gaze traveled around the cobblestone porte cochere with its ornate marble fountain in the center, up the facade of the gray stone mansion, from the French doors fronting the garden on the ground floor, up the line of balconied windows spanning the second story, up to the third story, and finally up to the gray tiled mansard roof with its four chimneys piercing the blue, cloudless sky. She ran through the interior pulling him along behind her, dragging him up and down the stairs, in and out of every one of the thirty-two rooms. He begged her to stop, but she tickled him in the ribs and ran away, her squeals of delight echoing through the empty rooms, leaving him laughing at the sound of her opening and slamming doors behind her.

She marveled at the crystal chandeliers sparkling in every room, at the marble fireplaces, at the curving banister of the sweeping staircase, at the modern kitchen with two sinks, at the stables out back. And most of all, she stood on the terrace and gazed at the line of trees marking her property and the sweeping green expanse of the lovely Parc Monceau just beyond.

Moving day for Victorine was both traumatic and joyful. She closed the door tenderly on her little apartment for the last time and leaned her forehead against the door. She had not expected this sadness to envelop her upon seeing the rooms empty and silent.

"Are you coming?" Philippe called up to her from the landing downstairs.

"I'm just saying good-bye," she answered.

Her hand stroked the front door and the tarnished brass knocker. Her first home, now bare and strewn with dust balls. Her first aristocratic lover, Rothschild, unceremoniously tossed aside by orders of the Duke de Lyon. Edouard? Better not to even think about him. She squared her shoulders. Well, this was what you always wanted, she told herself sternly. No use wasting time on nostalgia. A three-story mansion awaited her and a man whose generosity knew no bounds was impatiently tapping his cane on the marble floor down below.

Kaiser Wilhelm of Prussia was scheduled to arrive for an official state visit. In his capacity as vice president of the legislative body, Philippe had organized an outdoor reception in the Bois de Boulogne to welcome him. It was to be a glittering imperial spectacle for all four hundred of the *"gratin"* of Paris, and marked the beginning of Grand Prix week at Longchamp racecourse.

Victorine sipped her coffee and nibbled a croissant in her palatial boudoir, awaiting Philippe's arrival.

"Hello, my love." He breezed into the room and wrapped her in his arms. "This is bound to be a spectacular day, I can just feel it."

In a short time, she had learned to gauge his moods. She could see that today he was in fine spirits. He hummed a little tune as he adjusted his cravat in her mirror, then turned his attention to her wardrobe. He always arrived early to help choose her ensemble. He insisted on attending her fittings as well, and gave advice on details most men knew nothing and cared nothing about. "Monsieur Worth, I don't mean to interfere with the genius of your designs," he would interject, then take a sketchbook and show the couturier with a flourish of his pen how a certain dress should look. Philippe always wanted more ribbons, more lace, more adornment on the dresses. It was clear that he would tolerate no dissent. His orders were final. The famously temperamental designer could only hide his fury, nod agreement, and redesign his own creations to the duke's specifications.

Philippe consulted his pocket watch. "Reception time's two o'clock. Your hairdresser's due soon?"

Her hand flew to her coif. "He's already been here, Philippe. Don't you approve?"

He studied her with a serious air, pulled some tendrils down, and loosened some wisps to frame her face. "Better. Count von Bismarck's my guest of honor, and I want you to dazzle him, Victorine. You speak German, which will surprise and charm him. I want you to gain his confidence; make him trust you. That would be most useful to me."

Victorine regarded him curiously. What did he mean by "useful"? She felt a tingling of apprehension in her gut. "I've read about him in the newspapers. He seems like a formidable man, this foreign minister of Prussia," she said.

"Nonsense. He's a connoisseur of beautiful, clever women. Be sure to engage him in conversation about the Opera. Your past at the Opera ballet is a piece of luck. He'll be enraptured." He produced a black velvet box from his breast pocket and opened it to show her a horseshoe-shaped diamond brooch studded with midnight-blue sapphires.

"A little good luck charm for you."

She held it up and admired the exquisite workmanship of the House of Boucheron.

He pulled her close and playfully bit her earlobe. "You

mean the world to me, Victorine. Believe me when I tell you that. Now, what shall you wear?"

On the stately ride down the Champs-Elysées in Philippe's open milord carriage, Victorine felt resplendent in her lilac-and-white satin dress with parasol to match. She leaned back against the tufted silk cushions and watched the crowds.

The people too insignificant to attend the imperial fête set up folding chairs along the pavements to watch the passing parade of swells on their way to the Bois de Boulogne. The crowds pointed as a princess passed in her cabriolet pulled by eight gleaming horses, and when a famous author in a tall silk hat trotted by on his horse. They even applauded appreciatively at a particularly elegant equipage. The spectacle continued all the way down the avenue de l'Impératrice, past the Hippodrome, to the entrance gates of the Bois de Boulogne.

Victorine had been privy to Philippe's planning for the gala reception and knew what to expect at the site. One thousand spectators from the general public who could afford the twenty francs for admission tickets would be allowed to roam the grounds and watch the festivities from the grassy field area. They were provided with beer and sausages dispensed from kiosks dotting the staging area. The four hundred invited guests, a more selective phylum, were entitled to enter the actual premises of the Pré Catalan amusement center. Only the most elite specimens of the Faubourg Saint-Germain and Parc Monceau were welcomed into the cordoned-off private imperial enclosure. Within that area, the most exclusive section was Emperor Louis-Napoléon's dais with its turrets, canopy, and red flocked seats.

The carnival atmosphere of the spectators along the Champs-Elysées was reflected in the happy mood of the guests in Philippe's carriage. Beside Victorine, they were Princess Mathilde, her married lover, Alfred-Emilien Nieuwerkerke, and their friend Maxime Du Camp, the reactionary writer she had met at the Salon.

"I attended a gallery exhibition yesterday of those confounded avant-garde artists led by Edouard Manet! The emperor had better banish those anarchists," Du Camp grumbled. "Alfred-Emilien, you're the minister of fine arts, can't you do something about them?"

"But Monsieur Du Camp," Victorine said, "surely you'd agree that Edouard Manet's paintings are a mixture of elegance and sharpness. He presents things of everyday life, then turns them into poetry."

"Poetry! Is that what you'd call a painting of a woman exiting a cheap café, holding a guitar, staring blankly into space?" He was clearly referring to Edouard's first portrait of Victorine. Philippe shot her a warning glance.

"Maxime, you're such a tireless bore." Mathilde poked his trouser leg playfully with the pointed toe of her silk shoe. "I happen to adore the modern painters. Especially the handsome ones." She winked at Victorine.

"Never has the low world of gallantry reflected high society as it does now." Du Camp shook an arthritic finger at Victorine. "The prostitute is a businessman and the businessman's a prostitute. This decadence will not bring our country to a good end. Mark my words, this is an abnormal time; the brain and the heart of the country are too disturbed, I tell you. Society will explode." He glared at Victorine.

Victorine looked to Philippe to come to her defense, but he glanced away, staring at the crowds along the street.

"Where are you from, young lady? I'm afraid we don't know who your people are." Nieuwerkerke leaned forward in his seat.

"Yes, tell us about your people," Du Camp sneered.

"I don't care to discuss the past. I believe only in the future."

The two men exchanged smug glances.

Philippe said sharply, "That's quite enough, Victorine. Let's discuss something pleasant, like horse racing. I expect quite a few Brits in my box at Longchamp later this week. How I'd love to show them that a French horse can beat out their nags!"

Victorine turned her attention to the scenery and fumed silently. Du Camp was unworthy to even say the name "Edouard Manet." And the other one. He was just the sort of snob Edouard loved to mock. She suddenly longed to be anywhere other than in this carriage, with this insufferable company.

"Don't pay a bit of attention to Maxime. He's just a sour old goat. Doesn't get enough sex. That's his problem," Mathilde whispered.

Victorine laughed, despite her anger.

"*Darling*, weave your magic spell on the Prussian. It will make our Philippe happy, and you'll be doing a great service for your country," Mathilde said.

"How will I be serving my country? What do you mean by that?"

Mathilde raised her index finger to Victorine's lips to shush her. "Just trust me." She hooked Victorine's arm in hers and turned to watch the crowds watching them.

The carriage entered the Bois through the Porte Maillot. They pulled past kiosks selling picnic supplies and rolled by La Cascade waterfall before halting at the entrance of the Pré Catalan. The liveried groom jumped from his place on the boot and held the door as Philippe stepped down, then turned to offer Victorine and Mathilde his hand. Under a cloudless

Fragonard sky, Victorine paused to survey the vast crowds in their elegant ensembles.

Sheltered by the shade of white turreted tents, ladies strolled in elaborate dresses, their bonnets trailing colored ribbons down their backs. Gentlemen milled about the green fields in black silk top hats, binoculars dangling about their necks, no doubt to catch a better view of the Prussian kaiser and the emperor when they appeared together on the dais. Waiters passed trays of champagne, while buffet tables covered in white damask groaned with delicacies to fuel the energy needed for social climbing. The scent of crêpes suzette sizzling in butter and the smell of warm chocolate sauce bubbling in pots wafted on the breeze from the cooking tents. On the bandstand, the orchestra played Strauss waltzes, while across the meadow, geese honked from the banks of the Lac Inférieur. Philippe had planned everything to perfection, as usual. Victorine suspected that he had even arranged for the beautiful, warm sunshine with just the lightest wisp of a breeze.

Philippe acted his role as official host of the festivities, greeting diplomatic emissaries from many nations, keeping Victorine constantly by his side. She met ambassadors and cultural attachés. She met Siamese and Americans and Swedish and so many other foreigners, and engaged them all in pleasant small talk. Philippe introduced her to a contingent of British racing enthusiasts. The Brits conversed about their upcoming Ascot in impeccable French, which impressed her to no end.

"Our fillies aren't as fetching or as fast as your French ones," a young Englishman said, leaning across Philippe to flirt with Victorine.

"Fast and wild," his friend joked.

"I just love a wild ride," the more handsome of the two said suggestively.

Victorine shook her finger at them. "You two are really very naughty."

"In Paris, isn't it nice to be naughty?"

De Lyon registered his displeasure with the tone of this conversation and directed their attention to the imperial entourage, which had just arrived. Emperor Louis-Napoléon and Empress Eugénie made their entrance trailed by fawning courtiers and ladies-in-waiting. Someone remarked that the emperor looked rather well, having just returned from taking the waters in Vichy for his chronic bladder condition. Another whispered that his "therapy" consisted of midnight ministrations from his current mistress, the buxom and beauteous Countess de Castiglione.

As Eugénie snaked her way toward the royal enclosure, she called out to Philippe that she prayed with all her heart for his good luck at the Longchamp races.

Mathilde hissed, "Keep your Machiavellian hypocrisy to yourself!"

"Shhh, Mathilde, she'll hear you," Victorine said.

"What of it? It's only the truth. That woman's a white devil."

Victorine asked what she meant by that remark.

"A white devil, one whose hypocrisy covers a boiling cauldron of deception. Philippe and I are wise to her."

Victorine spotted André in the crowd. He had told her to look out for him and his visiting uncle Willie. William, the Duke of Alsopp, was a member of the wealthy British branch of André's family. He had crossed the Channel to watch his horse run in the Longchamp race. André had said that although Uncle Willie was a confirmed old bachelor, he had begged for an introduction to the international beauty Mademoiselle Laurent, about whom all of Mayfair society was abuzz.

In fact, there was a pilgrimage of husbands leaving the imperial enclosure and threading their way through the crowds for a chance to chat with Victorine. "Good afternoon, Mademoiselle Laurent!" The husbands of the imperial court pulled on waxed mustaches and puffed out little chests. "Always a pleasure, Mademoiselle Laurent!" They tipped their tall silk hats to her.

"Lovely to see you," she called out, tilting her parasol prettily.

"Look at you, you're magnificent!" André removed his bowler and kissed her cheek. "Are those the de Lyon stable racing silks you're wearing?"

"Oh, André, come here and let's chat. I've missed you so."

"You've been so busy, no one's seen you in weeks!"

"How is Baudelaire? And Julia? And . . . everyone?"

"Oh, *everyone* can't find a model who suits him."

Uncle Willie poked André in the ribs to catch his attention.

"Where are my manners? Victorine, may I present my uncle, William, the Duke of Alsopp."

Victorine flirted shamelessly, bringing a schoolboy's blush to his cheeks.

"Victorine," Philippe called out. "I'd like you to meet my distinguished friend Count Otto von Bismarck." Philippe presented Victorine with a flourish. "May I present Fräulein Laurent."

Bismarck bowed and presented her a view of his bald head, pink as the map of Prussia, crisscrossed with rivers of blue veins.

"Herr von Bismarck, a pleasure to meet you," she said in his native tongue.

Delighted by her perfect German, he monopolized Victorine for an animated conversation, while Philippe stood by, glowing with pride. Bismarck was so enraptured that he did not present himself to Eugénie in the royal enclosure. The arrival of Kaiser Wilhelm of Prussia was announced by a trumpet fanfare. One by one, the swells left Philippe and headed to their seats in the royal enclosure. Maxime Du Camp made a big show of bidding Philippe adieu. The minister of fine arts left. Victorine was annoyed to see even Mathilde deserting them. Philippe was obliged to remain behind because courtesans were strictly forbidden in the imperial enclosure. She noted his chagrin as his gaze followed his friends hurrying to find their seats in the exclusive area.

"Philippe, I'd like to join your friends in the imperial enclosure." She slipped her arm through his.

He looked at her as though she had asked him to stop the earth from spinning.

"Darling, you know if it were possible, I would." He glanced at the royal pavilion and the haughty faces lining the enclosure.

"Philippe, you can do anything, I know you can. Please?" She paused for a moment. "You're not ashamed of me, are you?"

"Of course not. It's just the rules, my love."

"It's ever so amusing to break the rules!"

With every step toward the private fenced-in area, Victorine's spirits soared. When they approached the entrance, the attendant's eyes bulged as comprehension dawned. With great aplomb, Philippe handed him his invitation. The usher pragmatically took a split-second consultation with himself and decided that the Duke de Lyon, the trusted adviser of the emperor, the vice president of the legislative body, the owner of several horses running at Longchamp, could go wherever he pleased. He smiled politely at Victorine and spun the turnstile with a whirl.

She couldn't actually hear whispers and gasps, but she could see them deflected off Philippe's face as they passed rows of imperial titles, both First and Second Empire. Victorine walked with the gravitas of Empress Joséphine treading the apse of Notre-Dame on Coronation Day, while Philippe marched like a man stepping up to the guillotine.

When Philippe exchanged glances with an astonished Eugénie, he halted. But a sudden blast of fanfare drowned out what he began to say. The great moment had arrived for the kaiser's entrance. Excitement squirreled through the crowd, and the audience swayed as one to have a better look. Philippe dragged Victorine by the wrist until they were back at the turnstile. He pulled her through and continued on.

The orchestra struck up a pompous march as the kaiser, followed by his retinue, waddled toward the emperor and the empress. The audience strained to view this squat, balding man over the crowd of tall top hats but could only glimpse a white plume passing by, swaying in the breeze above a pointed helmet. Despite the sprightly military march played by the band, the kaiser negotiated the steps with some difficulty, leaning on the arm of the trusty foreign minister von Bismarck to reach his imperial host on the dais. The public evaluated this jovial-looking grandfather with a chest full of colored ribbons and military medals glinting in the bright sunlight. He looked less the Teutonic warrior and more the jolly Christmas *Kuchen*.

Victorine glanced away, tears of mortification in her eyes. The entire imperial court had just witnessed her utter humiliation. The entertainment for the distinguished guests unfolded. Philippe had commissioned Jacques Offenbach to produce a spectacle showcasing the wonders of modern France: Science and Industry were portrayed by voluptuous showgirls and tumbling acrobats; the Arts by *tableaux vivants*—actors and actresses dressed as Fragonard *galantes* on a swing and as Géricault's shipwrecked survivors on *The Raft of the Medusa*. Victorine was sinking into her misery when she became aware that the crowd was chanting her name.

"Mademoiselle Victorine! Mademoiselle Victorine!"

She was startled to see an actress onstage in a flesh-colored leotard stretched out seductively on a chaise longue. Behind her stood an African beauty holding a bouquet of flowers. The scene was faithful in every detail to Edouard's painting. Philippe grabbed Victorine by both arms and urged her to step up on her chair seat.

"Wave to them," he insisted. "Give them what they want, darling."

He held her steady as Victorine raised her right hand and waved. The crowds applauded with a roar of approval that reverberated through the grassy fields. She had never experienced anything like it. The rest of the afternoon spun past in a blur. Faces crowded her, hands groped to touch her. Total strangers shook her hand as though they knew her. She clung to Philippe for dear life.

On the ride home, she heard Philippe rhapsodizing about how she had charmed Bismarck. He raved about Victorine, how the crowds chanted her name, how they roared when she waved to them. "Nieuwerkerke. Did you ever hear anything like that? They cheered her like a conquering hero. Wouldn't you love to hear that kind of adulation just once in your miserable, sorry political career?" Victorine had never seen him so elated. "Mathilde—did you see Victorine with Bismarck? He was won over, eh? That Teutonic sausage. We'll fry him and have him with our eggs for breakfast!"

In the sanctuary of her cavernous dressing room, Victorine collapsed on a striped silk hassock. Her gaze traveled around the room to the full-length mirrors, the gilt-trimmed furniture, the chandeliers and sconces dripping crystal, the heavy brocade draperies tied back with tassels, the Aubusson rug beneath her feet, the faux Boucher frescoes on the walls, and she was acutely aware of how very much her shoulders ached. Her sides ached from the stays of her corset; her head ached from the noise of the crowds.

She crossed her arms on the mirrored vanity table and laid her head down, unable to contain the tears any longer.

Toinette stroked her long hair and patiently murmured comforting words that Victorine could not hear, lost as they were among the sobs that reverberated across her bedroom, through the hallways, and down to the very foundation of her mansion.

Chapter Fourteen

The wise can never match the splendid dreams of fools.

—Charles Baudelaire (1821–1867)

Victorine waited patiently, shivering in her corset and pantalets. She hugged her knees and became conscious of the musical notes floating up from the ballroom as musicians tuned their instruments with a trill of a flute, a plucking of violin strings.

"This one would look splendid on you." Philippe pressed a red taffeta ball gown against his body and contemplated the reflection in Victorine's dressing-room cheval glass. The sight of the powerful Duke de Lyon swathed in a pouf of satin ruffles and velvet trimmings made her smile. Philippe tossed aside the red frock on the tufted bench and held another gown against himself. "This gray velvet is quite fetching. These silver threads accent the color of your eyes," he said in a serious tone.

"Ma'm'selle would look beautiful in either one." Toinette tapped her foot.

Victorine threw her a wink.

Toinette slipped Victorine's peignoir over her shoulders and stoked the fire in the marble chimneypiece, trying to keep the barrel-vaulted room warm. She sighed and glared at Philippe as he contemplated the two dresses.

"It's important to me that you look exquisite every time your public sees you."

He handed her the red dress. She seated herself at her dressing table and turned up the gas jets on either side of the cheval glass to apply her makeup. Philippe watched her intently.

"You're pouting. Is it about the misadventure at the reception today?"

Victorine hesitated to answer.

"I have enough conflict in my professional life. That is not what I come here for. Is my meaning clear?" His voice rose with irritation.

She nodded silently.

"Very well. Dress quickly; your guests will be here soon."

Victorine stood beside Philippe under a quarter-ton rock crystal and sterling silver chandelier and welcomed *le tout Paris* into her grandiose new home.

Compliments such as "magnificent decor," "sumptuous furnishings," and "perfect taste" gushed from the very people who had watched with horror as Victorine had almost scaled the walls of their private sanctuary hours earlier. Victorine exchanged meaningless pleasantries in the receiving line. She felt slightly ridiculous in her Marengo red frock and could only hope that the rivière of fiery-red rubies and diamonds nestled between her collarbones distracted attention from the vulgar crimson ball gown.

"What is this Chinese lantern of a dress you're wearing?" André whispered as he planted a peck on her cheek.

"I'm so glad you're here! You're the only person in this room I'd want to know." She squeezed his hand.

"We're the only two under the age of one hundred." André nodded toward the silver-haired dowagers and balding aristocrats around them. "Do you expect those fossils to crawl to the ballroom and dance after dinner?"

Philippe was ushering the guests from the marble foyer into the drawing room to sip champagne and marvel at the objets d'art he'd personally selected for her mansion. Her manservants passed elaborate platters of hors d'oeuvres, and a harpist in the corner accompanied the low murmur of guests' chatter. Then supper was announced by Ariel, newly made head butler of Victorine's household.

In the dining room, all flowed smoothly until the dinner service was interrupted by a servant delivering an urgent communiqué for Victorine. She read the note, rose from her place, and apologized to her dinner partners. Every head swiveled as she hurried the length of the long banquet table, stopped at André's chair to whisper in his ear, then continued to the head of the table. "I have to go," she said.

"What's happened?" Philippe's chair screeched against the parquet floor as he stood and grabbed her wrist. His dinner guests exchanged glances and smirked.

"It's Baudelaire. He's been ill . . ." She pulled her hand away.

"Go back to your seat. You may not leave now," he whispered.

"Yes, I can. And I will."

Victorine marched out of the room with André scurrying behind to catch up. She threw open the doors with such conviction that she startled her footmen in the hallway.

"My cloak! And instruct the groom to prepare my carriage. Quickly!"

In the parlor of Baudelaire's town house on the rue Mozart, Victorine found Julia at the piano playing Baudelaire's favorite Wagner. His beautiful Caribbean mistress, Jeanne Duval, sat beside Julia on the piano bench.

Jeanne rose to embrace Victorine and André. "I'm so glad you're here," she said.

"It started this morning." Julia looked tired and pale. "His face was flushed and his breathing became erratic."

"I was at Philippe's reception all afternoon . . ." Victorine felt a twinge of guilt.

"It's the pox. He caught it years ago, but this evening, his fever spiked and gave us quite a scare," Julia said. "The doctor was here and just left."

Baudelaire's bedchamber door opened and Victorine caught her breath—Edouard. So many months had passed; she'd forgotten the effect of his magnetism, that aura of genius he wore like a comfortable cloak. For several moments, they simply stared at each other. Edouard gazed at Victorine with a look of infinite tenderness until, in a flash, his expression changed. "How nice of you to take time from your busy social calendar."

"Please, Edouard. I came as soon as I heard."

"Who stopped the music? Play, goddamn it," Baudelaire's weak voice called from his bedchamber. Julia found her place on the music sheet and began to play.

"May we go in and see him?"

Edouard stepped aside for her and André.

Baudelaire's skin had jaundiced to the color of ancient parchment paper, and his cheeks were sunken, craggy hollows. He lay in bed surrounded by sheaves of half-finished scribblings; a bed tray holding an inkwell and pen lay beside him. He struggled to sit up in bed.

"Victorine . . . André . . . You needn't have come."

"So, this is what love's done to you? Well, I hope she was worth it, you old lecher." André tilted Baudelaire's nightcap to a jaunty angle.

Baudelaire attempted an appreciative smile. "I heard about the Longchamp reception today. Well done." He reached for Victorine's hand. "Invitations to imperial receptions, not bad for a little *lorette* from Saint-Roule."

"My poor darling." She tucked the counterpane under his chin and kissed his burning forehead.

"Edouard . . . did you see him?" he asked in a voice barely louder than a whisper. "He can't paint without you. You know that. Forgive him and reconcile. For my sake."

She nodded. Tears stung her eyes to see dear Baudelaire this way.

"Listen to that beautiful music." A peaceful smile floated across his face. "My pipe." He motioned to a hookah. She brought it to his lips and watched as he inhaled the opium, sighed, and laid back, a haze of contentment misting his eyes.

"We mustn't tire you," Victorine said.

"Send in Jeanne. I want her."

As she left Baudelaire's room, she motioned for Jeanne to go in, then glanced around the parlor. "Edouard . . . gone?" Julia stopped playing and nodded toward the library. She half rose from the bench, but André grabbed her arm and shook his head as though to say, *Let her go to him alone.* Julia reluctantly sat down.

Victorine found Edouard in the wood-paneled library stretched out on the leather chaise longue. In the dim firelight, she saw that he was engrossed in a sketch. He did not glance up as she entered. "I can't believe how he's changed," she said.

"We've all changed, haven't we?"

She approached the chaise and sat beside him.

Edouard contemplated the half-completed charcoal sketch of Baudelaire on his lap. "He never felt inclined to climb the mountains of India or sit by some lake in a faraway place, like certain other poets. He found both his heaven and hell right here in Paris." At last he raised his gaze to Victorine and observed the shadows of firelight flickering across her face.

"I remember once we passed an ex-paramour of his on the street. She barely acknowledged him, but he told me, 'I preserve the sacred essence and form of all my loves as they decay.'"

"The day Baudelaire met you, he predicted you'd conquer Paris. How right he was. Remember that day you first came to my studio? Seventeen years old. You bewitched three sophisticated Frenchmen . . . we were completely undone by one girl." He shook his head and laughed.

Suddenly, their long estrangement and angry words seemed trivial. He opened his arms and wrapped her up in them. She placed both hands tenderly on either side of his face and drew his mouth slowly toward her. His spine stiffened and he pulled back.

"I want you to . . . ," she whispered.

He brought her hand to his mouth, kissing her fingertips one by one, then pulled the diamond-and-pearl comb from her hair and let it fall free. The embers in the fireplace crackled and hissed as he lowered his mouth toward hers. He unclasped the ponderous diamond-and-ruby necklace around her throat and let it drop heavily to the carpet. She shivered as his fingertips slid her dress off her shoulders, and she felt those hands she had watched so often painting her body now caressing it like a familiar road down which he had traveled all his life. She was aware of a pounding in her ears that was her own heartbeat. The more tenderly he kissed her, the more desperately she wanted him. And then she panicked. "No!" She pushed with all her might against his chest.

He lifted his head, panting for breath. "Victorine, you can't stop this now."

"I have to—this will ruin everything."

"Tell me you don't love me and I'll stop."

"Stop," she said.

He looked like a man who'd stepped off a precipice. He pushed himself off her, walked several paces away, and clung to the mantelpiece for support. She watched him from behind, his shoulders heaving as he tried to catch his breath.

"Let me be part of your life as I used to be." Her voice was barely a whisper.

"Your master won't allow you to." A bitter tone sliced his words.

"I want to come back. Please?"

She'd seen few men struggle as mightily as Manet did with himself at that moment. "All right. Come back to me. We'll be as we were," he said.

They stared at each other, aware that nothing could ever be as it was before, but willing to pretend that it could. At that moment, the library door flung open and Julia stood silhouetted in the doorway.

"The fever's broken, thank God," she said.

A three A.M. melancholy enveloped the corner table at the Café Tortoni as waiters shuffled about performing the rituals of closing time. They turned chairs upside down on tabletops, bedding them down for the night, as the barkeep clinked newly washed whiskey glasses, stacking them neatly on shelves behind the gleaming mahogany bar.

"I remember a day trip to the beach at Argenteuil," Edouard said. "Baudelaire refused to skinny-dip with us. I'll never forget the sight of him sitting on the sand like a proper gentleman in a dowager's parlor, sweating away in his frock coat and cravat, while the rest of us frolicked nude in the surf."

Julia passed him her handkerchief to wipe away his tears.

"Will France ever produce another poet like Baudelaire?" André asked.

"Haven't you noticed since that stroke years ago, each time he has a relapse, he recovers yet a little worse than before."

Victorine checked her pocket mirror, dabbed her tear-stained cheeks, and excused herself for the ladies lavatory to wash her face. As she returned, she stopped for a moment before entering their field of vision.

"Baudelaire is dying, Victorine returns," she heard Edouard say as he stared at the parrot-green color of his drink, seemingly searching for the mysteries of life there.

"You're still in love with her," Julia said in a flat tone of voice.

"Aren't all of us in love with Victorine? It's just a matter of degree. Some less. Some more," he said.

"Pardon my straight talk, but I'll be there when you finally efface her imprint from your heart."

"Julia, I told you. What happened between us, it's no more than what it was. You were there and—"

Julia held up her hand to silence him. "I'll be patient."

Victorine took a step farther back into the vestibule to gain her composure. "You know, Monet adores you," she heard André say.

"Monet? I never noticed," Julia said.

"He'd be good to you," Edouard said. "He's the kind of man you ought to have."

"Edouard, I'm the safe road home. Victorine's the challenging mountain cliff. I know danger brings excitement, but it can bring disaster as well."

"Monsieur Manet," a waiter interrupted. "It's nearly three thirty. We're closing now, sir. I'm sorry."

"Quite all right, old chap. Here, take this." Edouard rose and pressed a five-franc bill into the waiter's hand.

Victorine waited a few moments before she made her entrance. They left the café and walked through the quiet streets as sadness settled around them. Even Paris seemed somehow to grieve in its slumber. Edouard recalled a poem of Baudelaire's, reciting from memory: " 'To be away from home, yet to feel oneself everywhere at home: to see the world, to be at the center of the world and yet to be hidden from the world—such are a few of the slightest pleasures of those with an independent, passionate, impartial nature.' Well, he's almost home now, dear Baudelaire."

Victorine returned to her mansion. She glanced through the doors of the ballroom and spied several stragglers still drinking champagne. Some guests in their evening cloaks passed her on the way down as she climbed up the stairs. They called out good night drunkenly and thanked her for a magnificent evening.

She walked into her dressing room. Philippe was waiting for her in the darkness, cigarette smoke curling above his head. "What were you thinking, leaving your own party like that?" His voice betrayed no emotion.

"Baudelaire needed me tonight. He's dying."

"I was humiliated. Everyone asked where you'd rushed off to." He clenched and unclenched his fist. "Never embarrass me again like that, do you hear?" His tone was still silky smooth, but his gaze threatened her. She continued to undress nonchalantly. Suddenly, he froze as his attention riveted to her bare neck.

"Where's your necklace?" he asked.

Her hand flew to her throat. A smile, a memory of a kiss.

"Manet. He was there tonight, wasn't he?"

She nodded. "I'm going to sit for a portrait tomorrow."

"I forbid it." His eyes narrowed as he exhaled an arabesque of smoke.

They stared at each other, each waiting for the other to capitulate.

"I can't sponsor you at court, Victorine, with your naked body on display all over Paris."

"Sponsor me at court?"

"I'll arrange the details through Louis-Napoléon. He can't deny me this small favor." He studied Victorine's face intently. "Once you've been presented, you'll be eligible to attend state receptions and imperial balls at the Tuileries Palace."

She slid her arms around his neck.

"Now I've made you smile," he said.

Edouard had left the studio door ajar for her. She stepped in and inhaled the tangy smell of oil paint. The paint-spattered floorboards squeaked beneath her shoes as she crossed the vestibule and flung open the double French doors. She stepped out to the balcony and leaned against the verdigris iron handrail. Her gaze embraced a jumble of russet and gray slate rooftops tumbling from the place de l'Europe up beyond Montmartre.

Victorine returned inside and glimpsed Edouard through the archway. He was bent over a recently completed canvas, touching his index finger gingerly to the tacky surface to determine if it was dry. A stray lock of hair fell across his forehead, and as he brushed it away with a familiar gesture, Victorine exhaled the sigh of a traveler dropping her suitcases on the floor, grateful to be home after a long voyage.

He straightened up and looked at her as though he could not quite believe that she was back. "I'm glad you're here," he said.

He helped her remove her cloak and laid it across his divan. They simply stood looking at each other. There were no words for this moment.

"DAMNED BIRD! DAMNED BIRD!" A shrill squawk pierced the air and Victorine noticed Edouard's new pet, a bright green parrot. "What do you call him?" she asked as she poked her finger through the cage. The parrot promptly tried to bite her.

Edouard said he had only bought him yesterday as a prop, and hadn't thought about naming him.

"Let's call him Bismarck. He reminds me of Otto von Bismarck with that bald head and screechy voice."

"You've met Minister Bismarck?"

"You can't believe the bores and snobs I have to suffer. Bismarck, that old lecher, you should see this funny monocle he wears. He clicks his heels like this, Edouard, when he bows—"

He interrupted her little pantomime.

"What exactly does de Lyon have in mind for you?"

"Oh, let's not discuss him. Better to tell me about this painting."

She successfully steered him off the subject of Philippe. "I found myself near the Luxembourg Gardens last week. There's a big department store near there, and I stopped to look at the window displays. They were showcasing boots, maybe twenty pairs, all factory-made perfection. Those mechanically produced commodities are the antithesis of individuality and spontaneity. That's when I got the idea for this picture."

"And what role do I play?"

"I envision an elegant woman in a peignoir; you'll be very demure. Except for that gaze, the famous look." His voice grew animated as he described every detail. "Courbet intrigued me with a brilliant picture he exhibited at the Salon recently. He painted a parrot hovering lasciviously over a supine nude woman. In Renaissance art, the parrot symbolizes Truth and Beauty. In my vision, a parrot perches on a tall stand to your left, watching you, just as demure as you."

Edouard handed her a peach satin peignoir and bustled about the studio gathering props. She undressed, chatting while performing a striptease that felt so natural, she was not even aware of its effect. "Shall I pull up my hair, or do you prefer it down?"

She heard no response.

She glanced at Edouard and was startled to see him poised to peel a prop orange, motionless, mesmerized by the sight of her. Surprised by the intensity of his gaze, she pulled the peignoir closed to veil her nudity. "We should get to work," she said softly.

He busied himself preparing his palette and setting the blank canvas on the easel. He then approached and placed his hands on her shoulders to turn her toward the afternoon light. Shivers flew up her spine at the touch of his fingertips through the satin fabric. He rearranged the folds of her gown, draping it to her body like the chiton of a Greek sculpture, evoking such tenderness, so opposite to Philippe's way.

"Stand here like this," he said. "Now, hold these violets like this." He placed a small nosegay of silk flowers in her hand, wrapping his fingers around hers.

He tilted her face forty-five degrees to the left and tucked a lock of hair tenderly behind her ear. His hand lingered a moment, caressing the scar on her cheek. "Will you tell me how you got this?"

"There was a man, Madame Goulue's most important client. When he found out I was only fifteen, he started asking exclusively for me. He wanted me to . . . wanted me to . . . perform Lachaise on him. I didn't want to. He forced me with the red, glowing end of a cigar."

"I'm so sorry. Forgive me for asking you. What kind of pervert teaches Lachaise to a fifteen-year-old?"

"Oh, he didn't teach me. I learned it at thirteen from Monsieur Kaye. When I ran crying afterward to Madame Goulue, she slapped me and told me no man would ever respect a girl like me. She said I should just remember that I'm an object provided for their pleasure to use in whatever way they choose."

"Never again." He tucked her head against his chest. "Not anymore."

She pulled away and looked into his eyes. Precarious dynamics balanced on the understanding that this consummation must not happen. He stepped back and took his seat on the little folding stool before his easel.

"Let's begin," he said, picking up his sketching chalk.

Chapter Fifteen

Hypocrisy is a fashionable vice, and all fashionable
vices pass for virtues.

—Jean-Baptiste Molière, *Don Juan,* 1665

You idiot, what are you doing?" Philippe shouted to his masseur.

"Monsieur le duc. How am I to ease the knots from your legs if you bellow? After a session with your fencing master, the muscles are always very tight."

Philippe waved him away and sat up gingerly, wrapping the towel around his waist. Victorine hid a smile behind her fan but was caught in the act.

"I've turned into an old man, Victorine."

She approached and wrapped her arms around his neck. "I'll take your saber thrusts over any younger man's," she whispered in his ear.

"Never leave me for a young lover. Do you hear?" He laughed and pulled her onto his lap.

"Why did you call me here so urgently?"

"I just received word that Prussia defeated Austria at Sadowa. They've added all the northern German states into their fold with Austria's unconditional surrender. Our ambassador traveled from Berlin to Sadowa to negotiate with your new friend, Count von Bismarck. As a trade-off for our neutrality, Ambassador Benedetti claimed land for France that Prussia took from the Austrians."

"Land?"

"Portions of the left bank of the Rhine, plus Luxembourg and Belgium. It was a damn foolish mistake. And worse yet, he brought Bismarck the request in writing. Bismarck refused him with a loaded revolver on the table."

Philippe took Victorine's hand and raised it to his lips. "I need a favor from you, my darling. I want you to pry some information out of Bismarck, just casually during the course of conversation. I'll give you some papers that will help guide you."

Victorine felt a stab of foreboding. "No thank you. I'll have no part in this."

"Victorine, France has been rescued by many noble ladies. Every schoolchild knows Saint Geneviève convinced Attila not to destroy Paris in the fifth century. And, of course, there's Joan of Arc."

"Philippe, I'd rather not be involved in matters of state. It's all too—"

"Germany's jealous of our status as the strongest power in Europe. Our country's like a beautiful woman, envied by her neighbors." He stroked her hair. "Bismarck's planning something. I'll give you a dossier outlining his military capabilities in simple terms. That way, you'll be prepared to coerce little secrets out of him."

"But how?"

"Use your intelligence and throw in a bit of your feminine charms, my dear."

"You're not suggesting I sleep with him!"

"Whatever's necessary." He shrugged.

She sprang off his lap. He might as well have tossed a match in a gunpowder factory. "Is that how you regard me—your personal play toy to be shared around at your discretion?" she shouted.

"Of course not. Please forgive me."

As the moments passed, Victorine recognized that frown across his brow. It signaled a strategy forming in his mind. "If I were to move forward the date of your presentation at court, in time for the emperor's music festival at Fontainebleau Palace, would that convince you to forgive me?"

"Is Bismarck attending, by any chance?" Her eyes narrowed.

"Yes."

"I ought to walk out right now." She stormed toward the door.

"Please, Victorine, wait. I'm sorry. I just want what's best for France." He grabbed her arm. "Can you ever forgive me? I truly apologize."

She glared up at him, struggling between two options. She certainly wanted no part of his scheme. Yet, given the prestige of being accepted at the Tuileries Palace, how could she resist? "Oh, very well. Give me the damn papers." She held out her hand.

Philippe approached a large marquetry armoire, turned the key, and extracted a cache of files. He handed her several dossiers stamped with the imperial seal. "Thank you, Victorine."

She replied with a colorful epithet and slammed the door.

⁓

Not long after, a convivial group shared the workspace of Edouard's studio on a steamy August afternoon. He had taught his parrot a bawdy drinking song, "Ferdinand with the Three Legs." Victorine and André laughed as the bird warbled the chorus. Julia clucked at their childish antics, distractions that broke her concentration on her latest painting, a portrait of two women taking tea in a cozy parlor. The theme of female companionship was exemplified by the solidity of the silver pieces juxtaposed against the delicacy of porcelain teacups.

She put down her brush and said, "Remember the patient at La Salpêtrière asylum I mentioned, Mademoiselle Marie? The one I'm assigned to by the volunteer committee? Yesterday, I asked Dr. Charcot if the mentally insane talk strictly nonsense or whether their thoughts are based on some sort of logic. He answered that their reality is different, that they live inside their minds. He plans to publish a paper about Mademoiselle Marie in a scientific journal."

"Why did he choose her?" Victorine asked.

"She's endlessly fascinating, Victorine. Time has no meaning for her. She's a woman in her forties, but thinks she's still twenty. Yesterday, she told me her baby had caught the influenza. She called for her maid: 'Gerthe! Take that blanket off, can't you see she has a fever.' She was so convincing, I almost forgot there was no baby."

"One of my aunts is named Gerthe," Victorine said to no one in particular.

"Victorine, turn this way, please," Edouard said. "Something's missing," he muttered to himself. His eyes focused intensely on the canvas while his hand stroked a day's worth of stubble shadowing his face.

"What are you aiming to achieve, Edouard?"

"I was thinking about private introspection and how it offers us a respite from the public spectacle we engage in every day."

Julia turned to listen.

"I've painted you and the background with no horizon line, so the viewer feels he can't relate to the pictorial space. I want him to feel uncomfortable, self-conscious, strangely disembodied, as we all feel in this modern age."

Victorine stepped around to the front of the easel. She studied her own image. "It exposes the chasm between our empty public persona and the meaningful private one."

"You understand my work better than anyone, Victorine," Edouard said.

Victorine remembered her first visit to his studio, how strange and ugly she had thought his work. Now, she saw only genius in each brushstroke.

Edouard picked out a cambric lace pelisse, placed it around Victorine's shoulders, evaluated it, then took it off. He perched a crocheted cap on her head. Again, he stepped back a few feet, mumbled something, and threw it down on the floor. His gaze flew over the props scattered throughout the studio until it settled on a monocle hanging from a silken cord.

"Why this?" Victorine asked, as he draped it around her neck.

"The monocle symbolizes a single focus. You're a modern, freethinking woman with foresight into the future."

"Someone told me lesbians wear a monocle to convey coded messages to each other," Victorine said.

He shrugged. "The viewer can interpret as he wishes."

"I'd rather avoid controversy, Edouard," she said. "I'm being presented at court next month."

Edouard and André exchanged astonished looks. Edouard asked if she was making some sort of joke. "You're a courtesan. You've no family name, no fortune, nothing that's required of a person presented to the emperor and the empress. They won't accept you, I guarantee it."

"We'll see about that. I will be presented, and you'll have to apologize to me."

Julia changed the subject and asked Victorine to accompany her on rounds with the Charity Committee. Wishing to prove to Edouard that she was capable of being a grand lady, one worthy to be presented at the imperial court, she graciously agreed.

⁓

After enduring a dull afternoon of visiting charity cases with Julia, Victorine met André at her dressmaker's, where he helped her choose designs for new ball gowns. He had the most exquisite taste, which he claimed to have inherited from his mother and grandmother, both famously well-dressed beauties in their day.

On the carriage ride back to her mansion at dusk, Victorine's driver brought the vehicle to a sudden halt in the circle of the place de la Concorde. She pulled aside the curtain to see several carriages in a tangle and bystanders in a circle pointing at an object in the street. Victorine called up to the groom to see what had happened.

He reported back that a pedestrian had been knocked down by a pair of horses and was awaiting the ambulance. He informed her that the woman was easily recognizable as the former courtesan Queen Mabille.

"That's the beggar woman I saw the first day I came to Paris!"

"There's an apocryphal story about Queen Mabille," André said. "During the height of her success, she had seven lovers, all friends from the finest families of the aristocracy. They decided to buy a chest with seven drawers for her boudoir, one drawer for each lover on his assigned night. Look at her now; she's just a cipher."

Victorine was contemplative for the rest of the ride home. She gazed out the window at the city streets flashing past, but her mind was elsewhere. Chancing upon Queen Mabille, she closed her eyes and saw the scene so vividly, herself as a young girl from the provinces finally arrived in the fabled city of dreams—Paris—to find not a dream, but a horrible nightmare.

Now, so many years, so many experiences later, she understood how perfectly Queen Mabille defined her Paris. The highest success could suddenly tumble into abject failure. The wrong lover, a mistaken motive, could spin an ally into an enemy and love into hate, precipitating a dangerous plunge.

Since that first day, Victorine's guiding principle was to never make the mistake that woman had made. To never spiral into the nightmare of that hell. Victorine had an inexplicable longing for Edouard. After dropping off André, she instructed her driver to take her to his place.

"So, you came face to face with Queen Mabille, that wraith from your past?" Edouard said.

"Yes. And I began to reflect on my journey from Alsace to where I am today. I've always believed that the past is dead, and best left buried, but I have so many questions. How shall I find the answers?"

"If you're prepared to discover the answers about yourself, engage a lawyer to conduct a search. I could recommend a good fellow. I'll write a letter of introduction."

Chapter Sixteen

The more one discovers about oneself, the more
there is to discover.

—Charles Baudelaire (1821–1867)

*E*douard had convinced her of the virtues in learning the truth, but on the way to the lawyer's office, Victorine wavered between optimistic anticipation and downright dread. She needed the moral support of André and Julia, as she still vacillated between discovering her true identity and leaving matters as they were, and so they had agreed to accompany her. She glanced down at the frayed purple velvet pouch she held on her lap. The little pouch contained scraps and fragments of her life, dragged from location to location as she was traded around by her relatives. It had accompanied her to Paris and held great sentimental value to her. It represented the only mementos she had of her childhood, and today it might serve some useful purpose for the lawyer, Maître Mollet.

Mollet presented Victorine with a yellowed document: her birth certificate. It revealed that Marie Laurent, age twenty-two, had been Victorine's mother.

"But it says my birthplace was Paris." Victorine held the document in her bejeweled hands. "I don't understand." André and Julia traded surprised looks.

Mollet rifled through a sheaf of papers on his cluttered desk. "Mademoiselle Laurent, may I be frank with you?"

"Of course. And these are my dearest friends. Whatever you need to say to me may be said in front of them."

Mollet cleared his throat. He said that Victorine's account of her childhood and humble origins in Alsace didn't match the facts presented in the birth certificate. He had corresponded as best he could with her caretakers in Alsace, and further research had uncovered letters of correspondence between her mother and her caretakers.

"Do you mean my aunts?" she asked.

He leaned back in his chair, assessing her. "The women whom you call your aunts were actually your mother's maidservants."

"What do you mean?" said Victorine.

"You were born in Paris to a young lady named Marie Laurent, address listed on the rue Turenne, near the Bal Mabille. After several months, you were sent away to live with her maid's family in Alsace."

A shocked silence greeted his revelation.

"I want to understand you correctly. My mother was a Parisian?"

"Yes. She chose to relocate you from Paris for her own reasons. I found no marriage record at City Hall. She decided to have no direct contact with you, although she did support you by sending generous sums of money to your caretakers."

"Generous! They were anything but generous. I was raised in very modest circumstances," Victorine said bitterly.

He squeezed a pair of pince-nez on the bridge of his nose and searched through a stack of papers under his elbow. From the crude accounting kept by Gerthe Zissner, he said, it appeared that they did not faithfully execute the trust placed in them.

"Well, who was my father?"

"On the line for father's name, it says, 'Pierre Pierre.' I can only conclude—"

"Yes, go on," she said.

"In cases where a young lady bears the illegitimate child of an aristocrat, the name of the father is customarily entered as Pierre Pierre, for obvious reasons of discretion."

Victorine inhaled a deep breath to steady herself. "An aristocrat? But I don't understand," she said. Then she remembered the velvet pouch. She emptied the contents onto his desk and an endearing pile of items tumbled out—the train-ticket stub to Paris, her acceptance letter to the Opera ballet school, other girlish keepsakes. Among them, Maître Mollet selected a lace handkerchief with the embroidered initials M.L. He unfurled it, and out tumbled a little bracelet of seed pearls, exactly the circumference of a child's wrist. From the bracelet dangled a tiny gold heart with an inscription.

"To my little *jolie*," he read aloud, then turned it over and read the reverse. "'Victorine Laurent, December 14, 1845.' Who gave you this?" he asked.

"I don't know; I've always had it."

Julia suddenly sat up. "Did anyone ever call you 'my little *jolie*'?" she asked.

"No, never. Why do you ask?"

"Mademoiselle Marie, the patient at the hospital, refers to 'her little *jolie*.' I assumed it was a little dog, but now it makes sense! Her little *jolie* is the baby she's been longing for all along. I believe the baby, her little *jolie*, is you!"

"Julia, that's ridiculous. You can't believe that madwoman could be—"

"But the baby lives somewhere with her *maid's family* . . ."

"Impossible," Victorine said. "My mother died in childbirth."

Maître Mollet's gaze darted between the two women. "Actually, she did not."

Victorine was stunned silent for a long moment. Then she asked, "Is she alive? Could my mother still be in Paris?"

"I've been unable to determine the whereabouts of Marie Laurent. She may have married and is known by a different name now. Or she may have passed away." He noted the crestfallen look on Victorine's face. "What would you like me to do, Mademoiselle Laurent?"

Her mind reeled. "I'm sorry . . ." She tried to rise but sank back down.

"Please forgive me if I caused you too great a shock," the lawyer said.

"No, it's quite all right." She took a sip of water from a tumbler Julia held to her lips. "Please continue your search for Marie Laurent's whereabouts. I suspect you'll need money to encourage my aun—my mother's maids—to part with more information. I authorize you to promise them whatever sum you feel appropriate."

"A wise tactic, Mademoiselle Laurent." He bowed politely.

"I can't thank you enough, Monsieur Mollet." She looked down at the copy of the birth certificate. "This little document has changed my entire life."

The trail of Marie Laurent led to the records of the Prefecture of Police for the thirteenth arrondissement. Maître Mollet informed Victorine that a Marie Laurent had been picked up by the police in January of 1856, wandering the streets and apparently homeless. She was admitted to Salpêtrière Hospital.

Chapter Seventeen

All men by nature desire knowledge.

—Aristotle (384–322 B.C.)

*J*ulia was convinced that the patient she looked after was
Victorine's mother. She insisted they visit Dr. Charcot
and present him with the string of evidence. She felt certain
he would release confidential patient records, reveal the
woman's name, and prove her right.

Victorine and André stepped down from her carriage
on the boulevard de l'Hôpital and walked toward the entrance of La Salpêtrière, just across from the Gare d'Orléans.
Victorine took each step with trepidation, preparing herself
for foul smells and frightening sights. Instead, she gazed up at
a building that reminded her of the Invalides hospital with its
classical dome floating above a geometrical Enlightenment
structure. They passed through a charming courtyard called
La Cour Manon Lescaut, and toward the entrance hall, where
Julia awaited them.

She led them through the hallways to Dr. Charcot's office. From behind a desk piled high with documents, books, and medical charts, a slight man with intense dark eyes pulled on a white lab coat and greeted them. "Hello, hello! Do come in, please excuse the mess." He removed some charts from three straight-backed chairs and motioned for them to sit. As they conversed, Victorine sensed him evaluating her every word and gesture.

"My career began here fifteen years ago after studying under the great Dr. Paul Janet, the father of modern psychology," he said by way of presenting his credentials.

"Mademoiselle Stanhope-Morgan is so impressed with your work, Doctor," Victorine said.

He regarded her seriously. "Thank you, mademoiselle. I've been interested for years in the manifestation of mental illness in women, often labeled erroneously as 'madwomen.' They're usually victims of unfortunate circumstances in their youth—abusive fathers, alcoholic mothers . . ."

"How do they come to be here?" Victorine asked.

"They resort to life on the streets at a tender age. The seamy streets of Paris become their 'home' until they're brought here by the police or committed by men who don't want them anymore. Anyway, that's enough about my work. Please tell me about yourself." He picked up his pen, poised to take notes.

Victorine briefly recounted her personal history in Alsace. "After an unfortunate incident at the age of thirteen, a former teacher helped me leave my village by placing me in the state-subsidized Paris Opera ballet school."

He assiduously scribbled these facts in a notebook and asked for specific dates.

"Shall we take Mademoiselle Laurent to see the patient now?" Julia asked.

"All in due time," he said to Julia. "Marie is a common name, and the fact that her baby lived elsewhere doesn't prove much." Dr. Charcot smiled at Julia.

"But I've come to know her. I have an intuition that it's so," Julia said. Victorine detected an undercurrent of affection in the man's gaze as he looked at Julia. "May we go to her room now, Doctor? I can't wait another moment for Victorine to meet her."

The doctor led the way down a winding series of hallways. Victorine peeked in doorways, expecting to glimpse wild women screaming and thrashing, chained to their beds. Instead, an efficient calm and an entirely humane atmosphere prevailed as they walked the polished floors of long corridors.

"Here we are."

Victorine glanced at the nameplate on the door: MADEMOI-SELLE MARIE. A fragile woman sat in a chair, hands primly folded in her lap, facing a window open to the courtyard. Her gray hair was neatly combed, and she wore a standard hospital gown. She didn't turn around when her visitors entered, but continued to stare out the window. When Dr. Charcot greeted her, she glanced at him with a blank expression. In her lined face, Victorine saw the vestiges of beauty, glimpsed the sadness of a discarded soul.

"Hello, Mademoiselle Marie! I've brought a friend today," Julia said. She grasped Victorine's hand to pull her forward. The woman seemed to see Victorine, but nothing registered in her eyes. Victorine felt unsure of what to do. "How do you do," she finally said, tentatively.

"We'll just stand back here out of the way," Dr. Charcot said. He nodded to André, and indicated to Julia that she and Victorine go and stand nearer to the patient. Victorine noticed his pen poised again over his small notebook.

The patient ignored her visitors and gazed out the window with her unfocused stare. Suddenly, she spoke. "Hurry, fetch the blue satin gown with ermine trim! I'll wear it tonight to the theater. And bring my jewel case!"

Victorine gave a start upon hearing the youthful lilt to her voice. "Remember, she lives in the past. She thinks she's a beautiful young woman in the happy period of her life. It's best to humor her or she becomes a bit ... obstreperous," Julia whispered.

"Have you any news about the baby?" the woman asked Julia.

Victorine and Julia exchanged glances.

"Baby's fine," Julia answered in a calm tone.

"When will she visit? I haven't seen her for months. My little *jolie*. My Victorine."

Victorine clenched Julia's forearm, her fingernails digging half-moons in the flesh. "Why did she say that?" Victorine hissed.

Julia gently unclasped her arm from the grip and held Victorine's hand.

"The baby's coming to visit soon, Mademoiselle Marie."

"The baron and I depart for the season to Biarritz, and I want to see my baby before we go. I miss her so."

"Where is your baby now, mademoiselle?" Victorine asked.

"She's in Schirrhoffen," she answered.

Victorine stared at this woman, unable to breathe. She had never mentioned the name of her village to anyone, ever. She searched the wrinkled face, the dull eyes, the gnarled hands—how could this be? She needed air. She felt herself choking. Victorine bolted from the room and ran down the long hallway. She turned corners, unsure where to go, then found an exit and burst into the courtyard.

The beautiful symmetry of the formal garden clashed against the chaos of her thoughts. This couldn't be. Maybe it was an elaborate confidence game of some kind? Maybe this woman had heard of Victorine Laurent and plotted to extort money from the young woman who was the favorite mistress of the Duke de Lyon? She stopped suddenly to catch her breath. That could not be her mother. She had no mother. She was an orphan. Everything could be explained away as co-incidence.

Except the name of her village.

There was no possible explanation for Schirrhoffen.

Victorine sat down hard on a garden bench. Nature mocked her with the lushness of trilling birds and the ob-scene voluptuousness of greenery dipped in a warm haze of sunlight. She had to think, but she could not. A shock so pro-found cannot be processed efficiently. Her entire life, her very identity, was a tangle of lies and obfuscations.

"Victorine! Victorine! Oh dear God! Are you all right?"

Julia ran to her, breathless and frantic, André close behind.

Julia handed Victorine the patient's medical record that Dr. Charcot released to next of kin. Victorine opened the folder to read the name on the top line: "Marie Laurent."

"So he knew all along. He should have warned me."

"Dr. Charcot told me not to prepare you. He wanted to record your initial reaction."

"Record my reaction? Am I a scientific experiment to him?"

Victorine's remark offended Julia. "No, of course not. He's preparing to publish a research paper about her and——"

"What about me? Is he going to publish a paper about a person who thought her mother was dead, then discovers that she's a madwoman who wandered the streets? That the 'rela-tives' she thought were her aunts had no connection to her other than a monthly stipend?"

"I'm sorry, Victorine. I thought you'd be happy to find your mother," Julia said in a quiet tone. "I didn't realize what a shock it would be." Tears welled up in Julia's eyes.

"What am I supposed to do now? Share old memories, reminisce with her?" She felt as hollow as an empty cistern.

"You could question her to find out the true story about yourself," André tried.

"I don't have to. Isn't it obvious? Some man had his way with her, she gave birth to me, unburdened herself of the annoyance, and continued her career unhindered."

"Maybe she had no choice, Victorine. I think she loved you and sent you away to protect you from her world."

"Well, then, irony rules this day. I'm afraid, Julia, that your penchant for seeing the best in everyone is misguided here. She rid herself of me with the maid's family, sent money—that is, as long as she was earning it. When she hit rock bottom, so did I."

Julia shook her head; pity and kindness rendered her almost beautiful. "She did love you, Victorine. You're just too agitated at this moment to see it."

"Coming here was a terrible mistake." Victorine rose.

Julia grasped Victorine's arm. "Wait, don't you want to ask her about your father?"

"I never want to see that woman again," she said.

A crisp sea breeze nipped Victorine's bonnet as she rode in Philippe's phaeton along the wide boulevard de la Mer on the oceanfront in Deauville. Seagulls squawked as they soared and dipped above the waves. She raised her parasol against the early September sun and squinted at the light reflected off the sand. Blue-and-white striped canvas cabanas dotted the seashore. Blue-and-white striped standards fluttered above the gabled roof of the Grand Hotel. On the boardwalk, white eyelet summer frocks billowed, and the azure sea met the horizon in one mellifluous blue line.

Philippe was sweeping the scene with binoculars like a lord overseeing his fiefdom. "Look over there." He pointed to open land. "A fisherman sold us all that acreage for a pittance," he laughed. "I profited very nicely from that little transaction."

"You took advantage of a simple fisherman?"

"Took advantage is putting it mildly. We stole it." Philippe chuckled. "I'll never forget the look of triumph in his eyes when he handed the deed to us. What a fool."

Victorine knew that Philippe and his friends had bought up land in the charming seaside village of Deauville, a sleepy little community located across the Touques River from the resort of Trouville. Those who owned banks put up all the money while Philippe exerted his political influence and obtained permission from the government to level the dunes, dredge the Touques to create a yacht basin, and build a railroad line to come to Deauville rather than Trouville. He also built a racetrack to lure tourists away from Baden-Baden. Luxury hotels and seaside villas added to the allure; now the oceanfront was dotted with ostentatious mansions and attracting pleasure seekers by the trainload.

Philippe proudly pointed out each new villa under construction, announcing the owner's name and how he had made his fortune.

"Monsieur Wainer, industrialist, neo-Gothic style. Monsieur Griguer, banker, neo-Renaissance style." He pointed. "Mademoiselle Laurent, beautiful enchantress, neo-Norman style."

"What did you say?" She suddenly sat up at attention.

"Your seaside villa, my love. Right there next to mine."

Philippe pointed a yellow-kid-gloved hand. Victorine saw early construction on a monstrous behemoth overlooking the ocean.

"It's lovely," she said, her tone flat.

"That's a subdued response. You've hardly said a word this entire day. Is something troubling you?" he asked. "Do you need money?"

"No." She turned away and looked far out to the horizon. Since meeting Marie Laurent, she could think of nothing else.

"Are you apprehensive about your presentation at the Tuileries Palace? All that stilted protocol, a bit daunting."

"No. I'm not worried."

"The day I pleaded your case for sponsorship, you can't imagine the screaming fight I witnessed between the emperor and Eugénie," he said, clicking the whip above the horses' heads. "It wasn't a pretty sight. But our little emperor stuck to his promise. He stood his ground against her and all's well."

He turned to Victorine, but she was impassive. "Aren't you pleased?"

"Yes, very," she said softly.

"Then what's bothering you?"

Should she tell him? She knew he barely paid attention to any of her doubts or fears. Unless they involved money. Then he would dispatch the problem swiftly by putting pen to check. The only man who truly cared about her and could assuage the pain and uproar in her heart was Edouard Manet.

"Nothing's bothering me."

"Well, we'd better head back to the train station. We have to choose your dress for court. You must look ravishing, but tasteful," he continued, while everywhere Victorine's glance fell, she saw herself digging through trash cans like Marie Laurent.

Chapter Eighteen

There are no little events with the heart. It magnifies
everything; it places in the same scales the fall of
an empire . . . and the dropping of a woman's glove,
and almost always the glove weighs more than the empire.

—Honoré de Balzac (1799–1850)

*P*hilippe was occupied at a session of the Corps
législatif, so Victorine chose André as her official escort to
the Tuileries Palace. He looked every inch the marquis
this day in his black frock coat, waistcoat, and gray trousers,
with the ribbon of the Légion d'honneur in his buttonhole.
He had impressed her on the carriage ride with his knowledge of palace protocol. His father was a Peer of the Realm,
and André had been a frequent visitor to the palace since
childhood.

"This was Catherine de Médicis' favorite residence," he said
as he galanted her on his arm past the line of Cent Gardes officers standing at attention. Philippe had told her that he had
created this magnificent corps in 1854 to serve as a symbol of
the imperial regime. Each man was exactly six feet tall, in perfect physical condition, dashing in sky-blue tunics and steel
breastplates. Horsehair manes adorning helmets swayed in the

breeze, and ceremonial swords gleamed against their white breeches and black boot tops.

Victorine glided past the officers, the train of her gown fanning behind her on the Savonnerie carpet. Philippe had allowed her to wear an elegant dress of her own choosing, a champagne-colored silk with subtle beading, sans the usual braiding, ruffles, and frills. Her hair was pulled into a sleek knot at the nape of her neck, the better to showcase a dazzling diamond *collier* worth five hundred thousand francs, Philippe's gift to mark this momentous occasion.

As she passed through the double doors to the entrance of the palace, she glanced up at the magnificent golden dome of the Pavilion de l'Horloge and took a deep breath to steady her nerves. The emperor was in residence, indicated by the tricolor flag flapping against the clouds in the azure sky.

As she progressed down the long hallway, she glanced at the pages standing at attention, gorgeous in their blue uniforms of the Household, with white knee breeches and white stockings.

Princess Mathilde greeted Victorine and André from a bench in the window recess where she had been waiting. "Darlings! Aren't we excited?" she gushed. "André de Montpellier, hello, you handsome thing. A kiss for Mathilde?" She offered her cheek. "Victorine, *mon ange,* my angel, you look absolutely beautiful!"

"As do you," Victorine lied. Mathilde's formerly red hair was now dyed a flamboyant shade of blond. Her magenta crinoline ensemble clashed horribly with the new color. Her makeup, as bold as her character, featured heavily mascaraed lashes and magenta-rouged cheeks.

They proceeded up a grand staircase, which brought them to the usher's room. Three ushers wearing maroon coats with silver trimmings stood at attention for the announcement of Princess Mathilde Bonaparte and her guests to the ladies-in-waiting in the Salon Vert. Mathilde and André breezed through, but Victorine stopped to stare up at the frescoes of green parrots painted above the doors and the trompe l'oeil tropical vines snaking around the crown moldings of the ceiling. A beveled mirror at the back of the room reflected the Cartesian symmetry of the Tuileries Gardens.

Victorine walked the length of the salon and stood before the mirror, awestruck at seeing her own reflection in those exalted surroundings. She gazed at herself and could not quite believe that she, Victorine Laurent, from an obscure village in Alsace, was now standing in the imperial palace, the seat of power of all France.

"Hurry, Victorine." She felt André grasp her elbow and steer her toward the next reception room. "You'll be presented to Her Majesty by one of the empress's ladies-in-waiting," he said as they caught up with Mathilde.

"There are two ranks of lady-in-waiting," Princess Mathilde explained to Victorine as they passed into the pink Salon Rose. "The senior rank consists of two ladies of the bedchamber." Mathilde led the way into the Salon Bleu.

Here was the final destination, where Eugénie would receive them, as well as several other visitors congregated there. As they awaited Eugénie's arrival, Victorine noted the arches above the doorways. They were decorated with portrait medallions of the famous society women she recognized from illustrations in the periodicals. *Les cygnes,* as they were called, were not actually as graceful as swans, but were the closest friends of the empress. André pointed out a stern portrait medallion of Baroness de Rothschild looming over the back doorway.

"Doesn't she look morose?" Victorine whispered to André.

"She's thinking about you screwing her husband!" André nudged her playfully.

Victorine tried to stifle a nervous giggle.

Perusing the salon, Victorine felt positively claustrophobic with the Sèvres and lapis lazuli vases as tall as her height, overstuffed chairs, ponderous brocade drapes, gilt boiserie walls, and enormous rock crystal chandeliers looming above.

"Terrible taste, Eugénie," Mathilde said. *"Quelle parvenue,"* she sniffed.

Victorine was aware of discreet sidelong glances from the other women waiting to be presented. "You've been recognized!" Mathilde glared ferociously at the voyeurs, who turned away with chagrin at being caught in the act.

"Prepare me, Mathilde. What happens next?" Victorine asked.

"When Eugénie makes her entrance, we all rise. One of her ladies-in-waiting will walk beside her and introduce each woman being presented by her sponsor. I believe my sister-in-law Princess d'Esseling is attending her today. When she was younger, she used to be Louis-Napoléon's favorite."

"Eugénie permits a former mistress of her husband's to serve as lady-in-waiting?"

"Eugénie endures the middle-aged ones. It's the young beauties like you she can't tolerate," Mathilde laughed.

"Ordinary husbands cheat, but this hypocrisy is disgraceful. They're the emperor and empress of France!" said Victorine.

She caught André and Mathilde trading amused glances. "Darling, your idealization of the imperial couple is so quaint, so bourgeois," Mathilde said. "The politics of pragmatism requires deception. The lies simply escalate as the position ascends." She noted Victorine's furrowed brow. "It's just a game, *chérie.*"

The rustle of silk and satin announced Eugénie's imminent arrival. The visitors rushed to rise and craned their necks for a better look. Her hair was swept high off her face, the better to display the famous swan neck, though a double chin sagged where there was once a chiseled jawline. Brilliantly white, artificially bleached teeth dazzled. She paraded slowly through the salon, greeting each guest, chatting amiably for a few moments before being gently urged by Princess d'Esseling to proceed to the next. She performed her duties with a practiced charm. The words and gestures were those of a beneficent monarch, but her skilled performance could not mask the malevolence behind her smile. When her attention turned to Victorine, a flash of anger sparked in her eyes. She raised a gloved hand and stage-whispered to Princess d'Esseling, "What is *that woman* doing here?"

Mathilde, in her capacity as sponsor, formally presented Victorine to Eugénie.

"Mademoiselle Laurent," Eugénie said, "it is indeed rare to have a person such as yourself at the imperial court."

Victorine sank to a deep curtsy as Philippe had taught her. "Thank you, Your Majesty. I've heard so much about you from the Duke de Lyon and Princess Mathilde. And every word appears to be completely true."

Mathilde raised her hand to her face to suppress a grin. André choked back a laugh and was overtaken by a fit of coughing.

Eugénie understood Mathilde and Philippe's contempt for her. Others in the room were oblivious to the subtle insult, but Eugénie's eyes narrowed and the pulse at her throat visibly throbbed with rage. She whirled around, the satin train of her dress slapping Victorine's shoes, and strode away with a brisk step.

The presentation ceremony now concluded, the ladies collected their cashmere shawls, a low murmur hovering above their coiffed heads as they proceeded to file out the double doors. Their voices rose out in the gleaming parquet hallway as they kissed and congratulated one another on their newly exalted status. A page pushed through the crowd with some difficulty to clear a path as he announced in a clear tenor, "Louis-Napoléon, emperor of the French!"

"This is most unusual. Louis-Napoléon never bothers himself with these petty ceremonies," Mathilde whispered to Victorine.

Victorine's heart began to pound. "May we leave, please?" She tugged Mathilde's arm.

"We can't go now." Mathilde looked at her as though she had gone mad.

As soon as he caught sight of her, Louis-Napoléon locked eyes with Victorine and strode straight toward her. His ceremonial sword slapped against his thigh as he walked; the gold buttons on his military tunic winked in the gaslight of the chandeliers overhead. Eugénie watched with mute anger as he stood expectantly before Victorine, and motioned Mathilde to present her to him.

"Well, well. This is the beauteous Mademoiselle Laurent. The Duke de Lyon is very fond of you, young lady." He took her hand.

Victorine curtsied deeply. "This is a great honor, Your Majesty." She rose gracefully and treated him to the full effect of the famous gaze of her silvery-gray eyes.

"They tell me the love of art has made you famous, mademoiselle."

"They tell me it's the art of love, Your Majesty." She flashed open her fan and raised it to her lips, allowing her gaze to travel down his chest and linger suggestively below his waist sash. The joy of antagonizing Eugénie was too much to resist.

"I shall have to discover your artistic talents at some future date." He pressed her gloved hands to his lips.

Predictably, Eugénie charged over, grasped her husband's arm, and angrily pulled him away down the hall.

"Bravo, darling!" Mathilde whispered and squeezed her hand.

The next morning, Victorine sat before the cheval glass of her vanity table, her reflection bathed in the sunlight streaming through the tall French doors. No longer was she simply the mistress of the Duke de Lyon. She dabbed her puff into the white rice powder, spreading it over her porcelain skin. No longer was she simply the muse of Edouard Manet, the subject of scandalous pictures. Two fingers dipped into the red rouge and painted the upper part of her cheek along the angle of the cheekbone. Now she was an official member of the highest strata of Parisian society. She selected a small pot of black kohl, touched the tip of a tiny brush in it, and painted a thin line around each eye. A sweep of inky mascara on her thick lashes and, finally, red lip color completed the picture.

The Red and the Black. Her brightly made-up face evoked the title of Stendhal's masterpiece, one of her favorites, and reminded her of something Baudelaire had once said: "Red and black represent life, a supernatural and excessive life of fire and earth." What an astounding achievement to be presented to the emperor and the empress, she thought, assessing herself in the mirror. I, an orphan from the provinces. Except that she actually did have a mother. And she did have a father. Victorine stared at her own reflection. Who was he, her father? She studied her high cheekbones and elegant nose. Her eyes, the faceted gray silver that fascinated so many men. Whose eyes were they?

"Toinette!" she called. "Tell the groom to bring round my carriage!"

Victorine sat across from Marie Laurent. Dr. Charcot sat beside Victorine to help negotiate the delicate interaction. "Mademoiselle Marie, this young lady would like to chat with you." The woman glanced at Victorine with an empty stare.

"Let's talk about your baby. How is she?" Dr. Charcot began.

"I don't know. They don't send me any news. I've written and sent a messenger, but there's no reply." She sounded dejected.

"Who is the baby's father?" Victorine asked.

Marie Laurent suddenly shifted her attention to Victorine but did not answer.

"Do you know who the baby's father is, Marie?" Dr. Charcot asked gently.

"No one must know his identity; it's a secret. But I told you once, don't you remember, Louis? It was at the New Year's Ball when the author and the Belgian count and the foreign ambassador all crowded each other for a chance to dance with me. Louis, don't you remember?"

Dr. Charcot turned to Victorine and explained, "To her, I'm 'Louis.' Apparently a confidant of hers from her past." He turned back to Marie. "Who is the baby's father? Could you tell me again?"

"I'll never tell." She made a motion to button her lip.

Victorine and Dr. Charcot exchanged pained looks. "Is he one of your lovers?" Dr. Charcot asked.

"He must never know he had a daughter. When I told him I was expecting, he became enraged. He told me to get rid of it. I said I would, but I lied; I was too far along. He cut me out of his life. I never saw him again."

"What was his name?" Victorine persisted, leaning forward.

"Who is she?" Marie Laurent demanded in a shrill tone. "I don't like her, Louis. You know I can't abide another woman in the room who's as beautiful as I am. Make her leave. Get out, you." She pointed a bony finger at Victorine.

The doctor nodded and urged her to wait outside.

As she stood up to go, Victorine took one last look at Marie Laurent. She detected no emotion in her eyes. As she waited in the corridor, Victorine wondered if she should have some filial feelings. The woman was a total stranger to her, and even now a small part of her questioned whether any of her story was true.

Dr. Charcot emerged from her room, all color drained from his face.

Victorine was startled by his display of emotion. "Did she tell you?"

He nodded.

"Well? What did she say?"

He crooked his finger and motioned for Victorine to approach. He put his mouth to her ear and whispered the answer.

"What! Could it be?"

"She gave me this." He handed her a poem scrawled in an elegant masculine hand.

"My God," she said as she read it.

"Tell no one, Mademoiselle Laurent." He glanced around. "Don't tell this man, either. I'm convinced he has no idea, and to disclose this now . . . there's no point. From what I know of him, he's not the paternal type, to say the least. Trust me, I know human nature. Keep this to yourself."

"I need to confirm this. I'll have my lawyer find out if this is truly my father."

Victorine banged on Edouard's door and called his name desperately.

"You must be in there," she whispered. "Edouard."

She held the lawyer's letter in her hand as she laid her forehead against the door, sobs wracking her body. She needed Edouard. She had to tell him now that the truth was confirmed. She knew who her father was, and she had to share this secret that was burning her up. Edouard was the only one she wanted to tell.

Victorine turned away and clung to the banister as she descended the stairs, afraid she would trip through her blur of tears.

On the other side of the door, Julia backed away quietly and returned to Edouard's bedroom. He lay sleeping soundly, his arm curled around his pillow, the indentation of her body still imprinted on his sheets.

Chapter Nineteen

From time to time, in every age, whores have
directed the affairs of kings.

—Catherine de Médicis (1519–1589)

I can't believe I'm here, André!"

Victorine and André strolled the Fontainebleau gardens at dusk, admiring the palatial residence with its gray mansard roofs and turreted towers soaring up against the silver-and-pink-streaked sky. The magical atmosphere encouraged properly behaved ladies and gentlemen of the Second Empire to gambol like satyrs and sirens. "Here, where kings of France have danced at balls and kissed their mistresses and hunted in the forest for centuries. It still seems a dream."

Rounding a bend in the pathway, they encountered Philippe and Count von Bismarck, enjoying a similar evening constitutional. As Philippe greeted her, Victorine felt his palm against the small of her back, gently urging her toward Bismarck. "Minister von Bismarck, would you kindly escort Mademoiselle Laurent back to the palace? I'm off to the boathouse."

"It would be my greatest pleasure. Fräulein?" He offered his arm with a curt bow. She laid her hand on his rough tweed sleeve as they conversed in German.

"Are you enjoying your visit, Herr Minister?"

"Between us"—he leaned in, the better to steal a whiff of her perfume—"I can't abide these French. Indolent pleasure seekers, the lot of them. We Prussians, thank God, are nothing like that, are we?"

"Not at all like these French idlers," she said.

"Alsatians are the very model of the Teutonic ideal. We're a moral, hardworking race who produce the finest composers, philosophers, and inventors in the world."

"I was at a musicale recently and met Herr Krupp. He fascinated me with tales of his new invention."

"The breech-loading cannon. It uses the same principle as the breech-loading gun; that is what led us to defeat the Austrians at Sadowa."

"We Prussians are not only the most noble of races, we're also the most scientifically advanced," she said.

"And our morals are unimpeachable, unlike these decadent French. When I was in Paris last May for the kaiser's state visit, I was propositioned by a common street prostitute. She offered me the rose leaf, the little Shanghai streetcar, Napoléon on the ramparts." He peered at her over his pince-nez. "I wonder what those all could be?"

"I think I know," she said with a smile and thought, Hypocrite! Dirty inside, sanctimonious outside.

"Frau Bismarck was unfortunately not able to accompany me to Fontainebleau, so perhaps later we could . . . that is to say . . . ," he stuttered.

"I'll flash open my fan." She stood on tiptoe and whispered. "That's the signal for you to meet me in the music room. I'll show you what 'Napoléon on the ramparts' is."

"I'll be counting the minutes, Fräulein," he whispered.

She left him standing in the darkening garden, and hurried up the pathway to the boathouse chalet, anxious to find Philippe. As she approached, she was surprised to see a woman rush past, her dress wrinkled and makeup smeared. At the boathouse, she discovered the double doors locked and called to Philippe to let her in. She heard rustling and scurrying inside before he opened the door. As he stepped out, she distinctly smelled another woman's perfume on his clothes. Victorine observed him closely. His hair was tousled and he was out of breath. She looked past him and saw chintz pillows askew on the rumpled chaise longue. "I have some interesting information for you." Her voice quivered with fury, though she struggled to maintain her composure. "But first, tell me, who is she?"

"Princess Romanoff," he said with a resigned sigh.

He was sleeping with the dissolute Russian behind her back.

"How dare you! I will not stand for this!" she shouted.

"Darling. Her family owns one of the largest copper-mining monopolies in Russia, and I'm in negotiations to buy it. She's completely obsessed with me. Last year she stalked me all over Europe." He followed Victorine down the steps. "It's a substantial windfall for my company and by extension you, too, my major stockholder." He stopped and grasped both her hands. "I want her gone more than you do, believe me. But I have to be diplomatic. She'll leave tomorrow, I promise you."

Victorine looked deeply into his eyes. It sounded so convincing. It was true that she had chased him across Russia last year; Mathilde had told her so. And standing in his arms, she felt her resolve weaken. "All right, I believe you," she said. "Bismarck told me that Krupp has developed a breech-loading cannon."

A long whistle of surprise escaped his lips. "Like their needle-gun. I'll send a message to General Vinoy. Excellent work, Victorine. Was it difficult to pry this information out of him?"

"As easy as that." She snapped her fingers.

"Then get more. Get everything you can. You'll be rewarded for your loyalty, Victorine. You have my word of honor."

A few hours later, Victorine watched from her balcony as servants set up rows of white wrought-iron chairs facing a pavilion stage on the Great Lawn. A string of vermilion Chinese lanterns glowed and bounced in the evening breeze, swaying above the heads of orchestra members tuning their instruments, slicing violin bows in the air and trilling horns. Victorine heard a crescendo of crickets in the nearby woods performing a competing evening concert. As night fell, servants stood by the edge of the lake and called to revelers in torchlit boats that the show was about to begin.

At nine o'clock, the Great Lawn began to fill with ladies splendid in magnificent crinolines and jewels accompanied by their escorts in elegant dinner jackets. A convivial buzz filled the air as friends discovered each other among the crowd. Victorine and Philippe strolled through the throng, greeting familiar faces. Her hair was fashioned into the newest style, partly swept up with tiny diamonds sparkling in it, and the rest free-flowing about her shoulders. And though everyone else was turned out in various carnival colors, she was ethereal in a white dress shot through with silver and gold threads, three lengths of fabric trailing behind her in a train. Diamond bracelets encircled both wrists of the white gloves that ended above her elbows. The top strata of Paris society officially numbered two thousand, but only the *gratin,* a mere four hundred, had been invited to Fontainebleau. Plenty of self-congratulations circulated among the elite, who surreptitiously tallied who was there and who conspicuously absent.

Victorine heard a familiar voice calling her name. "Edouard! What on earth . . . you . . . here?" She was delighted by his surprise appearance. She surveyed him, so handsome in his frock coat trimmed with satin lapels, black evening trousers cut to the perfection of a centimeter, a starched white linen shirt with watered silk waistcoat, and, the latest in fashion, a black bow tie replacing the traditional cravat. His usual white gardenia graced the buttonhole of his lapel.

"I'm here by invitation of a friend of yours," he said mysteriously as he adjusted his white gloves with a quick tug.

"I thought you disdain these palace snobs," she whispered behind her fan. "Isn't it you who loves to laugh at them?"

"The more exalted the title, the louder I laugh." He nodded at Philippe. "Oh look, our exalted vice president of the Corps législatif, the Duke de Lyon."

"Manet, good to see you," Philippe said.

"And you," Edouard said in a curt manner.

"I've heard a rumor that your family name was de Manet. Tell me, why did you choose to drop the aristocratic article?" Philippe asked.

"I don't ascribe to arcane class distinctions."

"Do you mean to say that you don't believe that the poor are born into their class by a law of nature, just as animals are arranged into their proper scientific phyla? So it's true, you *are* one of those leftist socialists?"

"If it were true, I should hope I'm not fool enough to announce it here, in the warmth of the imperial bosom."

Victorine stifled a laugh while Philippe's demeanor stiffened. She observed the two standing side by side. Philippe, silver-haired and slight of build, undeniably handsome, his supercilious bearing complementing the tight, nervous energy of a man of action. Edouard stood a head taller, sandy-haired, rugged, broad-shouldered, and wide of stance, as steady and firmly planted in his French soul as a great oak tree in the

Fontainebleau soil. One an intellectual, a creator of beautiful objects, a lover of women. The other a businessman, a collector of beautiful objects, a consumer of women. "Do tell me who invited you here," she asked.

At that moment, Princess Mathilde approached, resplendent in a turquoise satin and sequined gown. The diamond *collier* draped around her neck featured stones the size of pigeon eggs. "Good evening, Victorine," Mathilde said. "And my darling Philippe." She brushed a more than platonic kiss across Philippe's lips. She smiled up coquettishly at Edouard. "Shall we find our seats, Manet?"

"You two . . . ?" Victorine clapped her hand to her mouth.

"Too delicious, isn't it? He's mine tonight, *chérie*. Mustn't be jealous," she called back over her shoulder as she led him away.

Philippe motioned to a boy in the crowd and asked Victorine if she would like to meet the Prince Imperial. Prince Eugène, ten years of age, greeted Philippe affectionately and shook hands in a perfunctory way with Victorine. As he bowed and took his leave, Philippe looked pensive. "Eugénie intends to badger the emperor to abdicate and name her regent until their son comes of age. The strongest opponent of that plan is me."

"Why would the emperor agree to such a thing?" Victorine asked.

"He's sick, Victorine. He's weary and longs for some tranquillity. But I won't let him demolish everything I've built. Eugénie knows she'll never prevail as long as I sit in the cabinet and my allies control the Legislative Assembly." The determination etched on his face was fearsome.

André emerged from the crowd and kissed Victorine on both cheeks.

"André! You're so handsome tonight." She straightened his cravat. "Philippe, you remember my friend the Marquis de Montpellier, the dearest man in the world."

"Marquis de Montpellier . . . aren't you related to Prince and Princess Lafite?" He shook André's hand while mentally cataloging him in the Parisian social phyla.

"Yes, quite right, monsieur le duc."

"You're a writer of some kind, yes?"

"Yes, of some kind or another," he replied.

Victorine knew André felt completely intimidated; he preferred the company of artists and writers to men of political ambition.

Presently, the master of ceremonies appeared onstage and announced that the concert was about to begin. When Minister von Bismarck spotted Victorine, he sliced a path through the crowd straight to her. Philippe and Bismarck sat on either side of her behind Louis-Napoléon and Eugénie in the front row, accompanied by the king of the Netherlands and the ambassador of Siam in a red silk tunic and black culottes. Enthusiastic applause greeted the handsome maestro Johann Strauss as he strode onstage. A hush fell over the audience as he threw back his head, sent a haughty look to his orchestra, and raised his violin bow to lead the opening notes of "The Second Empire Waltz."

Louis-Napoléon nodded to the music, occasionally glancing back to smile at Victorine until Eugénie dug her fingernails into his arm. As the orchestra played on, Victorine scanned the audience for Edouard, finally spotting him with his eyes closed, transported by the music, a dream of rapture on his face. Her attention shifted to Mathilde, whose white-gloved arm snaked around his neck in a proprietary manner. The realization that they were sharing a bed caused her to become restless. She flashed open her fan and began to fan herself. Bismarck stood up and fumbled past annoyed audience members to reach the aisle. Everyone turned to stare at the Prussian foreign minister, including Eugénie, who noted that Victorine also rose and left her seat.

"I was afraid you wouldn't come, Victorine," he said, speaking in German. He grabbed her hand and roughly pulled her closer to him. "You're attracted to men of power." His hands, large as pinwheels, came toward her and held her face.

"Herr Minister, any woman would adore a man who can change history."

She watched with disgust as his shiny bald head lowered to kiss her breasts.

"Man cannot create the current of events, Victorine." He looked up at her. "He can only float with them and steer."

She looked into those gray eyes, cold and hard as bullets, and saw cruelty and genius in them. She slid down to her knees and gently pushed him back on the divan. "This is Napoléon on the ramparts."

When Victorine rejoined Philippe on the terrace, the concert had long concluded. Guests sipped crystal flutes of champagne served by liveried waiters. Philippe arched an eyebrow; Victorine nodded. They walked to the edge of the crowd for privacy. She glanced down at her finger adorned with a spontaneous gift from Bismarck—his signet ring. She raised her hand. "Look what he gave me." She showed off the gold ring engraved with the von Bismarck family crest. "After it was over, he proceeded to brag. He lit a cigarette and told me some amazing things."

Philippe was in a sparkling mood, not a hint of jealousy or regret about sharing her. "What sorts of things, my love?"

"He boasted about his success in unifying Germany, an important precursor to defeating France."

"Defeating . . . what did he mean?"

"War," Victorine said. She felt oddly triumphant as the color drained from his face.

"What else did he say?"

"He invited me to Berlin, where, in his words, everywhere you go, you'll hear the tramp of men at drill and the swinging pivots of monster guns. He said his army numbers half a million men, equipped and ready to march across the borders of Alsace and Lorraine."

Philippe was as a man hit by a carriage. "Louis-Napoléon's been talking disarmament while Bismarck's . . . my God, we're totally unprepared. The emperor must be alerted—you'll have to tell him, Victorine."

"But if Bismarck hears that I've informed to you?" She was alarmed.

"Bismarck's ego will never allow him to suspect your motives."

"It seems risky." She left him and stepped out to the balcony balustrade. As she gazed up at the night sky scattered with stars, the crisp forest air cleared her mind and becalmed her spirit. The entire palace, hundreds of windows, glowed behind gossamer drapes. Which one belonged to Edouard? she wondered. A picture appeared in her imagination of him making love to Mathilde. She closed her eyes, but it stubbornly lodged in her mind. She glanced across the vast, dark acreage to the lake shimmering in the icy glow of moonlight. She had once read about a wild child who was discovered in Fontainebleau Forest, raised by wolves. He had been rescued and brought to civilization, but ran away. She felt like that child, aching to run.

The next morning, Victorine sipped her coffee outdoors on the terrace overlooking the Le Nôtre gardens. She was stewing about Edouard and Mathilde. To think she was going to share the amazing identity of her father with him! What was she thinking when she had run to his studio, confident that he cared about her? That he would share the joy of discovery in her true identity? What a foolish notion. He cared about her problems and concerns as much as Philippe did. She would never tell him now, nor anyone else. She would keep the precious secret to herself, just as Dr. Charcot had instructed her.

When André joined her, he attempted to make conversation. "Remember when Edouard urged me to experience life? Well, I think I've found someone. One evening last week, a Chopin waltz floated through my open window; it was coming from the flat above where a new chap had moved in, Eric Chevalier. He's a student at the Paris Conservatory. His warm smile, bright eyes, the way his hair flowed over his collar and framed his features . . . I haven't been so affected since the first time I met Edouard—"

They were interrupted by Princess Mathilde.

"May I?" She dropped onto a chair, bleary-eyed, hair tangled, peignoir loosely tied at her waist. In short, she looked like she hadn't slept all night. They sat in awkward silence for several moments. "My thighs are so sore, I can hardly walk." She let out a throaty laugh. "He really is the *most amazing*!"

Victorine winced. "Spare us, Mathilde."

"But Victorine. Everything they say about him is true. I'm not exactly an ingenue, but oh, my dear! I'm madly, madly, madly in love with him."

Victorine glared at her. Would she not desist?

The corners of Mathilde's mouth curled in a smile and she threw André a wink. "Victorine, you're jealous of me," Mathilde laughed.

"That's ridiculous."

"You may as well know." She stood to go. "Edouard Manet's quite madly, madly, madly in love with me." Mathilde blew Victorine a kiss and left.

Victorine watched her walk away through narrowed eyes.

André was marshaling his courage. "Victorine, aren't you just a tiny bit in love with Edouard?"

She stood up so abruptly that her coffee cup crashed to the floor and shattered into shards. "Love! I never want to hear that word again. Ever!"

"I'm sorry I mentioned it. Don't be angry with me."

"I'm not angry!" she shouted.

André drummed his fingers on the table as he tried to think of something to lighten her dark mood. "What shall we do today?" he asked in a cheery tone.

"I don't want to do anything."

"Edouard is sketching down by the lake. Let's meet him and have a picnic?"

Some alchemy began to bubble in her mind. "Now, there's a wonderful idea. We'll go bathing. I'll meet you by the lake at noon." She rose and glanced back over her shoulder with a sly grin as she walked away. "Bathing costumes optional."

When she entered the palace, a man stepped out from an alcove as though he had been awaiting her. He was dressed in a scarlet tailcoat embroidered in gold braid and lace. "Pardon me, Mademoiselle Laurent?" he said in a deep voice.

"Yes?"

"I am Comte Bacciochi, first chamberlain to the emperor." He bowed. "Would you do me the honor of following me? The emperor of France requests a few moments of your time."

Here it is, she thought, the droit du seigneur.

He led her wordlessly down corridors, the stillness broken only by the echo of servants' voices in rooms they passed. Finally, they approached a massive set of double doors emblazoned with the imperial coat of arms. The count bowed formally to her and discreetly withdrew. She took a deep breath and knocked.

"Enter!"

She found Louis-Napoléon lounging comfortably in a silk dressing gown, smoking a pipe. She stood rooted to her spot, gazing at him. In this grandiose bedchamber of lofty ceilings and gold-trimmed boiserie, he seemed a small, diminutive man without his imperial regalia.

"Mademoiselle Laurent . . . May I call you Victorine? . . . Don't stay so far away; come sit here next to me." He patted a spot on the divan.

She tried to avert her gaze from the gold-and-onyx bed on a raised dais that dominated the room. They chatted for several moments, Louis-Napoléon speaking directly to her décolleté instead of her eyes, before he moved closer. "My, my. De Lyon has such exquisite taste in women." He stroked her cheek with a stubby finger.

"Thank you, Your Majesty." She shrank away as he leaned in.

"Relax, Victorine. Is it de Lyon you're thinking of? My dear, let's don't be concerned about him." He jerked her closer.

As he pulled her toward the bed, she suddenly understood. This had all been prearranged by Philippe.

So many official entertainments beckoned guests at Fontainebleau Palace that there seemed precious little time for them to become embroiled in scandal. Yet somehow the men and women of the Second Empire always managed to keep the gossipmongers busy. The story making the rounds in the drawing room at lunchtime involved a young lady, a popular actress of the Comédie Française, who had been invited that morning to take a carriage ride with an older woman, a princess who was close to the imperial family.

This outing took them deep into the woods, where the two women became quite indiscreet, kissing in the backseat, carrying on in a most sapphic way. When they were discovered in this compromising position, the princess simply laughed and told their interloper that love was in the air and he should mind his own business. André swore this story was entirely true, because it was he who had surprised Princess Mathilde and Sarah Bernhardt in the woods.

Victorine endured his retelling as they relaxed with Edouard on a blanket under a canopy of oak trees. The remnants of a sumptuous alfresco picnic prepared by the palace chef lay strewn around. André popped the cork on their second bottle of chilled Veuve Clicquot as Edouard opened his sketch pad to draw Victorine stretched out lazily on the grass.

"Well, Edouard, it appears your new love interest enjoys the pleasures of the female sex as much as you do." Victorine smirked at her own double entendre. "How unfortunate you didn't know."

"Actually, I did know. Last night, Mathilde and Mademoiselle Bernhardt kindly included me in a most intriguing ménage à trois," he said.

"They say good luck comes in threes." André chuckled.

Victorine cursed them and stood up. "I'm going bathing."

She pulled her bodice over her head and dropped it to the ground. Next, off came her corset. She stepped out of her skirt and slid layers of petticoats down over her hips, leaving a trail of lace and silk behind. Her audience stared, completely enraptured, as she had meant them to be. She tugged a tortoiseshell comb to shake her hair free and allowed it to tumble to her waist. Throwing a nonchalant smile over her shoulder, she stepped into the water. A Botticelli Venus could not compete with the tableau she had created.

"Why don't you join me?" she called to Edouard, as she swam a backstroke in lazy circles, floating like an ethereal naiad, her nudity shimmering through an arc of sunlight on the water's surface. When she came back to shore and stood up, Edouard looked as though his heart would stop. He brought a blanket to her and they stood together for several moments, chest and thighs pressed tight against each other. Victorine gently pushed against him and took a step back.

After she had dried off, Edouard asked her and André to pose for him.

She reached for her camisole, but he stopped her. "I had an idea this afternoon for a new painting, a luncheon on the grass. It will echo an earlier painting of mine, inspired by a Titian I saw in Venice. But this one will feature André as a fully clothed modern gentleman and you, Victorine, a nude allegory of the past."

A troubled frown crossed her face.

"Is that going to present a problem for you?"

They both knew what he meant. She stopped to consider for several moments.

"No. Another nude would be fine."

He arranged André on the grass, right elbow to knee, left hand on the ground, supporting himself. He instructed him to stay motionless while he posed Victorine; after five minutes, André complained that the numbness in his arm competed only with the tremulous pain in his leg. "May I drop the pose now?" he pleaded with Edouard.

"It's going to shock those conservatives to see a man in modern-day dress seated beside a nude. This hearkens back to classical painting, yet the setting is familiar to all."

"The past kisses the future in your work," Victorine said in a soft tone. Edouard stared at her. Had she allowed tenderness to color her words?

Chapter Twenty

Good heavens! How indecent! The public has taken good care
not to judge *Luncheon on the Grass* as a true work of art.
The only thing it has noticed is that some people are eating,
seated naked on the grass after bathing.

—Emile Zola, *Revue du XX Siècle,* January 1867

ootsteps rushed up the marble staircase two at a
time and approached Victorine's boudoir from the hallway.
The door burst open and Philippe stormed in. "Get out!" he
shouted at the frightened hairdresser, who scurried away, leaving
behind his valise of brushes and combs. He glared at a
footman who was bent over the grate in the fireplace repairing
a loose piece.

"Who's that?" He pointed.

"That's Fouquet, my new footman," Victorine said.

The man turned around and stared at Philippe.

"I've seen you somewhere before," Philippe said.

"Yes, sir. I was employed at the Tuileries Palace previously,
sir."

"Well, I don't care who you are. Get out."

The footman laid down his tools and left. Victorine
knew what was coming. The Salon had opened at the Palais de

l'Industrie, and Edouard's painting of the picnic on the grass had shocked all of Paris. She folded her hands and composed herself as she watched Philippe pace from one end of the room to the other. "Explain yourself." He struggled to modulate his voice, controlling his rage.

"It's a masterpiece," she said.

He stared as though he meant to strangle her. "You promised no more nudes."

"I'm not portrayed as a nude. I'm depicted as an *allegory*. Didn't you gather the reference to Titian?"

"Do you know what they're saying out there?" He pointed to the French doors, which opened out to a balcony. "They're calling it indecent. An outrage. They're calling Manet a seditionist. They're calling you . . ." He stopped.

"Philippe, please listen to me. Edouard juxtaposes the classical against the modern. I'm an allegory in the purest sense. The painting says, 'Look at how the past and present are like us, rubbing shoulders with each other in our modern city, and yet so isolated from each other.'"

"Stop. I don't want to hear all that. Why the devil did you do it? Isn't this home enough for you? The trust fund, the servants, the jewels and dresses?"

She dared not say what she was really thinking: *How else could I wound you, repay you for sleeping with that Russian woman, for offering me to Bismarck and Louis-Napoléon like a common streetwalker?* "I did it because I believe in his art. Because I'm fortunate to be a part of something that will be immortal."

He selected a cigarette from a silver case; a match flared, and smoke blew out through his nostrils. He watched her as she continued to dress her own hair in the mirror. "How do you think it affects me? How do you think I felt today at the cabinet meeting when Eugénie threw it in my face that your naked body—"

"Nude, not naked."

"...your *naked* body's on display in the Palais de l'Industrie? She insinuates to the other cabinet ministers that France spirals downward due to low morals exemplified by you, a courtesan, and by me, the illegitimate son of the Comte de Gabbay."

Victorine winced. "Surely those ministers know you put Louis-Napoléon on the throne. They know who the real power behind this empire is."

"I'm the illegitimate son. I will always be that to them." His shoulders slumped in a way that alarmed Victorine. He sat down in a chair and stared at the carpet.

Victorine approached and knelt before him. She stroked his hair and cupped his face in her hands. He refused to look in her eyes, staring instead at the arabesques in the Persian carpet as though in them was the answer to his despair.

"You're the most powerful man in France. No one can deny that."

He allowed himself to be drawn into her arms. She murmured soothing words as she rocked him gently. He seemed to remember himself and squared his shoulders, exhaling a long sigh. "You must come with me to a palace event this morning. That will show her and the other ministers I'm not intimidated, will not be shamed into weakness."

"On behalf of the Widows of the Veterans of the Napoleonic Wars," said a nervous little girl in the grand Salle des Maréchaux of the Tuileries Palace, as she offered a bouquet of roses with a shaky hand. "In gratitude for Your Majesty's patronage," she finished, and performed a sweet curtsy.

One hundred fifty aged pairs of hands broke out in enthusiastic applause echoing up to the coffered ceilings. Empress Eugénie smiled and stepped forward to accept the bouquet, and acknowledged the adoring ovation by nodding her perfectly coiffed head and waving a white-gloved hand. "Thank you, thank you, ladies. I'm grateful for your kindness. As you know, I am a tireless worker for the underprivileged and downtrodden of our country—" She was interrupted by another burst of applause. "You have given so much. Your very dear husbands lost their lives in the military service of their country. You have made the ultimate sacrifice, are the true heroines of our imperial regime."

"*Vive* Empress Eugénie!"

Her short speech concluded, Eugénie touched their outstretched hands as she passed. Victorine and Philippe exchanged looks as they followed her to the exit, engulfed by a horde of Widows of the Veterans of the Napoleonic Wars.

Victorine became Louis-Napoléon's current obsession, just as Philippe had planned. She was surprised to discover that the little emperor had a romantic side to his nature. She was amused to receive daily flower bouquets accompanied by love letters full of poetic sentiments and odes to her "beauteous thighs," which he daydreamed about in his spare hours. She read the love notes, then carefully secreted them away in a safe place. Victorine's coachman often found himself ferrying her to the emperor's private entrance of the Tuileries Palace, her barouche so familiar to the palace guards that they waved it in without the usual security checks. After the emperor's years of clandestine rendezvous with different mistresses, the routine was familiar to his pages and ushers. With utmost discretion, they led Victorine toward Louis-Napoléon's private study, ushered her through a secret door, up the narrow, winding staircase to his apartments, and quietly withdrew the moment their master appeared to greet her.

Chapter Twenty-one

Power is evil.

—Louise Michel, Communard leader (1830–1905)

Victorine sat in her cozy library. She wore a burgundy velvet peignoir sprinkled with gold star appliqués with a gold rope belt cinched around her waist. Her hair hung loosely about her shoulders and cascaded down her back. On her tiny feet, she wore burgundy velvet kitten-heel slippers embroidered with the de Lyon crest. When she heard Philippe's voice in the foyer, she laid aside her etui. Philippe handed his cape to the butler, Ariel, and gave him instructions as though he were still his own employee.

"Ring the footman, direct him to set up the game table, and get the cards out of the sideboard for bezique."

Victorine glanced at the clock on the mantelpiece: eight thirty. Louis-Napoléon was due at nine o'clock. Philippe was desperate to spur the emperor to action; he had arranged for Louis-Napoléon to visit Victorine this evening, and instructed her to divulge Bismarck's secret plans in the erotic and opulent surroundings of her boudoir. With the German army so formidable, Philippe could ill afford to waste any more time.

"Toinette visited every fruit seller in Les Halles to find tropical pears for a beautiful *poire belle Hélène*." She kissed Philippe's cheek. "Philippe, you're certain that's his favorite?"

Philippe assured her, then caught sight of his crest on her slippers. "You'd best take those off and change into others," he said.

She glanced down at them and realized that the de Lyon crest was a blunt reminder that Victorine was the property of Louis-Napoléon's trusted adviser. She went upstairs to change the slippers. When she returned, she was startled to find a strange man in her drawing room.

"This is Lieutenant l'Aiglon of the palace police," Philippe said. "He surveils every private residence before the emperor arrives."

The officer tipped his hat and proceeded out to the foyer.

"He'll stand guard with a loaded revolver in your hallway until the visit is over." He noted her concerned expression. "Don't worry, it's all routine. Louis-Napoléon's assignations are orchestrated with the precision of a Strauss waltz." He flipped open his pocket watch. "Now I go."

"I'm still worried that it will be me on the grill if something goes awry . . . ," Victorine said.

"It won't. Trust me. That's my good girl." He kissed her forehead.

"I am *not* a good girl." She arched an eyebrow. "Don't you dare call me that."

As Philippe had instructed, Victorine recited what Bismarck had told her, and then offered Philippe's subsequent analysis. Louis-Napoléon listened as he swirled an excellent Armagnac in a crystal snifter, raised it to inhale the aroma, and swallowed it whole. He regarded her with admiration as she rattled off facts, respect mixing with lust in his eyes. After supper, she invited him upstairs. He swayed up the stairs, leaning on the butler's arm for support. He was clearly unwell, and the rouge applied to mask his illness had worn off, giving him a ghoulish appearance.

A few minutes past midnight, she escorted him toward the front door. She slowed her pace to match his sickly gait. Ariel held the door as Victorine watched Louis-Napoléon limp down the marble steps to his waiting carriage. A blaze of light exploded out of the darkness and the crack of gunshots rang out. Two men in black capes jumped from her bushes and rushed toward Louis-Napoléon, pistols aimed point-blank. Louis-Napoléon's guards jumped, but the two assailants slipped their grasp and bolted. The palace police pulled their revolvers and chased after the intruders. The emperor was bundled into his carriage and sped out her entrance gates as Victorine watched, stunned.

Toinette dashed out to the portico in her nightshift. "Did I hear firecrackers? What's happening, ma'm'selle?"

A detective grabbed Victorine's arm.

"What are you doing?" She jerked her arm out of his grip.

"Come with us for questioning, Mademoiselle Laurent."

"What!"

"It's routine, ma'am." He pulled her down her own steps. "Just following orders."

"Whose orders?" Victorine demanded.

Two officers scooped Victorine under the arms and shoved her into the police wagon. "Ma'm'selle! What should I do?" Toinette cried.

"Hurry to Monsieur Manet! Tell him what's happened and to come help me!" Victorine called out the window as they drove her away.

Victorine awoke in Edouard's bedroom. She sat up slowly and glanced in the cheval glass, surprised to see her reflection, her hair matted and tangled, the burgundy velvet peignoir smeared with grime. She found Edouard asleep in his parlor on the red divan, his body twisted like a contortionist's, an arm dangling to the floor, a leg draped over the armrest. André was snoring in the armchair across.

"Edouard. Wake up," she whispered as she knelt beside him.

He rubbed the sandy blond stubble on his chin as his blue eyes squinted against the sunlight streaming through the window. He had slept in the fancy dress shirt he had worn to the Opera, and an odor of cigar smoke and expensive female perfume still clung to him. "Oh my God, Victorine." He sat up as the events of a few hours earlier focused in his mind.

"Thank you for rescuing me last night," she said. "If not for you . . ."

"Don't thank me, thank my father's influence at the Ministry of Justice." He smiled, but noticed that she remained grave. "What exactly happened? Tell me now that I can think." He ran his hands through his tousled hair.

"These men, palace detectives . . . They said it was an 'interrogation.'"

"What sort of interrogation?"

"They asked me why I spied for Prussia. And why I wanted to assassinate Louis-Napoléon! I was . . ." She could not continue. "It was worse than a nightmare. They promised to release me if I'd agree to turn over evidence against Philippe."

"What did you say?" Edouard asked.

"I told them to go to hell. I wasn't an informer."

"That's my girl," André said.

"Who else knew that Louis-Napoléon would be at your house last night?" Edouard asked.

"I don't know. Philippe and the bodyguard and . . . I don't know."

They heard urgent pounding on Edouard's door. Julia rushed in with the morning newspapers. "Look at this!" She flashed open the political daily *Le Figaro* to a twenty-point headline, ASSASSINATION ATTEMPT ON EMPEROR, and, in smaller type below, VICTORINE LAURENT SUSPECTED.

Victorine sat down hard on the divan.

"Read the story to us," Edouard said.

Julia took a seat on a silk tufted hassock and read aloud. "'Mademoiselle Victorine Laurent, the famous courtesan and favorite model of Edouard Manet, is a suspect in the violent assassination attempt on the life of Emperor Louis-Napoléon.'" She paused and looked at each of them, then continued. "'The emperor escaped with no injuries and is resting comfortably. The Alsatian was allegedly acting as an operative for Prussia and is said to have close ties to an important minister of Kaiser Wilhelm's government.'"

"What?" Victorine cried.

"'She is a personal friend and confidante of Foreign Minister Otto von Bismarck and was recently spotted in Berlin with him.'"

"That's a lie! I've never been to Berlin in my life!"

"'Sources close to the palace confirm that she will be prosecuted as a Prussian spy and charged with treason for selling military secrets to a foreign government.'"

"How can a newspaper print rubbish like that?" Victorine said.

"Political pressure and bribery," Edouard said. "Villemessant, the publisher of *Le Figaro*, is a particularly loyal mouthpiece for the imperial couple."

"Bribery? Money in exchange for lies?" Victorine asked.

"Not necessarily money; that would be too overt," Edouard said. "They're bought off with political access or exclusive news items unavailable to their competitors. I've seen it many times."

"I'll go to Philippe. He will straighten this out." She rose.

"If you venture out, the police will arrest you," Edouard reminded her.

"This can't be happening." She shook her head. "Philippe is likely terribly worried about me. I must get a message to him and tell him I'm safe."

"I'll go," Edouard offered.

"You? I thought you detested him," André said.

"I have nothing but contempt for the man. But I understand a little of his political world."

"Quite the understatement," André said, "considering the number of illustrious diplomats and magistrates in your family. I'll go with you."

Victorine and Julia waited anxiously for their return until they heard voices in the foyer.

"Well? What did he say?" Victorine asked, half rising from her seat.

"He told us that if he admitted he sent you to spy for France, the consequences would be grave for himself," André said. "A minister of the government using a girl to seduce the foreign minister of an adversarial nation? It could precipitate an international incident. Maybe war."

"He's a politician out to save his own neck. Does it surprise you?" Edouard said.

"But he promised he'd protect me—"

"Edouard called him a cur, said he was a coward using you for his blatant political purposes then throwing you to the dogs . . ."

Edouard laid a hand on André's arm and shook his head.

"He's going to stand by while they destroy me," she said slowly. "How could I have trusted him?"

"You're exhausted, darling, and your nerves are frayed." Edouard pulled her to him and stroked her long hair. Suddenly, sobs wracked her body. "What's this?" He held her by the shoulders and tried to meet her eyes, but she looked away, ashamed of her tears. "Is this my Victorine? Is this the girl who told all those aristo snobs to go to hell?"

She laughed, wiping her cheeks of tears.

"You need to rest," Edouard said.

He took her hand and led her to his bed. Edouard tucked her in and drew the counterpane under her chin, caressing her cheek and lips with his index finger. "Try to sleep," he whispered.

Victorine lay on the pillow and watched through the open door as Edouard gazed out the balcony window to the Paris rooftops beyond. André had left, but Julia stood behind him and encircled his waist with her arms. She laid her cheek against his back. "Edouard, Victorine needs you, but I need you, too."

He turned around and looked down into her face. As he closed the bedchamber door, Victorine saw Julia unbutton her basque. She closed her eyes and tried to squeeze the image of them out of her mind.

~

All of Paris was caught up in the unfolding scandal.

Incredible stories appeared daily in the papers. "Sources close to the palace" accused her of possessing official memos stamped "For your eyes only." These documents were reported by the newspapers to be state secrets stolen by Victorine to sell to the Prussians. The two would-be assassins, Prussian nationals, were in police custody but refused to talk. A signet ring bearing the crest of the von Bismarck family was cited as further evidence of treason. Edouard called in his late father's considerable political connections and contacted an old family friend to help Victorine.

"I've sent an electrical telegram asking him urgently to advise us. This persecution is growing worse." Edouard sat down beside Victorine. She was dressed in Julia's borrowed clothes.

"I wonder what he will do?" Julia asked.

"My father maintained good relations with the current regime. Don't worry, we can depend on Judge Manet's contacts."

"But who's *behind* all this?" Victorine asked.

"We'll find out. Patience."

The next day, while Edouard stepped out for an errand, imperial guards stormed in, demanding Victorine Laurent. Before André and Julia could react, they kicked in the bedroom door and cuffed her wrists. They dragged her away, struggling, as Julia followed them down four flights of stairs, screaming that Victorine was innocent.

The police vehicle whisked her down the boulevard Haussmann. Shopping arcades whizzed by, the chocolate sellers, the perfumeries, the leather goods dealers, the jewelers, all her usual haunts. The police wagon swerved around a corner onto the avenue Marigny, slowed as it crossed the Seine over the Pont-au-Change and turned hard left onto the quai de l'Horloge. She heard gates clang shut and cobblestones bumped beneath the wooden wheels as they pulled up to the front entrance of her new home, the Conciergerie, the jail reserved for the most notorious prisoners of the state.

When the carriage door swung open, she stepped down and squinted against the bright morning sunlight. She shaded her eyes and gazed up at the formidable gray stone facade of the medieval fortress until she felt a rude push from behind and stumbled forward.

"Keep moving," a guard said. Her eyes adjusted to the dark hallway of the Prisoner's Corridor. A shiver traveled up her spine at the damp chill seeping through the stone walls as guards escorted her through the mildew-dank hall. They stopped at the concierge's office to register her. A group of guards gathered around to gawk by the flickering light of wall torches at the famous Mademoiselle Victorine.

"Well, well! Mademoiselle Laurent. It's a pleasure to welcome you," the concierge leered. "We've had many notorious assassins here, but never one so beautiful."

The guards standing around her laughed.

"I'm not an assassin," she said.

"We'll have to wait for the trial to judge that, won't we? Until then, take her to the women's wing." He waved her away.

She stumbled up a narrow stone staircase and down another corridor with ceilings low as a crypt, until the guard stopped before a wooden door. The keys jangled in the rusted lock, the door creaked open, and she stepped in. Victorine raised her handcuffed forearm to her face to block the stench of urine from the chamber pot in the corner. A straw cot occupied one wall, while a worm-eaten desk and straight-backed chair stood opposite. The width of the room could be spanned by holding out one's arms fingertip to fingertip. The guard turned up the flame in the gas lamp. When he turned to face Victorine, she realized he was a young man, perhaps twenty, the same age as she.

"Now, then, I'll remove those," he said. He reached to uncuff her and pulled her hands toward him in such a curiously tender gesture, tears welled up in her eyes.

"Don't worry, mademoiselle. You won't be hurt," he said.

"I'm so frightened," she whispered.

"Everyone who comes here is frightened."

After hesitating a moment, he slammed the door shut with a decisive clang.

Chapter Twenty-two

Digging down among the small is the surest way
to make oneself the equal of the great.

—Cardinal de Retz (1613–1679)

Centuries of fear permeated the damp prison air. Victorine trembled uncontrollably, from the cold and from the bad dreams that plagued her throughout the night. Condensed water trickled across the ceiling of her cell and dripped to the floor like a ceaseless finger tap against her temple, threatening to drive her mad. Dozing alternated with violent waking; she was in the midst of an improbable dream of Baudelaire sitting by her bedside when the clanging of metal woke her.

"Prisoner Laurent. You have visitors."

The door swung open. Edouard, André, and an older gentleman whom she did not recognize stood in the doorway.

"Victorine?" Edouard stepped in.

She ran to him and buried her face in his chest. She sobbed so violently that it appeared she was having a convulsion. When she gained some control of herself, Edouard introduced Victorine to her lawyer, Comte Jules de Briac.

A colleague of Edouard's late father had contacted the distinguished count, who had agreed to take her case. He was not only the scion of one of the wealthiest families of Napoleonic times, but his entire lineage consisted of advisers and lawyers to the aristocracy. De Briac had personally extricated many a title from legal disaster during his storied career. Most important, he knew where the secrets were buried and who had interred them there.

Calmer now, Victorine accepted Edouard's pocket square to wipe her tears. She turned her attention to the gentleman standing beside him. "Thank you so much for taking my case," she said sincerely.

"Mademoiselle Laurent." He bowed officiously. It was obvious that he did not approve of Victorine or her reputation. "Judge Auguste Manet was my dear friend and a respected colleague," he said icily. "I suggest we conduct our consultation in less-cramped quarters. I believe there is a Women's Courtyard where we may breathe a bit of fresh air and commence our interview."

They followed the jail keep down the Prisoner's Corridor, their footsteps echoing as in a tomb, and stepped out to a garden courtyard. The flash of bright daylight stung Victorine's eyes. She took a seat on the stone bench and glanced up at the five-story edifice surrounding them. Three stories were built above a portcullis that ran around the structure, enclosing the courtyard. Although every window was barred, this narrow, outdoor court was quite pleasant, with a small, rectangular garden of rosebushes and boxwood hedges in the center, a fountain for washing clothes, and a stone table where the women prisoners could take their meals in the fresh air.

De Briac was watching Victorine. "As a matter of interest, Mademoiselle Laurent," he said, "our own emperor Louis-Napoléon was incarcerated here for a short period by King Louis-Philippe after his first coup attempt back in 1840."

He asked Victorine to relay every detail of the events leading to her arrest. She recounted each step of her entangle-
ment with the imperial family, the Duke de Lyon, and Count
von Bismarck. He took scrupulous notes as she spoke, his
bushy white eyebrows rising expressively at certain pivotal
points in her narration. He asked trenchant questions, and as
he refined his understanding of the events, his punctilious
handwriting filled page after page of a weathered green-
leather notebook. When Victorine reached the conclusion of
her story, he closed the notebook and stroked the leather
cover, regarding her thoughtfully, but saying nothing for several moments.

"There is one obvious way to exonerate yourself, Mademoiselle Laurent." He rubbed his forehead. "Expose the truth
about the Duke de Lyon, that it was he who ordered you to
spy on Prussia."

She remained silent for several moments. "No. I won't ruin
him," she said.

"I don't see him worrying about you," André blurted out.
Edouard grabbed his arm and propelled him to the side. Victorine heard Edouard whisper to André, "Stop reminding her
that de Lyon's sacrificing her to save his own skin. It devas-
tates her each time she hears it."

"Giving the authorities the evidence they want against the
Duke de Lyon—"

"I won't betray him." She crossed her arms.

"Your motives may be personal," de Briac said, "but it *is*
the wisest course in view of the diplomatic repercussions for
our country." He rose and performed a formal bow with the
stiff perfection of a military man.

"I can't thank you enough, monsieur le comte," Edouard
said as they shook hands. "Will you begin by requesting bail
for her?"

"I took that step yesterday. Bail denied."

"But why? I mean, by whose authority?"

"By the highest authority," he said. "Normally, the judge appointed by the *cour d'assises* would decide the question of bail. But in this particular case, the supreme prosecutor has gone directly to the palace. The emperor has the power to pardon or withhold. He has chosen to withhold the right to bail in this instance."

"She'll have to remain here?" Edouard waved his hand around the prison. "Can you contact the Duke de Lyon? Surely with his influence . . ."

"I have already tried. Philippe de Lyon has left the country on a diplomatic mission to Italy. He plans to distance himself from this scandal literally and figuratively. He has called in his favors with newspaper publishers and successfully kept his name out of the news reports. If the blame and public outrage can be centered on Mademoiselle Laurent, he will be able to skillfully save his political career."

"Maître de Briac, she *is* innocent. I assure you, she's being used as a pawn by powerful people!"

He nodded and patted Edouard's shoulder. "Your young lady is in grave jeopardy," he said.

Toinette and André arrived the next day with a carriage load of her possessions. The concierge said none of it would fit in her tiny cell. Discussions ensued and a compromise was reached. Victorine was moved to a larger cell, one on the first floor, close to the director's office in the Prisoner's Corridor.

"Oh, this is ever so much better," Victorine said as a guard opened the door to her new quarters. "There are two windows up there, so I'll have air and more light."

"You'll end up like the last famous prisoner who stayed in this cell," he said.

"And who was that?"

"Marie Antoinette. They took her straight from here, loaded her on the tumbrel, and carted her off to the place de la Révolution, where they . . ." He drew his hand across his throat. Toinette shrieked.

André tried to distract Victorine by sharing the latest fashion periodicals he had brought. Together, they perused the illustrations of familiar society names in their elaborate ensembles. His rude, insulting critiques did make Victorine smile. As they chatted, Toinette shuffled about, transforming the cell into a lady's boudoir, to the best of her ability. She had brought lace portieres for the windows and satin pillows for the straw-filled bed. Toinette suggested that she could sleep on an extra cot in the corner of the cell to look after her mistress, wash her clothes, and dress her hair. Victorine doubted she would be allowed such a concession and assured Toinette that all would be well.

Victorine spent the long hours embroidering or reading Balzac outdoors in the Women's Courtyard, though she read the same page repeatedly without comprehending, unable to concentrate. Meals were taken at a rough-hewn table in her dark cell. After three days of this routine, Victorine received a message from de Briac indicating that he had collected important information and asking for an immediate meeting.

A driving rain prevented them from meeting in the outdoor courtyard and forced them to have their conference in the Chapelle des Girondins, situated adjacent to Victorine's cell, a peaceful, deserted place where they enjoyed some bit of privacy. After a few perfunctory remarks, Maître de Briac called Victorine aside to join him in the small, private alcove called the Chapelle Expiatore. Hour after hour passed; Edouard and André left to dine at a nearby brasserie, and their footsteps were not heard again on the stone floors until after dark. Finally, Victorine and her lawyer emerged. "They've charged me with lèse-majesté, high treason. High treason carries a sentence of death."

Edouard sat down hard on the wooden pew.

"Maître de Briac learned that last month, Philippe convinced Louis-Napoléon to bar Eugénie from all future cabinet meetings. Eugénie entrapped me to ensnare Philippe; she expected him to step forward and exonerate me. She misjudged him, too."

De Briac spoke up. "Eugénie now has changed her plan. Victorine is charged with the more serious crime of lèse-majesté. Faced with high treason, she testifies under oath in a court of law, implicates de Lyon, and lands him in the center of this sex-and-espionage scandal. He's disgraced, and Eugénie wins."

"Maître de Briac's assistants found a blank cartridge near my front steps," Victorine said.

"Of what significance is that?" André asked.

Edouard said, "It means the 'assassination' was an elaborate charade. The bullets were blanks, unable to harm Louis-Napoléon. All orchestrated by—"

"Eugénie." Victorine completed the thought.

"What's to be done now?" André asked, glancing up at the white marble statue of the Virgin Mary looming above in the shadows of the chapel. Her outstretched hand seemed to wave a blessing over Victorine's head.

"I shall have to use my only leverage," Victorine said.

"Which is?" Edouard asked.

"Louis-Napoléon's letters. I'm to tell Eugénie that I'll offer his love notes to the scandal journals for publication unless she calls off this sham prosecution."

"That's excellent strategy. The general public doesn't know the imperial marriage is a sham," Edouard said.

André paced the narrow aisle of the apse. "No newspaper or even scandal sheet would dare publish such incendiary letters.

The government censors would shut them down before the presses began to roll."

"The Marquis de Montpellier is a journalist," Edouard explained to de Briac.

André said, "The London papers, however, would be thrilled to publish such salacious proof of our emperor's libertine ways. Word travels fast across the Channel, and we could get the same results."

"Yes!" Edouard said. "Ingenious, old sport!" He clapped André on the back.

De Briac asked how they would deliver the letters into the anxious hands of the British press barons. All three turned to André. He shrugged. Then suddenly comprehension spread through him like a virus. "No, no, no! Not I. No, I couldn't possibly," he stammered.

Edouard told André that he was the only one. It wouldn't be appropriate for de Briac to do it. And Edouard, himself, was now followed by the palace secret police every time he left his studio.

"But it's a dangerous mission. Fraught with peril." André dabbed his forehead with his pocket square. Just the thought of it caused buds of sweat to blossom on his brow. He suggested that they hire someone. But Edouard reminded him that they needed a person who could be trusted, an insider immune to bribery, someone who would not be suspect traveling the Channel. "You have an uncle in London, don't you? How natural to pay a visit to old Uncle Angus, the Duke of Marmalade."

"Uncle Willie, the Duke of Alsopp. But I couldn't possibly be the courier. I couldn't take the stress of such a dangerous mission." He added, for good measure, "I also suffer from a mild form of scrofula." André glanced at each of them and noted that they remained unconvinced. "Victorine, you know I would do anything for you . . . ," he began. Victorine threw her arms around his neck and planted kisses all over his face. And one on his lips. "I must say, for that alone it's worth risking—"

"Where are those letters at this moment?" de Briac interrupted.

"In a safe place," Victorine answered. "I hid them."

De Briac said that palace police had been to her house and searched it. André replied that every day they came and tore apart rooms searching for evidence. De Briac corrected him. "They have all the evidence they need to charge Mademoiselle Laurent. Those secret police are searching for the emperor's letters. He realizes how priceless they are, as do we. Where exactly are they?" he asked Victorine.

When she told him that one volume in her library of four hundred books was hollowed out, with the letters hidden inside, she thought the man would literally dance a jig. "You are a brilliant young lady!" he exclaimed.

Over the next few days, every detail of the clandestine mission was planned. They met daily for whispered conferences in the privacy of the chapel, where de Briac instructed André. First, André was to telegraph his uncle Willie and inform him of his intention to visit, asking for a reply by post. This ensured a letter in Uncle Willie's own hand inviting André to dine with him at the Union Club the first evening of his arrival in London. Here was the alibi in tangible form for André's voyage.

André must obtain letters of credit from his Paris bank to be presented at a financial institution in London, more proof that his trip was as natural and lacking in suspicious motives as that of any ordinary tourist. De Briac suggested making a reservation at the posh Hotel Brunswick in Mayfair, and told André to request that theater tickets be ordered in his name. All of this detail was absolutely vital for verisimilitude. De Briac anticipated every possibility; Victorine pitied any adversary facing him in court. André was instructed to buy up all four seats in the private compartment of his Calais-bound train to ensure complete privacy. The steamer at Calais would then deliver him to his port of call, the Admiralty Pier in Dover. De Briac told him to assume that surveillants hired by the imperial palace would shadow him, and that he should visit the usual sights to allay any suspicions. "Above all, protect those letters. They're Mademoiselle Laurent's only hope." He was to visit the press baron Sir Geoffrey Black at his offices at the London *Times*. De Briac had used Sir Geoffrey's niece as a go-between: the young lady wrote a letter to her uncle asking him to meet her friend, a French journalist looking for a little extra money as a correspondent in London. All of these precautions were necessary to dupe the palace secret police, who opened and read all correspondence emanating from Victorine, de Briac, and Edouard.

André had been gone three days when Edouard stepped into Victorine's cell, waited until the footfall of the guard died away, and grasped both her hands in his.

"It's finished. You've won," he said.

De Briac had met with Empress Eugénie under the most secret circumstances, shown her the blank cartridge found in Victorine's driveway, and warned that even as they spoke his "operative" was offering for sale to the British press love letters from her husband to Victorine. Eugénie had requested some time to formulate her response. According to palace gossips, Eugénie's fury was frightening to behold. The entire palace was subject to screaming outbursts and foul language. It did not take very long for her to interrogate her husband, for she quickly informed de Briac that there had been an unfortunate mistake, that the true assassins had confessed and exonerated Victorine of any guilt.

Victorine's friends convened for a joyous fête to welcome her home from the Conciergerie. The banquet table was decorated with garlands of fresh flowers, her favorite meal was prepared, and Dom Pérignon flowed in crystal goblets. Jules de Briac sat in the place of honor, hailed as a hero by all.

"I'd like to propose a toast to the comte de Briac." Edouard stood and raised his glass. "To you, sir, and to Victorine, who had the stomach to fight the good fight. We toast this victory with the champagne sent by the empress, as sweet to the palate as the official apology from the Tuileries Palace."

The toast was echoed with cries of *"Salut!"*

Victorine raised her glass. "I would like to propose a toast to all my friends who supported me during this awful ordeal." She toasted de Briac. She thanked André for his courage. She mentioned Julia for her kindness. She blew a kiss to Baudelaire. "To our dearest Baudelaire. You mean more to me than you will ever know. But most of all"—she turned to Edouard—"I wish to thank the artistic genius who made me famous . . ."

"Infamous!" André called out.

She laughed. "Infamous then, by painting me more beautifully than any woman has ever been. And who has also saved my life. I owe you everything. Thank you, Edouard Manet."

Julia's glance darted between the two as they raised their glasses to each other, oblivious to the entire company.

Applause rang through the dining room, and dessert was served.

The party broke up in the early hours of the morning. Edouard and André were the last to leave. "A ride home, Edouard?" André slurred. He and Edouard were both tipsy, having emptied a few bottles of Dom Pérignon between themselves. Victorine helped Edouard stagger to his feet. He leaned heavily against her, draping his arm around her shoulder. She laughed and swayed under his weight as she helped him toward the front entry. She held his black evening cape for him, but he simply stood looking down into her eyes. Slowly, he began to move closer, as though to kiss her. She turned her head away.

"Edouard, please, you're drunk," she said.

"I'm not drunk. I love you," he slurred, lifting a lock of her hair to his face and inhaling her perfume.

"You don't love me, you're drunk."

"I'm drunk with love. Kiss me."

"Stop it." She stepped back.

"Don't be so shellfish."

Victorine laughed.

"*Self*ish. You kissed me once. At Baudelaire's, remember? De Lyon's gone now. Run away. He's gone. Gone. Gone." He swayed toward her and grabbed her by the shoulders.

"Please let go."

"Why?"

"Stop it, Edouard."

"Don't you believe me? I love you."

She looked up at him for a moment. Could she believe him? He hiccuped and burst out laughing. Then she remembered who this was. Edouard Manet. What a ridiculous notion.

"I *do* love you," he said.

"Yes, yes. Now your carriage is waiting outside. Give André a lift home and get some sleep." She stood on tiptoe and draped his cloak over his shoulders.

He suddenly gathered her in his arms and kissed her on the mouth. His kiss was so deep and so long, she thought she would faint.

"There. That's something I've wanted to do all night." He swayed, and André caught him under the arms. Edouard managed to fumble the gardenia out of his lapel.

"Here, a gift for you." He handed the flower to Victorine.

"Good night, darlings," Victorine called from her doorway as she watched André struggle to help Edouard into his carriage. He turned, touched his top hat, and climbed in after Edouard. "Good night," Victorine whispered and closed the door.

She lifted the gardenia and inhaled the scent.

Chapter Twenty-three

Man's love is of his life a thing apart,
'Tis woman's whole existence.

—Lord Byron, *Don Juan*, 1819–1824

On a blustery late November afternoon, Edouard pushed Baudelaire in his wheelchair as Victorine walked holding his hand and André strolled beside him. They approached the pont d'Alma with the first early snowflakes of winter drifting around, melting soft as kisses against their cheeks. Victorine shivered and implored Edouard to walk faster toward their destination, the warmth of the Café Guerbois.

"If only there were some method for the public to see an artist's work by circumventing that heinous Salon system," Edouard said.

Victorine noticed young women casting sidelong looks at Edouard as they passed by. He wore a long red knit scarf wrapped several times around his neck and a black woolen greatcoat, which gave him the look of a romantic hussar. "By God!" He stopped suddenly. "Why not exhibit directly to the public and eliminate the Salon altogether?"

Victorine tugged on his sleeve and urged him to keep walking.

"How do you mean?" Baudelaire asked. His illness was progressing; he was wrapped in a cashmere coat with a lap blanket across his knees to keep out the chill.

"What if an artist created his own exhibition space and invited the public?"

"But an 'exposition' is genteel, well mannered," André said. "An 'exhibition' sounds vulgar, like a display of commodities at Le Bon Marché department store."

"To hell with distinctions like that. I'm willing to gamble that people will come see my paintings with an open mind."

"Everyone knows of the Salon; how would they hear of your exhibition?"

Manet said he would buy advertising space in art journals and put up handbills around town. He pointed out a parcel of land at the corner of the avenue Montaigne and the rue d'Alma as they passed and said that he could rent an empty lot like that one, owned by the Marquis de Pomereu. "I could have a little pavilion built."

"You'd charge admission?" André asked through chattering teeth.

"A token entrance fee. I'll ready it for the hordes of tourists at the Universal Exposition. It opens the first of April. I have almost five months. Perfect!"

At that moment, a beautiful young woman in her mid-twenties stopped them. She had lovely long brown hair and dark Spanish eyes set off by a peach complexion. "Excuse me, aren't you Monsieur Edouard Manet?" she asked, twisting her hands. "I'm sorry to accost you, but I've been following you for several blocks and . . ."

Victorine traded glances with André.

"I've loved your paintings ever since I first saw them at the Salon in 1863. Your pictures sang to me."

"Thank you. You don't know how much that means to me, mademoiselle . . ."

"Gonzales. Eva Gonzales. I'm an artist, too. Not like you, of course. But I try in my own way to paint modern life." She shivered as a cold blast of wind whipped right through her thin cloak.

"Mademoiselle Gonzales, allow me to buy you a hot chocolate? A fellow artist is always welcome in our circle," Edouard said.

He was so smooth. Victorine watched with annoyance as he eased this beauty right into his life. They continued along toward the Guerbois, Victorine stewing, recalling his false words about how much in love with her he was.

Whenever she received an invitation to a soiree that November, she inquired if the Duke de Lyon was expected. If so, she declined to attend. She received frequent letters from Bismarck, who indicated that Berlin would be honored to be her new home if she chose to leave Paris after the treatment she had received from her own government. Messages of support continually arrived from leaders in the fields of industry, the military, and the diplomatic corps. Countless times, messengers arrived at Victorine's door. Countless times, she turned them away with no response to Philippe's urgent messages. One morning, her manservant announced a visitor, and stepped aside to reveal a footman liveried in lilac and white, the de Lyon colors. He bowed and presented Victorine with a gift box and a handwritten note in a familiar masculine scrawl. She took the note, tore it to shreds without reading it, and threw it in the fireplace. She then unwrapped the gift box. A necklace of luminous black South Sea pearls, as rare as flawless diamonds, lay nestled in a cream satin bed. She set the box down and rang for Toinette, casting a glance at Philippe's footman.

"Ma'm'selle?"

"Toinette, this"—she opened the box—"is for you."

Toinette and Philippe's footman gasped in unison.

"I couldn't . . ." Toinette started to back away, her eyes round with shock.

"I insist. A gift for your loyalty and kindness to me. Come and take it."

Toinette swallowed hard and approached. She stared at the pearls, suspicious that this was some sort of madness. "For me? Are you feeling quite well, ma'm'selle?"

"Keep them or sell them. They're worth at least fifty thousand francs. If you're worried someone will accuse you of stealing, I'll go with you. Knowing you, you'll sell them and invest the money wisely."

Toinette hugged the box to her chest and curtsied.

"Now." Victorine turned to Philippe's shocked servant. "Go home and report exactly what happened here to your master."

Victorine and André descended the marble steps of the opera house in a stellar mood after enjoying a rousing performance of Rossini. As they waited in the throng for Victorine's coachman, an elegant carriage pulled up and a look of horror crossed Victorine's face.

"Victorine! Please, a moment."

Victorine pushed through the crowd of theatergoers pouring out the doors, while Philippe threaded his way through them to reach her. She rushed into the darkened foyer of the opera house and bolted up the grand staircase. He followed her, taking the red-carpeted steps three at a time. At the top of the staircase, he reached for her white-gloved arm and spun her around. "I've tried for weeks to send you letters of apology. Please listen to me!"

"No!" She pulled her arm away.

"I had to do what I did."

"Go away." Her throat constricted, and she could barely manage a whisper.

"Victorine, please forgive me. I've been miserable without you."

"They would have destroyed me, and you let them. You abandoned me."

"What else could I do? I had to protect my name, my reputation."

She turned her back to him. He placed his hands on the shoulders of her satin evening cape. She flinched as his touch seared through the fabric. "What am I if not a politician?" His voice caressed her. "My whole life has been devoted to this one passion, politics. I've realized something these past weeks. I need you. You give me something priceless—"

"Go away." She tried to stop the tears, not wishing to appear weak or emotional, but they spilled over her cheeks and betrayed her.

"Victorine, I love you."

She was stunned. Never had she expected those words from him.

"How do I know it's true?" She turned now and faced him.

"I've never said it before. To you or to any woman. I love you, Victorine."

He had lied, betrayed, deceived her, she stubbornly reminded herself. She remembered how adroitly he manipulated and controlled her, but she knew that she was as much a creature of his creation as she was of Edouard's. Her gaze traveled every feature of that face she knew so well. She loathed the self-satisfied curve of his mouth, the world-weary expression in his heavy-lidded eyes. Yet she longed for the familiar feeling of belonging to him, the comforting knowledge of being owned by him that she both hated and craved. It was perverse, she knew, but she allowed herself to be enveloped and felt herself collapse physically and emotionally into him.

When she told her friends that she had accepted him back, they reacted with amazement. Edouard did not take it very well. He vowed that this was the final blow and the absolute end of their relationship. He announced that he was leaving Paris for an extended stay in Spain with Mademoiselle Gonzales. There, he intended to visit the Prado and pay homage to his gods, the Spanish painters El Greco, Velázquez, and Goya.

Chapter Twenty-four

1867

Chance is a word void of sense; nothing can
exist without a cause.

—Voltaire (1694–1778)

The Universal Exposition, set to open in three short
months, was the topic of conversation in practically every
quarter of the city. Philippe told Victorine that it would be
the most elaborate and unrivaled event of Louis-Napoléon's
reign, designed to showcase French achievements in manufac-
turing, weaponry, and the arts. It was also a way of distracting
Louis-Napoléon's constituency from the rumblings of discon-
tent among the leftist factions of the population. Seditious socialist "clubs" were springing up in the eastern *banlieues,* the
poorest sections of Paris, organized by Emile Ollivier and
Henri Rochefort, Edouard's anti-imperialist friends. By 1867,
France had lived under the glittering yoke of Emperor Louis-
Napoléon for sixteen years. Everyone knew that he had first
swept to power on a wave of nostalgia for the drama and glory
of his uncle Napoléon I. The public was in a restless mood,
as Philippe often told Victorine, and the obvious solution,

proposed by de Lyon, was to distract them with a grand spectacle, the 1867 Paris Universal Exposition.

~

A few minutes past midnight on January 1, 1867, Victorine and Philippe were among a throng of revelers on the ballroom floor of the Tuileries Palace. As they whirled around the ballroom, Victorine debated whether this was the moment. Noisemakers blared, couples kissed, and she decided tonight was the night. "It's so crowded in here," she said. "Let's go up to the roof of the Louvre. I want to be alone with you and hear the New Year rung in from every bell tower in Paris."

They stood on the deserted rooftop of the Louvre Palace as the lights of Paris flickered down below them. The stars above shimmered as though blown by the chilly wind. Ancient bells clanged from every cathedral in the city, a symphony fit for heaven itself. Victorine shivered from the cold wind whistling past the turrets. "Happy 1867." She planted a light kiss on his lips, then whispered into his ear.

"It's not mine." Philippe took a step back and regarded her with a wary expression.

"Of course it's yours!" she said.

"It's not mine," he repeated.

"You're the father, Philippe," she said, exasperated.

He turned his back to her. "Then I'll pay your expenses to get rid of it."

"I will not," she said quietly.

He whipped around. "Victorine, be reasonable. This is not the way things are done between a man like me and a woman like you."

"A woman like me? What precisely does that mean?"

"I have a name to protect. I have a reputation. An illegitimate child . . ."

"You were an illegitimate child."

"My mother was an aristocrat. She wasn't a—"

"You said you loved me," she said softly. The starlight threw flickering shadows across her pale face.

"I can't marry you," he said simply.

"I'm not interested in marriage. But I'm having this baby."

"Why? I've had to fight my entire life against the fact that I was born illegitimate. I will not support it, Victorine. Not one sou. And don't expect me to acknowledge the child as mine."

"Well, it's mine. I've never had a soul in the world who belonged to me, Philippe, but now I finally do. With you or without you, I've made up my mind to have this child."

"I'll never acknowledge it as mine. I warn you," he repeated.

She turned to go. "Good-bye, Philippe."

Edouard's private exhibition pavilion was set to coincide with the Universal Exposition of 1867. He had finally relented and invited Victorine to attend the opening. After all, as André pointed out to him, his most brilliant masterpieces all featured Victorine. How could Edouard hold a grudge against his model and muse? At the same time, a most curious avalanche of good luck befell André. He received a telegram informing him of the sad news that Uncle Willie had passed away. But to André's great surprise, he had been remembered in his will, and had come into quite an astounding inheritance. The very first thing he did was to march down to the offices of *Le Moniteur* and quit. The very next thing, he marched to Boucheron's and bought Victorine the most gaudy, ostentatious piece of jewelry on display in the shop.

In early April, the opening of the 1867 Universal Exposition, the crowned heads of state from all over Europe converged on Paris. The night of the premiere of Offenbach's *Grand Duchess of Gerolstein,* Philippe, a major backer and the producer of the show, was seated in the front row in the best house seats. At his side was his new mistress, Princess Romanoff.

Victorine awaited her escort in the foyer while he was delayed in the throng checking cloaks. She raised her opera glasses and peeked in the auditorium of the Théâtre des Variétés. First, she spotted Madame McMillan and Princess Mathilde, accompanied by the actress Sarah Bernhardt. The number of dignitaries and luminaries was awe-inspiring. She saw Jules Verne, Hector Berlioz, Gustave Flaubert, Louis Pasteur, Emile Zola, Georges Bizet, Baudelaire, George Sand, Stéphane Mallarmé, a young friend of Edouard's she had met before called James Whistler, and so many more. But when her escort finally stepped to her side and Victorine made her entrance through the double doors, all conversation halted seemingly in midsentence. The theater fell quiet as a temple. Victorine wore a dazzling cream satin gown sewn with crystal and black jet beading. A floor-length silver chinchilla cape draped her shoulders. The necklace sparkling at her throat was worth millions, but that was not the cause of astonishment. For she glided down the center aisle of the theater on the arm of the tall and very distinguished-looking chancellor Otto von Bismarck.

This was a daring and provocative act. Furious whispering erupted through the audience as Victorine and Bismarck found their seats one row behind the Duke de Lyon and the imperial family. Even the king of Prussia and Czar Alexander could not resist a sidelong glance at the beauteous Mademoiselle Victorine, whose fame had reached across the capitals of Europe. De Lyon's companion whispered to him, but his gaze remained stoically focused ahead, refusing a backward glance at his former mistress.

"Shocking, simply shocking," Eugénie hissed to the Russian princess.

Victorine pretended to peruse her program, but could not hide the delicious smile sliding across her lips.

"She couldn't have done anything more calculated to steal the spotlight." Princess Romanoff meant the comment to reach Victorine's ears.

Nothing could have made her happier. The overture began, the curtain went up, and the whispering ceased as a hush rolled across the house.

～

"You should have seen the expression on Eugénie's face!" Victorine snuggled in the corner of Edouard's big velvet divan as she relived the evening's highlights.

Edouard watched Victorine in silence.

"What?" she asked.

"There's still time to . . . you don't have to have the baby, Victorine."

"Not you, as well! Everyone tells me not to have it. But I will."

"Let's assume you do. How will you raise it? What will you tell people?"

"Do you propose I give it away to a servant, have the child ignored, abused? Have her grow up believing she's unworthy of the love and attention every child craves?"

"Of course that's not what I meant! Shh. Stop crying. You shall have your baby. And I'm sure you'll be the most dazzling mother sitting on the park bench in the Tuileries."

She laughed through her tears. "I'm going to give her my surname. She'll go to a proper school and learn proper manners, too."

"You're certain it's a girl? Well, boy or girl, you'll spoil it something awful, unless Uncle Edouard hasn't done it first."

"Uncle Edouard!" She burst out laughing. "What do you know about babies?"

"I know how to make them," he teased.

"Why are you so good to me? I don't deserve it, you know."

"I know. I suppose I'm just perverse," he said.

Chapter Twenty-five

Artist Edouard Manet's private exhibition in his self-constructed pavilion has created a sensation. The prestigious Mayfair Gallery of London has invited Manet to exhibit his pictures in the fall. In a major breakthrough for an American artist, Miss Julia Stanhope-Morgan of Boston, Massachusetts, a protégée of Mr. Manet, will show four of her paintings as well.

—*New York Tribune*, 1867

I'm not showing yet, am I?" Victorine turned sideways and inspected her image in the full-length cheval glass of her boudoir. She ran her hand along the curve of the bulge under her Empire-waisted dress.

"You're as fat as Nadar's balloon."

André dodged Victorine's fan hurtling toward him.

Julia glanced up from her knitting. "Victorine *embonpoint*. It's hard to imagine." She held up a dainty square of pink wool. "Do you like it so far?"

"It's beautiful, Julia. But pink. Suppose it's a boy?"

"Oh, it *is* a girl, I'm certain. I can tell by the way you're carrying. I predicted the gender of all my nieces and nephews without a miss."

"Victorine!" Edouard's voice called out from the staircase.

"We're in here."

"Terrible news about Mexico." Edouard waved a clutch of newspapers in his hand. "Emperor Maximilian's been executed, shot by firing squad. This is de Lyon's doing. Maximilian's blood is on his hands." He dropped down in an armchair and extended his long legs. "I'm going to paint the execution, and the firing squad will feature the faces of de Lyon and Louis-Napoléon."

"Edouard, you know the government censors—"

"I have to do it, Victorine. This regime is rotting from within. It's my way of condemning this stinking imperial family and their ruthless tactics."

"I couldn't agree with you more," she said and gave a start, clutching her stomach.

"What's wrong?" Edouard sat forward.

Victorine laughed. "If this is a girl, she certainly has a powerful kick!"

By July, Victorine was in her seventh month. The pregnancy was now difficult to disguise under her voluminous dresses and shawls. It was time to leave Paris for her villa in Deauville to await the arrival of the baby. Before leaving, she had one important matter to take care of. She composed a letter to Dr. Charcot at the Salpêtrière Hospital. She enclosed a five-hundred-franc note and informed him that she would be sending that amount every month to be used for the special care of Marie Laurent. She asked him to provide proper dresses for her and use the money to make her life as comfortable as possible.

Victorine took Toinette, the chef, and several servants with her to Deauville, to wait out the final trimester of her pregnancy. She also invited André to accompany her. After all, an *enceinte* woman could maintain respectability only if escorted by a male companion.

"So, let's hope it's a boy, eh sir?" The train porter winked as he led Victorine and André to their first-class coach compartment.

"Boy or girl. I'll be happy either way," André said.

"Naw, you'll be wantin' a son, I'd wager."

"Oh, I'm not the father. I'm the uncle."

The porter moved off with a shrug.

Once they reached Deauville, Victorine and her household settled into her great, rambling neo-Norman-style mansion behind a boxwood hedgerow on the avenue Strassburger. Following breakfast every morning, Victorine took constitutionals by the seashore, fueled by deep breaths of brisk marine air tinged with the tang of salt. She and André trooped through local medieval battlements and tasted the locally produced Calvados at nearby wineries. When they toured the twelfth-century Chapelle Saint-Laurent, Victorine claimed it as proof that she was the descendant of a saint, after all.

But after several weeks, this rural life began to lose its charm. Victorine and André became restless, finding precious little to occupy the long days. Except for their early morning walks along the oceanfront on boulevard de la Mer, there was no socializing outside the home; etiquette forbade a woman in Victorine's condition to be seen on the streets. Carriage rides down country lanes were pleasant enough, rolling through the countryside past acres of apple orchards and Camembert-producing farms, but where were the crowds? Where were the *grands passages,* the brasseries, the carousels, the *café concerts?* As time passed, the only form of entertainment was watching the seabirds catch fish.

Edouard and Julia steamed across the Channel to their Mayfair Gallery show. Victorine lived for letters from them and for her Paris newspapers delivered by post. She and André shared news from the gossip pages, particularly relishing the stories reprinted from the British newspapers about Edouard's escapades in London.

"Oh, listen to this!" Victorine settled down next to André in the drawing room, folded her arms over her belly, and read aloud. "From the London *Times.* 'The French painter Mr. Edouard Manet and the American artist Miss Julia Stanhope-Morgan caused a "to-do" in White's restaurant on the Strand last night. Mr. Manet filled the grand piano with champagne to prove it could act as an aquarium, apparently to win a wager against his companions . . .' "

As August slipped by, Victorine's doctor called on her weekly and stroked his beard, predicting the child would come at any moment. Each week he was wrong.

"One never knows with the first baby." He waved his hands in a Norman version of the Gallic shrug. "My sister's first child was so late he was born with a mustache and goatee!" He regaled Victorine with case histories of babies who came two, sometimes three weeks late. Somehow, she didn't find his stories amusing.

"This child is going to stay in the womb forever," she sighed.

Interrupting the deadly ennui, on the last day in August, an urgent electrical telegram arrived.

TODAY BAUDELAIRE DIED IN HIS MOTHER'S ARMS. DEVASTATION. SADLY, EDOUARD.

Victorine and André mourned together. "He's finally found the inner peace he searched for," André said. Victorine dabbed her red-rimmed eyes with a lace handkerchief and quoted lines from *The Flowers of Evil:* "'O death, old captain, it is time, let us weigh anchor. To the depths of the unknown to find something new.'"

The next day, a rush of fluid oozed down Victorine's thighs. For thirty-six hours, she writhed and clenched the bed-clothes in her fists to withstand painful contractions. Toinette stayed by her side, dozing in the bedside chair at night, and providing a hand to squeeze during the contractions. Finally, on the morning of September 3, the doctor caught a slippery bundle who entered the world with a hearty wail. Victorine wept tears of joy when she heard that first cry.

"Congratulations! You're the proud mother of a healthy, beautiful baby!"

She held out her arms for the doctor to gently hand her son to her. She gazed down at the little creature with such tenderness; tears fell like kisses on the baby's face. She stared in wonder at his little hand, each tiny fingernail delicate as a seed pearl. She ran her fingertip across his forehead, dipped down his nose, and giggled as his tiny breaths tickled against her bare neck. She would build a fortress of love around him. And she knew exactly how to raise him. She would do the opposite of everything ever done to her in her own childhood. He would grow up to be a great man, secure and confident in himself. His birthright was established. It mattered not in the least that he had no father or paternal surname. Greatness flowed through his veins.

Victorine heard muffled voices outside her door. The wet nurse was arguing with André, preventing him from disturbing Victorine. She called out to allow him in.

André burst into the room, anxious to see his "nephew." He had stayed in the far wing of the house the entire time of her labor, unable to withstand her screams of pain. But now he rushed to Victorine and fell to his knees at her bedside. Victorine held up the baby for André to kiss.

"He's perfect! I see he's inherited his hair from me." He stroked the fine tufts of blond fuzz on the baby's round little head. "What will you name him?"

"I'll call him Alexander, the name of kings." Victorine kissed the baby's head. "The nobility of aristocrats and poets runs in your blood, my little man." She caressed the curve of his cheek with her index finger. The baby yawned, and as she watched him drift asleep, she felt content and finally at peace. "André, you are my most loyal friend. The one who has always been at my side, never disappointing me. I'm going to tell you a secret that you must swear you'll never, never reveal to another soul. Not even Edouard or Julia."

He promised.

"Baudelaire was my father."

André seemed unable to comprehend the enormity of this disclosure. After recovering his composure, he began to review the similarities between father and daughter. It all made perfect sense, he decided. Baudelaire's affair with Marie Laurent and the consequences for their child were predictable as well. "This damned society of ours. You were never allowed to enjoy the privilege of your birthright. This society condemns Edouard's paintings, and it's precisely this society, this theme, that inspired Baudelaire! Aren't you angry, Victorine, at what was stolen from you?"

"I feel at peace now. In the balance of the scale, I feel as though the loss of a father was compensated by the birth of a son."

"Did Baudelaire know he was your father?"

"I never told him, and he never mentioned it to me. It was best that way."

A month passed, and the doctor pronounced the baby fit and strong enough for the rail journey back home. The household devolved into an uproar, servants busy all day packing steamer trunks full of baby clothes, baby accoutrements, newly acquired artifacts, and presents for everyone back home in Paris.

Chapter Twenty-six
1869

Parisians do not reason, they feel;
they do not discuss, they are carried away. Paris is a
nervous aggregation, governed by impressions.

—Maxime Du Camp (1822–1894)

Two years passed quickly. Victorine resumed her social life, entertaining illustrious admirers at her mansion on the rue Van Dyck, presiding as gracious hostess for her weekly literary salons, music recitals, and fancy-dress balls.

Edouard began a new painting featuring Victorine, inspired by his hero, the Spanish painter Goya, and his famous painting *Majas on a Balcony*. Victorine was the seated central character; André and Julia were depicted standing next to her. The picture was magnificent; Victorine's smoldering glance announced her sexuality although clothed in a virginal white muslin dress. Edouard joked that his vision was inspired by her new status as a mother, but, in fact, the contrast between her overt sensuality and the innocence of her attire provided an erotic charge that leaped from the picture. Julia was most dissatisfied with the way Edouard depicted her—as a pale, secondary figure. André stood between the two women on the balcony, a typical young dandy of the Second Empire. The painting was denied for the Salon of 1870; no doubt the palace played a role in the painting's rejection.

The Tuileries Palace seemed a remote dream to Victorine now. She barely paid mind to the stories in the press about Empress Eugénie's official visit to Egypt for the opening of the Suez Canal. Editorials hinted that Louis-Napoléon's regime faced mounting political challenges from the left. A friend of Edouard's, the dashing leftist aristocrat Henri Rochefort, debuted a seditious newspaper called *La Lanterne*. In it, he lampooned the Bonaparte reign and criticized the Mexico fiasco. Before he could be arrested, he escaped to Belgium, where he continued publishing. The paper was smuggled into France and turned up on street corners, Victorine suspected, with Edouard's assistance. When the authorities confiscated all copies off the boulevards, it was distributed by post in plain brown envelopes to subscribers.

The elections of 1869 brought bad results for Philippe in the Corps législatif. Not only was the radical Rochefort elected to the chamber by a working-class constituency, but the Liberal movement swept the country. Democracy was the new cause of the day. Victorine heard, through well-connected friends, that Philippe had proposed a change in tactics and a move toward democracy. He recognized that this was a necessary evil to hang on to power. Eugénie disagreed and tried to dissuade her husband. But as long as Philippe sat at the emperor's right hand, her reactionary voice was shouted down. Victorine smiled to herself when she heard insiders predict that the emperor's political aspects looked dim and the future of his regime looked doomed.

One day, Victorine and André sat on a bench in the Parc Monceau sharing a bag of burned almonds under the shade of swaying poplar trees as Alexander and his nanny sailed a toy boat on the pond. Victorine sat up at attention when she noticed a familiar figure strolling the pathway. The gentleman walked with difficulty, leaning heavily on a cane, yet presented a picture of elegance in his top hat, yellow gloves, gray morning coat, and striped trousers. He stopped suddenly and stared at her. It was Philippe.

Victorine called out, "Alexander, come to me."

Her darling boy in his white sailor suit obediently left the water's edge and toddled into her open arms. With his blond curls and muscular little body, he was the unmistakable image of his father. As Victorine pulled him close, Philippe took a few steps toward them, thought better of it, and turned on his heel. Hugging her little son protectively, Victorine watched as he turned a corner and was gone.

A few weeks later, Princess Mathilde came to call. "I've just returned from a visit to New York. Oh, darling, what an exciting place. I found myself a steel tycoon who fell madly for me. He couldn't speak a word of French, but we managed to communicate through the language of Eros."

"Mathilde, you and I have grown apart for obvious reasons. May I ask the purpose of your visit?"

She alighted on Victorine's silk damask divan. "I think you've guessed at whose behest I'm here. Victorine, it's about your—"

"I don't want to discuss this."

"Please. Philippe begs your permission to visit the child. He's changed; you wouldn't recognize him. And he's ill, too."

"Nothing you say about him could alter my feelings."

"He just wants to see his son."

"He made a decision about this child and told me clearly that it was final."

"Victorine, people change. He's changed."

Victorine rose to indicate that this meeting was over. "Thank you for your visit."

Mathilde rose with a sigh. "Please reconsider his request, darling."

Chapter Twenty-seven

1870

Paris changes, but in sadness like mine nothing stirs;
new buildings, old neighborhoods turn to allegory
and memories weigh more than stones.

—Charles Baudelaire, "The Swan," 1859

Alexander and his British nanny, Miss Rosedale, returned from the park with an inlaid marquetry box in the nanny's hand. Victorine was sitting in her library at her writing desk composing a letter to Degas in New Orleans when Alexander ran in and jumped on her lap, wrapping his arms around her neck.

"Hello, madam. Look at the lovely present Alexander's got." Miss Rosedale untied her bonnet and held up the ornately carved box.

"Where did you get that?" Victorine asked, running her fingers through his blond curls and inhaling the milk-and-biscuits scent of his breath.

"The gentleman gave it to him. He said he'd like Alexander to have it."

Victorine hugged Alexander closer to her. "What gentleman?"

"A kindly, aristocratic gentleman. We always see him on the bench nearby when we play. He knows we come to the park every day at the same hour, and he's usually there waiting for us. He's become quite fond of Alex and today brought him this. He said they were the toys he used to play with and that he wanted Alex to have them." She opened the box and displayed a set of Napoleonic toy soldiers, hand painted, of the finest quality.

"Look at my new soldiers!" Alexander pointed with a chubby finger, his little voice rising in pitch with excitement.

"You shouldn't have allowed a stranger near Alex," Victorine scolded.

"Oh, madam, no worries. This gentleman's a fine, upright type. Top hat, yellow kid gloves, that sort. He's been rather ill lately, and watching Alex at play seems to cheer him a bit. Today, he came in a wheelchair pushed by an attendant."

"Nevertheless, I don't want you to go back to that park anymore. Alexander can play in our garden from now on."

"But madam, he loves the swings. Please, madam—"

"I said no! He plays at home from now on. Is that understood?"

"Yes, madam." Miss Rosedale lowered her eyes.

Bismarck had been searching for years for the perfect excuse to declare war on France. His opportunity arrived in the unlikely personage of Leopold, an obscure nephew of Kaiser Wilhelm's. When Queen Isabella of Spain abdicated her throne, Prince Leopold was the next in line for succession. After years of diplomatic wrangling, all Bismarck had to do was to sit back and watch the French erupt into typical Gallic histrionics as the Tuileries Palace faced the prospect of a Prussian ruler on France's southern border.

In July, word officially reached Paris concerning Leopold's ascension. Many statesmen were on holiday and had to be called urgently back to their posts. Rothschild returned from Biarritz and visited Victorine at her home. After a sumptuous dinner, he lingered over a fine snifter of Armagnac, and told her that Louis-Napoléon had requested that he telegraph the London branch of his family to pressure Prime Minister Gladstone to join the protest against Leopold. He also told her that Louis-Napoléon had dispatched Ambassador Benedetti to the elderly kaiser to urge him to renounce his nephew. After much jockeying, the Prussian prince's name was withdrawn and the crisis seemed over.

But, according to Rothschild's sources, Eugénie and Foreign Minister de Gramont refused to let the affair rest. They sent a telegram to the old king demanding that he strongly condemn the choice of his nephew and insist his name never be resubmitted. Wilhelm politely refused to take orders from the Tuileries Palace. Ambassador Benedetti pushed for another audience. The king politely declined to meet with him.

Victorine said that she was certain the withdrawal of Prince Leopold caused Bismarck deep disappointment, but she knew him well enough to know that he would not be deterred so easily. Rothschild agreed that this was probably not the end of the matter.

Surely enough, a few days later, a copy of a private telegram from Kaiser Wilhelm to Bismarck mysteriously appeared in the newspapers of all the capitals of Europe. In the telegram, the king insulted the French by dismissing their envoy, Benedetti. It was "the red rag to the Gallic bull" that Bismarck had bragged to Victorine he would wave.

On July 14, Bastille Day, Parisians awoke to read in the morning papers that a French ambassador had been insulted by an "old Kraut king." The press, ever loyal servants of Eugénie, whipped the public into a frenzy. A council of high ministers met while crowds milled around outside the Tuileries Palace calling for war against the Prussians. The honor of France was at stake.

Victorine predicted that Philippe would stand firm against the warmongers: He knew how well prepared the Prussians were. Philippe would be the voice of reason; he would say, "I have indisputable information, gained from Bismarck himself, that General von Moltke has efficient rail lines for transport plus steel artillery and field guns that far outrange ours."

But Victorine could well imagine Eugénie shouting him down.

Philippe would insist that they were falling into Bismarck's trap, but Louis-Napoléon would listen to the shrill voice of his wife.

The headlines in the papers declared, in twenty-point type, WAR AGAINST PRUSSIA.

On a humid, stifling day in August, Victorine sipped her morning coffee and perused the papers for the day's news. There were discouraging reports from the military front. France's brave troops had fallen back from Metz to Verdun. A dashing regiment of cuirassiers on their gleaming horses had charged down a little street in a village near Strasbourg to be blown to pieces by German artillery. In Washington, D.C., the French ambassador to the United States had shot himself in the head with a revolver. But she choked on her coffee when she read the headline below the fold in *Le Figaro*. The Duke de Lyon had died last night of complications from pneumonia. The paper slipped to the floor as she stared out the window. A chill came over her, and she began to tremble. No tears formed in her eyes, but she felt as though a curtain had closed, and the room seemed to suddenly turn dark.

Victorine received a summons to the offices of a respected solicitor, a trusted member of the imperial family's inner circle. On the day of her appointment, she promised to meet everyone later at the Café Riche.

When Victorine entered the restaurant that evening, the fawning maître d'hôtel led her to the table. Edouard, Julia, and André were all eager to hear her news. "Bring me a *coupe de champagne* right away," she said as she dropped into a chair, flushed and in a daze.

"Well? What was the mysterious summons all about?" Edouard asked.

"It was the reading of Philippe's will." Victorine was served her champagne flute and downed the entire glass.

"Victorine, what the devil?" Edouard said.

She glanced at each of her friends sequentially. "He married me posthumously. I'm the Duchess de Lyon, the sole owner of his companies, his railroads, his palace on the Champs-Elysées, his Château de Beauvois, his racehorses, and . . . Alexander is entitled to his name and is heir to his patrimony."

Stunned silence greeted this announcement.

"Oh, darling!" Julia rushed to hug Victorine.

"So, that blackguard actually had a conscience after all," Edouard said.

"Madame la duchesse." André bowed an exaggerated sweep. "Now that we're fellow members of the aristocracy, we shall eschew this common rabble." He waved his hand at the table full of friends.

Victorine didn't laugh. She held a sealed envelope in her hands and stared at it.

"What's that?" Edouard asked.

"He wrote me a note to be read after his passing." She broke the wax seal and began to read aloud.

> *Dearest Victorine,*
>
> *I write this as a man regretful of many things he's done in his life. But the biggest regret is that I cheated myself out of my son. And I regret my pride, which kept me from you. Until faced with my own mortality, I didn't know what is truly immortal. It's too late to make amends for myself, but at least I can provide for you and the boy. Although I'm not worthy of your forgiveness, please speak kindly of me to our son and know that I love you.*
>
> *Philippe*

Droplets of tears fell on the paper as she repeated the last line.

"And know that I love you."

Chapter Twenty-eight

The wine is poured, we must drink it.

—Empress Eugénie (1826–1920)

French troops headed off to the battlefields to confront the deadly Prussian war machine featuring the breech-loading cannon Bismarck had bragged about to Victorine. The palace-censored newspapers fabricated optimistic reports about the war effort, but Victorine heard the true account from Rothschild, who was privy to events at the front. He told her that supplies didn't arrive when needed. Generals lacked maps of the terrain. When villagers called out asking where they were going, soldiers routinely gave the same reply: "To be butchered."

The presence of Louis-Napoléon began to infuriate the troops; they slogged though the countryside, mud up to their knees, while a convoy of imperial carriages splashed past them carrying the emperor's entourage. The rain doused their campfires while the emperor's tents blazed with light. Soldiers gobbled meager rations while the scent of Louis-Napoléon's meals prepared by imperial chefs wafted to them on the breeze.

Morale plummeted further when Louis-Napoléon became too ill to ride on horseback. Instead of leading the army into battle like Napoléon I on his white charger, he followed behind in a carriage. His high command thought it would be best if he returned to Paris, but Eugénie telegrammed him: "Under no circumstances. It will be seen as defeat. It would be better if you were killed in action than bring on me a humiliation like this!" In her capacity as regent, she became more delusional about her place on the world stage. At the end of August, when she was informed that General MacMahon had ordered the troops to retreat to Paris, she immediately sent an urgent telegram countermanding his orders, forcing them to turn back.

When the Prussian commander, General von Moltke, heard this bit of news, he encircled his two hundred thousand men around the French army and ordered an offensive at a town called Sedan. A French general at the front wrote to his wife in Paris, "We are in a chamber pot and will be shat on." Rothschild told Victorine that the disintegration of the army of the Second Empire was due to Prussian superiority, but also to the incompetence and arrogance of French leadership.

On the second of September, the inevitable happened. Louis-Napoléon surrendered to the Prussians. Bismarck took him prisoner and held him in a little farmhouse near the battlefield. News of the humiliating defeat reached Paris the next day. Mobs stormed the *hôtel de ville,* City Hall, and shouted, "Down with the emperor. Down with the Spanish woman!" The mob was calling for Eugénie's head. Victorine laid down the newspaper. The woman who had tried to destroy her was now herself destroyed.

There was justice, after all.

Prussians were on the march, headed toward Paris. André was in a panic and suffering from an egregious case of nervous hives. "We must leave, Victorine. It won't be safe when those Huns break down our walls. Especially for Alexander. Who knows what's ahead?"

"This is my home, André. I'm not leaving."

"Julia, tell her," André said.

"Victorine, darling, Alexander is as dear to me as if he were my own. I'm worried about his safety."

"I'll send him with the nanny to Château de Beauvois. He'll be safe for the duration."

A servant announced the arrival of Lieutenant Manet. They glanced at one another as though to ask, *Who?* Edouard entered the room dressed in a midnight-blue military tunic complete with gold-trimmed epaulets and double rows of gold buttons, red braiding, and crisp white breeches with gleaming black boots. He held a kepi in the crook of his arm, and a saber slapped his side as he walked toward Victorine.

"You've joined the National Guard?" Victorine asked, as André threw up his hands and rolled his eyes.

"I've signed up with an artillery unit to defend Paris from the Hun at our gates." Edouard performed a smart salute.

"You could be wounded!" Julia cried.

"Don't worry. I'm a crack shot." He threw André an arch look. "Considering your family and the number of illustrious military heroes among your ancestors, why don't you join up and help defend France's glory?"

"Me? Not with my nervous disposition."

"They'll take anyone at this point, even you."

André declined vehemently, citing numerous digestive disorders and a serious weakness of internal organs.

Victorine approached Edouard. "Why must you put yourself in such danger?" A premonition of disaster kneaded her gut.

"Now that Louis-Napoléon's gone, I'd be a hypocrite if I didn't fight to protect what I believe in. I'll defend Paris to my last breath."

"Oh, a pretty speech!" Victorine stamped her foot. "Don't go, Edouard."

"Please don't," Julia echoed.

Little Alexander toddled into the room and gasped at the sight of Edouard in his uniform. "Are you a soldier, Uncle Edouard?" he said, his eyes sparkling at the military regalia. Edouard bent down and flung open his arms. The boy bounced joyfully onto his lap, pudgy fingers examining the shiny gold buttons on Edouard's tunic.

"A soldier!" he repeated with great respect.

Edouard kissed him good-bye and rose to leave.

"Wait, Lieutenant Manet . . . ," Victorine called out. She crossed the room and encircled her arms about his waist. "Be careful, please?" she whispered urgently.

He was so taken aback he glanced at André and Julia as though to ask, *What is the meaning of this?*

Degas patriotically joined up, but discovered during target practice that his right eye was completely useless. He was disappointed to be assigned a clerical job in Provence. Renoir was conscripted into the cavalry. Monet and Pissarro decided they wanted no part of valor—Monet quit Paris and left for Holland, while Pissarro sailed off to England. Cézanne moved far away to a small town called L'Estaque in the south. Many others fled the city rather then stay and defend her.

It became increasingly unpleasant to be in Paris as the weeks wore on. The Prussians tightened an embargo around the city, allowing no food or supplies to flow in and no mail to flow out. The few friends who remained in Paris gathered in Victorine's ornate banquet room to welcome the New Year, 1871. To keep up spirits, Victorine requested that everyone dress in their most elegant finery to recall happier days. She wore a silk satin dress of emerald green and a choker to match of diamonds and emeralds. Julia had borrowed a gown from Victorine of canary-yellow velvet with capped sleeves that featured pearl and jet beading in floral patterns on the skirt. The gentlemen wore white tie and waistcoats with their evening frock coats. The contrast struck everyone as quite amusing: dining on a gleaming mahogany table under crystal chandeliers, off porcelain and sterling silver, while chewing with great difficulty scraps of mysterious, stringy meat accompanied by some pathetic turnips and potatoes.

"Toinette went to the English butcher's today, the one on the boulevard Haussmann," Victorine said. "She didn't have much enthusiasm for the choices: camel, kangaroo, and zebra."

"I heard the zoo's completely cleaned out of deer and antelope." The table shook as Edouard's knife tried to saw his meat with some difficulty.

André said that Bismarck was ensconced in Baron de Rothschild's Château de Ferrières, drinking his way through the very best vintages in his *caves*.

"Well, maybe the New Year will bring us happiness." Victorine raised her crystal goblet. "A toast to 1871 and better times."

"To better times. And better donkey meat!" Edouard said.

Chapter Twenty-nine

1871

There is only one happiness in life, to love
and be loved in return.

—George Sand, letter to a friend, 1862

The first week of January, Victorine was surprised to receive a letter in the post from Bismarck. He wrote that the surrender of Paris was the Prussian goal, but he and his generals disagreed on how to bring this about. Bismarck stubbornly refused to shell the city, believing a blockade would suffice to force Paris to surrender. He confessed that every night he climbed alone to the top of a hill and watched the lights of Paris shimmering like a dream, and tried to imagine her in her elegant silks and satins in her mansion behind high courtyard walls. But Bismarck could no longer constrain the generals. They ordered a shelling campaign of Paris. The boom of Prussian cannons replaced the waltz as the music of daily life.

When Edouard learned his unit had received orders to move out, he decided to transport his precious masterpieces from his studio to Victorine's care for safekeeping. No matter if all Paris burned to the ground, Edouard felt sure Bismarck would protect Victorine. She watched as he carried in canvases, setting them down on the marble floor of her foyer. "Here's the last of them." Edouard tore the brown wrapping paper off *The Street Singer*. With the passage of years, the beauty of the painting glowed more incandescently. "Remember when the critics called it 'strange'?"

"Baudelaire answered them best," Victorine recalled. "'The Beautiful is always strange.' Baudelaire wouldn't have approved of this perverse notion to be a soldier. He would tell you to save your talent for your art."

"Don't scowl, Victorine. Have you no patriotism?"

He wrapped his arms around her and playfully danced her around the foyer. An outsider looking in would have seen a handsome young officer in a dashing uniform and a beautiful, aristocratic woman in a striped silk dress; in better times, they could have been practicing a waltz for the imperial ball at the Tuileries Palace.

"Edouard, if anything happens to you—"

"You told me once I wasn't what you *needed*, remember?" he laughed. "Have you changed your mind?"

"I didn't know what I needed. I didn't know anything back then," she said softly.

He paused, trying to ascertain if she was joking. Then, gathering her again in his arms, he held her as dearly as a man embracing all the colors of the world.

Victorine urgently riffled through the mail. She had been devastated to learn that Bazille, just twenty-nine years old, had been killed in action. "A letter from Edouard!" Victorine called out to Julia, who rushed down the staircase from her bedroom on the second level; Victorine had convinced her to leave her flat in the rue Visconti for safety's sake. "He's been wounded, and his right hand is bandaged . . ."

Victorine suffered a miserable night, dozing and waking from a series of horrific nightmares until she screamed out and sat up, her heart pounding, her nightdress drenched in sweat. Even as she sat trembling in her bed, the image in her dream was seared in her mind: a soldier's bloody corpse crumpled in a ditch on a muddy battlefield. It was three in the morning; she went to the drawing room, lined up a dozen of Edouard's paintings, and huddled on a divan, hugging knees to chest, contemplating them. When she heard footsteps behind her, she motioned for André to join her.

"You can't sleep either?" she asked.

He shook his head. "Not with those infernal cannons thundering out there."

"On our carriage ride to my first meeting with Philippe, I told Baudelaire that all I wanted was financial security." She smiled ruefully. "I thought money made one secure."

"So what is security?" André asked.

She shrugged. "I don't know. But surrounded by Edouard's pictures, I feel safe. André, I'm going to find him."

"How?"

"I'll visit the military staff office. I'll wager they can tell me Edouard's whereabouts. Will you come with me?"

After a few inquiries, she learned that Edouard had participated in the final valiant military stand against the Prussian army.

"So he's at Versailles?" Victorine asked.

"Yes, wounded and recovering in the field hospital there."

The carriage clattered over cobblestones and careened around corners toward the rue l'Impératrice, the route out of the city through the Porte Dauphine. A detail of soldiers on duty at the gate called to the coachman to halt.

"You can't leave the city; turn around and go back!"

Victorine opened the door and stood on the step. There was a general murmur of recognition. "I'm going to our troops at Versailles."

"It isn't safe, madame. Orders are not to let anyone in or out of the city."

"It's Victorine Laurent! It's Mademoiselle Victorine."

"She's the stinking Duchess de Lyon now!"

"I'm not an aristocrat, I'm a working girl!" she shouted.

There were cries of assent. "Let her go! Let her go through!"

The crowd parted, and the frightened coachman snapped the reins above the horses' heads. They passed through unharmed. As they left the protection of the city walls, the carriage picked up speed along the white road toward the Versailles countryside. They didn't proceed far before sniper fire whizzed past the carriage windows. "Halt!" A small party of Prussian soldiers appeared on the road, bayonets pointed, flushed with excitement. Victorine affected her most dazzling smile and addressed them from the window in fluent German. An officer stepped forward and questioned her. A bit of bantering, a bit of flirting, a wink, and the young officer waved her on her way.

André crossed himself.

"What did you say to them?"

"Never mind," she said.

At dusk, they reached their destination. A congregation of white muslin tents bivouacked on the edge of a farm served as the field hospital. André took the carriage to a nearby inn with instructions from Victorine to secure two rooms for the night while she set about to find Edouard. When she lifted the flap of the hospital tent and stepped inside, she saw exhausted medics and crowded rows of cots bearing wounded soldiers.

"Manet? Does anyone know Lieutenant Manet?" she called out.

Some patients stared up at her with glazed eyes; others cried out, "I'm Manet!"

Finally, she reached the last row and halted. Her throat constricted, allowing only a whisper to emerge. "Edouard." She ran to his bedside and dropped to her knees beside him. He slowly rolled over in his bed, and stared at her for several moments, unsure if he was hallucinating. "Victorine?" He seemed not to trust his vision. He reached out his hand to touch her; was she real or a dream?

She cupped his palm to her cheek and nuzzled it. She couldn't speak for several moments. "Edouard, what happened?" she asked, eyeing the bandage wrapped around his right hand.

"Some shrapnel, that's all." He struggled to sit. His right foot was also bandaged. A coughing spell convulsed him. The acrid odor of chloroform mingled with the stench of rotting flesh consumed all the oxygen in the room. "I can't stand this place another moment," he said. He stood shakily, placed his arm around her shoulder, and limped toward the exit. None of the nurses or medics cared to stop him. One less patient suited them fine. As they stepped out of the hospital tent, a blast of crisp winter air hit them like a slap. Edouard inhaled and exhaled a visible stream of white breath.

A rutted dirt pathway cut through the mud. Clouds drifted overhead, alternately exposing and obscuring an icy moon hovering over the frost-encrusted fields. They struggled to walk, his weight bearing down on her, footfalls crunching on the frozen mud.

"Why did you come all the way here?"

"I was frightened. I dreamed that a soldier was lying dead on a battlefield." She closed her eyes. "I couldn't see his face. But it was so real. I had to come find you."

They were near a stable. Edouard indicated they should go inside, so he could rest for a moment. She unbolted the rusty latch and pushed against the door with her shoulder. The dry, yellow aroma of hay drifted around them up to the rafters. He limped to a lantern, touched a match to the wick, then lowered himself down on the hay, gingerly stretching his wounded foot in front of him.

"I'm not dead. I'm quite alive, as you can see." He smiled.

"When I thought I'd lost you . . ." Tears ran down her cheeks.

He sat up slowly and studied her face in the yellow glow of the lantern light. He seemed barely able to breathe for the words he was hearing, unable to believe she was saying them.

"It was always you," she said simply, raising his hand and touching it to her lips.

"But de Lyon . . ."

"Philippe was like me, afraid to love. All I ever wanted was security and thought his money would provide it. I wanted money desperately and never knew what it is. It's trash." She whispered, "I was always afraid I'd become like the others to you."

"I knew that. I knew I had to wait for you to change, to grow up."

"I thought if I loved you, I was certain to lose you."

"Never." His lips touched her cheek. "My paintings, my life, would be a blank canvas but for you, Mademoiselle Victorine."

Softly, tenderly, he began to make love to her. There was nothing frantic or rushed about the way he caressed her. His fingertips brought every nerve of her body to the very edge, then halted, seeking only her pleasure, unmindful of his own. For the first time, she began soaring into ecstasy.

Chapter Thirty

The great questions of the day will not be decided by
speeches and resolutions but by blood and iron.

—Otto von Bismarck, speech delivered to
the Prussian legislature, 1862

The locomotive from Provence inched to the platform of the Gare de Lyon and exhaled a sigh of steam like a
portly dowager settling into an easy chair. Crowds of passengers
eager to see Paris after self-imposed exiles burst down the steps,
like horses at Longchamp bolting out the starting gate. Victorine and Julia strained to spot Degas among the hordes, all of
them jostling one another as they brushed past with their
steamer trunks and valises. Victorine ran beside the long line of
shiny green and brown coach cars straight into his open arms.
Degas dropped his portmanteau and pressed her against his
scratchy tweed jacket, his beard tickling her cheek. He linked
arms with the two women, and they exited the station among
the other fashionably dressed refugees streaming back to Paris
after the lift of the Prussian blockade.

Victorine's open landau joined the heavy flow of horse-
drawn omnibuses and vehicles vying for space on the Champs-

Elysées. She leaned closer to Degas, to be heard over the creaking of wooden carriage wheels and the clatter of horses' hooves and the shouted epithets of hackney-cab drivers all around. "You wouldn't believe it, but the Prussian army marched right past here to the Arc de Triomphe and up the Champs-Elysées."

As they rolled through the streets, a crowd of angry social-ists marched around the corner of the boulevard Sébastopol shouting rude slogans and waving red banners.

"What in God's name?" Degas pointed to the scruffy band.

"Since Minister Thiers won the election, we've had the working classes turned against the upper classes," Victorine said. "Now that Louis-Napoléon's exiled to London, the Reds blame the new government for losing the war." She remem-bered that Karl Marx's manifesto, which Edouard had intro-duced to her, had predicted that the bourgeois Bonapartist class of the Second Empire was fated to suffer the same doom as the French aristocracy of 1789. "It's probably best for you to stay with me, Degas. We've all been safe, so far, behind my high walls."

On March 16, President Adolphe Thiers demanded that two hundred cannons, paid for and cast during the Prussian siege by the fractious Montmartre district, be turned over to the government. The left-wing residents of Montmartre village re-fused, claiming ownership. On Saturday morning, March 18, Victorine opened *Le Figaro* to find that the citizens of Mont-martre had proclaimed themselves a "Commune" with the mandate to overthrow the government of President Thiers.

"Here's the proclamation." Victorine read aloud to André, Degas, and Julia as they breakfasted together. "'Soldiers, chil-dren of the people! The men who brought us defeat, dismem-bered France, delivered up our gold to the Prussians in exchange for armistice, wish to escape responsibility. The only remedy is'"—Victorine's voice broke—"'civil war.'"

Forks ceased to clink against plates. Coffee cups paused in midair.

She traded glances with them, then continued reading, "'The people of Paris wish to preserve their arms, choose their own leaders, and dismiss them when they have no more faith in them. No more permanent army, but the nation itself all armed!'"

Victorine glanced at a young manservant standing quietly by the service buffet in the corner of the dining room, his expression a mixture of excitement and a nascent realization that perhaps he could tear off his white gloves and join his comrades in arms.

"What's to become of our city?" Julia said.

"Paris will be an armed camp," Victorine answered. "This is class warfare. It's just as Marx envisioned it." She laid down the newspaper and stared past the manservant, out the window past the brocade portieres, past the leafy green acacia trees, envisioning the restive neighborhoods of Montmartre on the hill.

"Isn't Edouard's former battalion posted up on Montmartre?" Degas asked.

That very thought had occurred to Victorine. If he was in the city, he was in as much danger as he had been on the battlefield.

Victorine left her house only when absolutely imperative. All of her necessities were delivered or she made do without. Most of the serious fighting flared around the Montmartre hill as armed citizens, including women, confronted loyal government soldiers at gunpoint. But newspapers reported that barricades, that age-old symbol of insurrection, had been thrown up across many other neighborhoods, from the Faubourg du Temple to the rue de Rivoli across the rue Royale. When the Commune successfully took over the city hall and legislative buildings, Parisians were shocked to learn that the government had decamped and fled to Versailles.

Yet despite the daily upheavals, Julia resolutely refused to cancel her exhibition at the prestigious Galerie Jordan. On May 16, she walked down Victorine's marble staircase holding a sheaf of handbills. "Now, please don't be late." She kissed Victorine on the cheek as she threw a shawl around her shoulders. "Here's a copy for you and André. I'm going up to Monsieur Jordan's." Julia tied her bonnet ribbons in a bow under her chin. "The show begins promptly at four o'clock."

Victorine followed her to the foyer. "Julia, perhaps you shouldn't venture out today."

"Don't worry. It's afternoon, and we'll be back before sundown."

"But the newspapers warned citizens to stay off the streets," Victorine said.

"Victorine, please, understand. I won't cancel this exhibit. There are plenty of pedestrians out and about; it's quite safe if you're not a government soldier or a Communard. Today's no different than any other day."

Julia twirled her umbrella. "Bye, darling. Now be there by four o'clock, or I shall be very cross," she said, and slammed the door behind her.

Victorine slipped on her fur-trimmed cashmere cape, and then thought better of it. "I don't suppose we should look quite so bourgeois," she said, and selected a modest wool capelet to drape across her shoulders.

"We'll buy several of Julia's paintings, and return home, posthaste." André was standing before a cheval glass in the foyer surveying his neck and forehead for hives. Straightening his cravat, he tilted his bowler hat at a rakish angle, emulating Edouard. Victorine broke off a gardenia from her bouquet on the piano and placed it in André's buttonhole. "There, now we can feel Edouard is with us today to share in his student's success."

When Victorine's gates swung open, she was surprised to see throngs of people surging everywhere. Her coachman halted halfway down the block and informed her that he didn't think a carriage would get through the crowded streets. Victorine and André decided they would set off on foot. They made their way toward the boulevard des Batignolles, but were redirected by the municipal police due to a disturbance up ahead. They turned down the boulevard Malesherbes and passed agitators waving placards and singing the outlawed "La Marseillaise," some chanting, "Death to the bourgeoisie!"

Victorine stared at the bizarre sight of a group of Communards herding nuns and priests at gunpoint. As they continued past shuttered storefronts and closed vegetable stands, Victorine nudged André and pointed to the only establishment open for business, a workingman's tavern. A popular Offenbach tune poured out the doors, accompanied by the raucous laughter of drunken customers and prostitutes, *filles de joie,* carrying on as though nothing unusual was happening. Suddenly, shells exploded across the street. Victorine grabbed André's hand and ducked inside the tavern for cover.

"Holy mother of God, what was that?" An inebriated patron weaved past Victorine, sloshing beer on her silk skirt.

All the customers followed and crowded around the soot-caked windows. The working girls leaned their elbows on the men's shoulders, trying to get a good look.

"This is it, lads! That old bugger Thiers and his troops'll beat those Reds senseless up on Montmartre," the tavern keeper shouted.

"I heard the Commune's gonna burn down Notre-Dame Cathedral."

"Unless the soldiers massacre them first."

"Oooh, there's gonna be bloodshed today!" A customer rubbed his hands at the prospect of a gory spectacle.

Outside the windows, a double column of infantry with bayonets crossed marched past the tavern.

"Victorine, let's turn back," André said.

"And leave Julia up there on Montmartre? André, let's hurry." Victorine slid her arm through his as they ventured on. They turned a corner to the rue de Castiglione and halted, astounded by the sight of a hundred workmen straining with ropes attached to the statue of Napoléon I at the top of the Vendôme column. A circle of bystanders shouted encouragement. "Pull, brothers! Pull!" a voice shouted. "Destroy the monuments of every regime that ever exploited the workers and the underclasses!"

Victorine pointed to the leader. "Isn't that Gustave Courbet?"

They heard a massive crash and saw the head of Napoléon I rolling eerily past them toward the gutter. "Well done, lads!" Courbet cried and ran toward his comrades.

Victorine gazed in wonder at the headless statue at the top of the Vendôme column and looked up at the sky, darkening with thunderclouds. "What time is it?"

André flipped open his pocket watch.

"It's five thirty."

They trudged uphill around the place de Clichy, one of the liveliest areas of Paris, and encountered nothing but darkened shop windows and deserted cafés boarded up with discarded remnants of advertising tablets. The atmosphere in the eighteenth arrondissement was electric with the static of violence. Down below, the crowds were simple amateurs satisfied to sing "La Marseillaise" and build barricades from paving

stones; up here, the mob was armed en masse with rifles, revolvers, and drawn swords. Victorine led André by the hand
around barricades and past armed gangs shouting obscenities,
until they reached a level terrace on Montmartre hill, a quiet
spot where they stopped to catch their breath. She looked up
at the heavy, leaden sky, so close she felt she could stand on
tiptoe and graze it with her fingertips. Glancing eastward,
she saw thunderclouds gathering energy above Notre-Dame
and beyond, to the Salpêtrière Hospital. The golden dome of
the Tuileries Palace seemed a dull hump in the midst of a
dark patch of garden, while the bridges nearby arched across
a black snake that was the Seine. All seemed eerily quiet.
Looking down on her city from the vantage point of a bird in
flight, she missed Alexander and Baudelaire and felt a burden
of remorse, heavy as a brick, for Philippe. And where was
Edouard? Was he somewhere on the hill among that hateful
rabble, playing the brave soldier? She tried to shake off this
sorrow; they had to keep moving.

Once they reached the place des Abbesses, it was even
more difficult to push through the throngs of agitators. They
turned a corner smack into a rowdy band of Communards
brandishing torches and surrounding a bewildered, white-
haired general on a horse. "It's my grandfather's chum, General d'Amboise!" André pointed. Mobbed, the famous
general, a veteran of the Algerian war and the Italian campaign, desperately wheeled his horse while grimy hands
pawed him, trying to pull him down. His elite guard of officers, far outnumbered, tried to push back the attackers, to no
avail.

"Seventy thousand of my troops are on the march from
the pont du Jour." The general's voice sounded frail. "You
traitors had best surrender to me now!"

Victorine watched in morbid horror as, enraged and egged
on by a crowd of bystanders, the Communards pulled the

general off his horse and dragged the distinguished eighty-year-old up against a wall. One Communard pulled a dirty handkerchief from his breast pocket and offered it to the general. The general turned his head and refused.

Victorine felt a sickening pitch in her stomach. Rifles raised to shoulders, shots blasted, and a cheer roared. As a grande finale, several women Communards stepped forward and jammed their rifle butts into the general's twitching body, crushing his skull.

Victorine ran to the gutter, doubled over, and vomited. The mob surged and Victorine was separated from André, he pulled one way by the crowd, and she propelled toward the place du Tertre. When Victorine finally broke free of the horde on the rue Saint-Eleuthère, she spotted Julia. Victorine shouted her name, but gunshots and screams filled the air. Julia began to run. Victorine pushed past crowds of people until she finally grabbed a handful of Julia's skirt. Julia whipped around and readied her umbrella to strike, then gasped, umbrella in midair. They embraced and clung to each other for several moments. Victorine shouted to her above the din, wondering where to flee, when a squadron of armed women marched around the corner. A woman elbowed Julia and thrust a torch in her hand.

"If you're not with us, you're against us!" Their leader, Louise Michel, pointed her rifle at Julia's head. Julia could do nothing but accept the torch and fall in behind her.

A squadron of soldiers under the command of General Martin came around the opposite corner. "We challenge you to fire on your own citizens," Louise Michel shouted, and her followers waved their rifles and pistols in the air. "Go ahead, shoot us if you dare!" she cried.

The general ordered his troops to fire. The youthful National Guardsmen raised their rifles, housewives and prostitutes in their crosshairs. They hesitated, reversed direction, and began firing on the general and his government soldiers.

The women's brigade cheered as the National Guardsmen fell in behind them. "To the arsenal!" they cried and marched off, pulling Julia with them, swept along by the frenzied mob. Victorine pushed her way toward her, but was buffeted by shoulders and elbowed aside. The women's brigade was met by more government troops and engaged in a heated shouting match while Victorine turned and headed toward the arsenal. She stepped back as a wagon rumbled by, piled high with dead bodies, their ideological differences irrelevant now. André, limping up the road ahead of her, was also making for the arsenal. She cried out his name, ran to him, and clasped both his hands. They laughed with relief at finding each other and promised they would not be separated again. Victorine asked if he had been wounded, but he confessed that he had merely twisted his ankle, running to escape a crazed band of women fighters.

Night fell before they reached the arsenal. As they approached, Victorine spied a figure standing guard, leaning against a partially demolished stone wall. She would know that form anywhere. As she watched, Edouard swayed against his bayonet, seemingly tired beyond exhaustion, then sank down to the ground and extracted a sketch pad from his soldier's knapsack. Victorine wondered how in heaven's name he could sketch in the shadows. She saw the flare of a match and the glow of his cigarette.

Smoothing her filthy dress, she walked calmly toward him. She saw him raise his head and stare as she approached. There were no words for a moment like this, only a silent prayer of gratitude to have found him and relief that he was alive. She wrapped her arms around his waist and held him. The screams and boom of cannons receded far away as she closed her eyes and felt herself enveloped in him.

"Halt, rabble!" a soldier's voice shouted out from behind Edouard.

The crowd of women, a mass of dark outlines against the torchlight, was moving raucously toward them brandishing their weapons. "Drop your weapons!" the soldier cried to the women. "Halt where you are!"

They didn't obey. Instead, they brandished their rifles. Victorine could just barely make out their shapes in the flickering light. Suddenly, a barrage of shots rang out from the ranks behind Edouard and his comrade. Women crumpled to the ground. "That'll show those dirty Communards," a young soldier snarled.

The commanding officer ordered his men to pick among the dead. Edouard grabbed a torch and directed Victorine to wait against the wall, then crossed the street and walked toward a woman's body lying face down on the cobblestones. He knelt beside the woman and saw that she clutched an umbrella in her hand, not a rifle. "You idiots! This one was unarmed. It wasn't a rifle, it was a . . . ."

He turned the body over and stared into the lifeless face.

Victorine was alarmed by the slump of his shoulders, the arc of his head bowed so heavy with sorrow. She felt a premonition like an icy hand gripping her shoulder.

She ran toward Edouard. His comrades stood in a circle above the motionless form sprawled in the street. Julia lay where she was felled, her blood-soaked shawl covering her body and her head languishing in a pool of blood. Her umbrella was beside her. Victorine screamed, dropped to her knees, and cradled Julia's slack head in her arms. She cried Julia's name over and over, as if that would wake her.

"Victorine, don't." Edouard tugged at her skirt, soaked with Julia's blood. He dragged her away, past a speechless André, to a quiet promontory that overlooked the city. She buried her face in his chest. "Why?" she repeated over and over. "I told her not to go out today," Victorine said. "I told her . . ."

He murmured soothing words until she finally fell silent with exhaustion. His arms encircled her tighter as he surveyed the scene down below. Suddenly, she felt him give a start. "God help us," he whispered.

Frightened, she opened her eyes and gasped. Fires were spreading through every arrondissement in Paris. From the Tuileries Palace to the Palais de Justice, flames lapped at the city like an inferno. The Seine itself was a river of fire. The wind fanned the flames, and angry clouds of black smoke funneled up to the sky, now lit by the phantasmagoric glow of fires crisscrossing neighborhoods. They heard screams all around them.

Edouard whispered in Victorine's ear, "Look, the Tuileries Palace. They've ignited it." They watched in morbid fascination, then a heard a horrific explosion. "The Pavilion de l'Horloge, it's caving in!"

Victorine remembered triumphantly passing under that golden cupola the day Philippe had arranged her presentation to Empress Eugénie. Now Philippe was dead, Baudelaire was dead, the city was in flames, and only Edouard stood between her and the chaos of hell all around. He held her tightly as they turned to watch the inferno below. He was the only security she'd ever had, and ever needed. "Our great city," he whispered, "clothed in purple and scarlet and decked with gold and precious stones . . . the smoke of her burning."

Epilogue

Seagulls swooped and skimmed the waves of the beach at Deauville on a warm June day. Edouard had rigged his easel on the dunes to apply the last finishing touches to a painting, oblivious to the grains of sand blown by the wind and embedded for posterity in the wet paint. André and Alexander walked barefoot near the shoreline.

The painting was of Victorine, her diaphanous white scarf billowing in the wind, her white dress swirling about her, as she stood at the top of a hill overlooking the beach. The pure light filtered around her and actually seemed to glow from within the painting. His life was now fulfilled by her. His palette, suffused with light, had grown more brilliant.

She tiptoed silently behind him and surprised him with a kiss.

He grasped her hand and pulled her onto his lap.

"It's almost finished," she said, admiring the work. "What

did they say when they presented you the Legion of Honor? Oh yes, Baudelaire's phrase, the 'Painter of Modern Life.'"

"The Legion of Honor," he scoffed. "Ten years too late."

"The painting's beautiful," she said.

"If it's beautiful, it's because of you," he said softly.

"Why did we waste so much time running from each other?"

"Life can't be measured by time," he said. "It's merely a series of impressions."

Author's Note

The main character in this work, Victorine Laurent, is a fictitious composite of two scandalous and fascinating women: Countess Virginia de Castiglione, an aristocratic courtesan, and Victorine Meurent, Edouard Manet's favorite model and muse. Duke Philippe de Lyon is based on Duke Charles-Auguste de Morny, who was the true brains behind the successful reign of Napoléon III. The character of Julia Stanhope-Morgan was inspired by the American painter Mary Cassatt.

One of the major plot points is based upon an assassination attempt on the emperor's life that actually took place on April 6, 1857. Napoléon III's beautiful Italian mistress Virginia de Castiglione was accused of plotting to kill him on behalf of an arcane Italian nationalist cause. The entire ruse was orchestrated by his wife, Empress Eugénie, to ensure her young rival's banishment from France.

The identities of models in some works by Edouard Manet are still debated by art historians. The titles and some dates of some paintings in this work are fictitious. Several Manet paintings described by critics in contemporaneous reviews have disappeared, perhaps to be rediscovered.

Reader's Group Guide

About This Guide

Rich and evocative, *Mademoiselle Victorine* is a novel of changing times, of the powerful intersection of art and politics, and of how one determined woman made her place in history. The questions in this guide are intended as a framework for your group's discussion of *Mademoiselle Victorine*.

About the Author

Debra Finerman began her career in journalism, and later attended the prestigious Christie's Graduate Program in Connoisseurship and the Art Market. This is her first novel.

1. Describe your first impressions of Victorine and Manet. What was your initial opinion of each of them, and in what ways did your view change as the novel went on? How did it stay the same?

2. Prior to reading *Mademoiselle Victorine*, what did you know about the French Impressionist painters? Was there any knowledge of their work or lives that illuminated your reading of the book?

3. How would you characterize the relationship between

Victorine and Julia? Are they allies and friends, or rivals? If you were Victorine, how would you feel about Julia, and vice versa? Did you find yourself identifying more with one than the other?

4. Consider the character of Queen Mabille. What does the old woman represent to Victorine, and in a larger sense, what role does she play in the Paris of this novel? What did her story add to your understanding of the world these characters inhabit?

5. Several of the characters in *Mademoiselle Victorine* came from wealthy backgrounds, but had shunned their privileged existences to live a bohemian life. What does Victorine think of this choice? Is it something she understands and accepts? Why or why not? What about you? When you hear of modern-day children of wealth "giving it all up" to become artists, what assumptions do you make? Would any of those assumptions be valid in the case of these characters?

6. Throughout the novel, Victorine continually reinvents herself and refines the story she tells of her background. What are some examples of the different stories she tells, and is there anywhere you see her getting caught in her own web and having to shift on a dime when she forgets what she's told whom? Why do you think her story is so complex and changes so much? Were there places you thought she had gone too far, beyond the point of lying for understandable reasons?

7. Discuss the character of André. What role does he play in the lives of those around him? André writes a popular society column. Did it surprise you that Paris in the 1860s had tabloids that reported gossip? Can you think of equivalent magazines or newspaper columns today?

8. Did Victorine remind you of any other literary or historical figures? If so, who, and in what way? Where else have you seen the story of a young woman pulling herself up by her bootstraps to find herself living at the pinnacle of society? Of artists' muses? Of the courtesan made good? What, if anything, makes Victorine different?

9. Were you surprised by the revelation of Victorine's line-

age? Why or why not? How did this news change your view of the man who turns out to be her father? Did it change Victorine's opinion of him, or her ideas on life and love in general? What, if any, lasting effect did you see the knowledge of the story behind her conception and birth having on Victorine?

10. What do you think inspires Philippe's ultimate change of heart? Did the transformation take you by surprise? What effect does it have on Victorine?

11. Discuss the portrayal of the leftist rebels in *Mademoiselle Victorine*. In the world of this novel, did you find their cause just? How did you feel about their methods? What part did the Communards play in the plot of the novel, and what did you think of this picture of them?

12. Philippe's liaison with a much younger, beautiful woman was common knowledge and not socially unacceptable. But when it became a political liability that threatened to ruin his career, his actions and attitude toward Victorine changed. Is this a familiar scenario? Why do you think political figures of all eras get caught in such situations though they know the risks?